A STRIKING TRUTH

HELEN McNEIL

A STRIKING TRUTH

First published 2016
Published by Cloud Ink Press Ltd, Auckland
PO Box 8988, Symonds Street, Auckland, 1150
www.cloudink.co.nz

ISBN 978-0-473-36782-4

Cover design: Robin Charles (robincharles.com)
Book design and typesetting: Greg Simpson

This book is dedicated to Harold Appleton and Garry Mace,
for providing both sides of the story

I've invented you to read these words. They're slippery. They break down and change into something else. Take a pine log; it gets pulped into chips, chemicals get added and it's no longer pulp. It's on its way to being paper. One day I'll write on it and I'll write the facts.

Once there was a town, with a mill. If you drove in from the west, with your own eyes, you might see this:

The log pile shifting. The stripped trees nudging each other as they roll and bruise. The hammerhead crane with its logs swinging over to the left side and then swinging to the right. There's no secure place for these twenty logs.

This is true. I think.

Last week these logs were pine trees, minding their own business, until chain saws ripped into them and front-end loaders pushed them on to huge trucks which held the traffic up, all the way to this site. Here they'll be minced to pulp and flattened to paper.

Each one of these logs has its own truth to tell. One holds the thin rind of a dry summer; one has a deep scar where it was almost flattened by a rooting pig. Each log has a signature set of rings.

That's true too. I know.

They'll journey through the mill to become blank, white paper. Just one week it could take. Or a year. That depends on the story written in the corporate reports about production costs and profit. It also depends on the story told by the men who work the mill, about dirt money, demarcation, and job retention. They're all written on the blank, white paper.

All these stories are true, possibly.

The crane driver places his load of logs and eases the jaws out from under them. One sticks, trapped between the forks on the left side. He jiggles the jaws. The log falls. For a moment, the pile stays. Then it collapses and, like dominoes, the logs collide and push each other over, sending up a cloud of bark and sawdust.

It was that last log that did it. There's always one maverick that destabilises the whole shebang.

That could be true. Depends what you see with your own eyes.

I'm the keeper of truth. I'm the librarian who protects all those paper books full of truth. It's often dangerous and it doesn't always set you free.

So promise me, if you find these notes, you'll burn them.

Chapter One

Miriama McLay

"Start again, from the top, Miriama. And Peter, give it some guts, boy!"

"Yeah, Peter, don't be such a pussy."

He blushed when Davey said that, his whole face went real red and his pimples stood out. He'd been squeezing the one on his cheek and it was all swollen.

Miss looked a bit pissed off and May and them were starting to give Pussy Peter the evils. When Miss pressed the play button, the opening chords were real loud and Peter jumped. Stupid prick missed his cue again but I just picked up my bit about summer love. I sang it twice. He still didn't join in.

"Peter, come on," said Miss.

He was so red he was nearly purple and I thought he might cry. That would be too much. No one wanted to watch Pussy Pete cry.

"Miss, I need to go to the toilet," I said.

"All right then, let's take A five-minute break."

Miss headed outside to have a smoke. I reckoned doing this musical was making her smoke twice as much and she pulled on that cigarette like the smoke'd fill her up so much there'd be no room for Pussy Peter and his pathetic voice. May and June came with me. We smoked in the toilets so Miss couldn't see. I was always the one who got to sit on the sink, with the cold water tap stuck up my bum.

"Fuck, Miriama, whad'ya reckon? Shall I promise him a blow job or something? Might give him a bit of life," said June. She's

May's older sister and she's tough.

"Pass the smoke. You don't want to do that. You'd scare the pants off him."

"Well, he'd need his pants off, wouldn't he?" said June.

"Maybe one of us could be the boy part too, I reckon I could do a better job," said May. May's little and flat-chested. She could do a boy part but she's shorter than me.

"Come on," yelled Miss. "Put your fag out. Get yourselves out here."

So we jammed the cigarette butt down the plug, just to keep up appearances, and pushed open the door.

Miss had someone with her. With his white shirt and flash pants he looked like one of those Mormons who ride around town. He'd even got a jacket with shiny buttons. A Moron Mormon. They're real wankers with their big white smiles and they say Ma'am even to me, at only sixteen, well, nearly seventeen. Makes me want to puke. We had a cool game, you called out to one of them, "The devil's up your bum" or "Don't run that angel over" or something like that, to see if you could make him fall off his bike. You got ten points for a wobble, twenty for a foot on the ground, fifty for a complete wipeout. They never swore at you, ever, but, if they did, that would be one hundred points. Game over.

"This is Ray," Miss said. "He's a visitor in town and he's come to have a look. So let's get on with it, get this song under our belts. Peter, you start from under the windows this time, a change in place might help."

So Pussy Peter went over the other side of the hall and it sort of worked, he was only a beat behind and I picked up my bit without losing it. We got to the chorus when we were supposed to be singing together but the other voice wasn't Peter's squeaky one, it was deep and IN TIME. I was kind of confused but what the hell. Maybe Davey finally got up the guts to do it; he'd just kept saying no way.

Everyone was singing the chorus, finally sounding like music.

Then it was Peter's turn again but that deep voice was back and it was coming from over by Miss. When we got to the soft bit when everyone else shuts up and me and him take turns, I knew who it was. It was that Mormon. He knew all the words and he could sing. Even the last notes, we made them fly. We just worked.

The track finished and Miss clapped. June and May were raising their eyebrows at Davey and Jason. Peter was sort of drooping and everyone was leaving a big space round him. He was still bright red and I reckoned he was holding his breath so he wouldn't cry.

"Gotta go," he muttered and grabbed his bag from the side of the hall and ran. No one tried to stop him.

Miss finally stopped clapping.

"Right," she said. "We've got a new Danny."

There was a long silence. I got a closer look at the Mormon. He was skinny and real pale, like a super Pākehā and he'd got stuff in his hair, like Danny in our musical. It looked like he made it fall over his face on purpose. Made me want to go to it with clippers and do him a good number one. I imagined him with his little bobbly head on his skinny neck, he'd look like an alien. You know, like ET in the movie with his head all naked and his neck all long.

"Haere mai, tāne Pākehā," I said. "Haere mai ki toku kāinga ātaahua."

"Good evening. Miriama, is it? Nice to meet you."

And the wanker put out his hand. Like he meant me to shake it. Really. Like old people.

"We don't do shaking hands in this country. 'Specially if we're brown. We do this."

And I turned him round with one hand on his shoulder, and pulled his head down to press his nose on mine. His eyes were coming at me, all wide and scared. I think he thought I was gonna kiss him or maybe even bite him and he jumped back with his arms all waving and nearly got to sit down on the hard wood floor. There was a snigger behind me.

"Now, Miriama, behave yourself," said Miss. "Tell us a bit about yourself, Ray. What are you doing here?"

So he told us that he was doing a year after finishing school, called a gap year, like there's a year with a hole in it or something, and that he was going to go to London University next year to study computers in industry. It sounded real flash.

"Yeah, but what're you doing here, in this little place?" Davey asked.

"Actually, I'm staying with my mother's cousin. Her husband works at the mill and he said I might get some work experience with the big computer."

His accent was real Pommy. The Old Man would call it toffee-nosed, but it wasn't like he was pretending, which some people do. It was sort of cool.

"Who's your cousin?" asked June.

"Mrs Hopewell. Her husband is Colin Hopewell. They live in Bell Street."

There was a silence. June's mouth went all monkey's bum and Davey and Jason were shuffling their feet but we needed a fulla with a voice and he had A VOICE. Miss interrupted the awkwardness. She looked straight at him. Not at us, we were all looking at our shoes.

"We all get along in this town," said Miss. "No matter what's going on. You're most welcome, Ray, and we all want to invite you to join the cast. What do you say?"

So he said yes and we all shrugged our shoulders and started the song again. Miss made us do it five times. She gave us the little talk again, about getting our mates to come and join in because we need more in the chorus and it would keep more of us out of trouble and blah, blah, blah.

It was nearly six by the time we finished and it was dark. Miss kept me and skinny boy for a while. She wanted to know about Ray's music background. Turned out he'd been in school stuff like me and he'd sung at a café where his mother lived. In London. Miss got all excited and by the time we'd finished talking Davey and June and them had gone.

"See you tomorrow, Miriama," said Miss. "She's our star, is Miriama. Good at English, too. My best pupil."

I was too whakamā to stay there and let Miss talk about me so I headed for the door but he was right behind me.

"I have to say you've got a beautiful voice, Miriama," he said. "I think I'm going to enjoy singing with you."

"Yeah, right."

"Shall I walk you home?" he asked.

I was even more whakamā but I wasn't going to let the Mormon know that. So I put my head up and looked him in the eye.

"No one needs to walk me home," I said. "Not me. I'm staunch. No one messes with me."

"I just thought we might talk a bit more, you know, the two stars getting to know each other a bit better."

Weird fulla. Thinking he can be like in the song, making out. No way. His cousin's one of my old man's big enemies. He'd kill me.

"Nah, got my bike," I said.

"Right. See you tomorrow then."

I was out of there real fast and on my bike before Miss had turned out the light. I didn't look back, just in case he was looking, but I did stop round the corner and have a jack. He was still there, talking away to Miss, like he wanted to get in good with the teacher.

I rode home slowly on the footpath because it was dark and my light was busted. I had the words of the song so stuck in my mind, like a broken record. Halfway home, I couldn't help it, I was singing to the hedge, singing about summer love when there was prob'ly gonna be a frost. Anyway I didn't need a summer love, not me. No one messes with me. I was thinking though, that maybe I'd dream about him, that skinny Pākehā with his sexy accent.

I came round the corner of my road, no hands on the handle bars, just getting the high note and almost crashed into Leo's ute up our drive. Him again. I always have to squeeze past that bloody old ute of his, it takes up so much space. I put my bike in the shed so it wouldn't get pinched.

Inside it was warm and the windows were all running with the condensation from their hot air. Leo and the Old Man were having a session at our kitchen table. It'd been going for a while, there were half a dozen bottles leaving brown rings on the table. Leo's home brew tasted like the mill smelt, a mix of sweaty football socks and dead rats. Even me and my mates never asked him for some, it was that bad. Him and the Old Man were well on the way.

"Now laddie, you know as well as I do that the bastards'll do the self-same line. You think we're here to line your pockets, they'll say. What they mean is, you're just the hired help."

"So we're still not going to the meetings then?" slurred Leo.

"Och, it'll be the selfsame stuff. How we need to accept that management knows best and how important the paper industry is to The country. We already know we're important, laddie, they're not telling us anything new. What they'd really like to be saying to us is that we're a pack of commie bastards."

Mum was messing around in the kitchen making bread and I could smell the first batch cooking, hot and homey, made my belly rumble. You could tell how the Old Man was by the amount of banging Mum did: cupboards, oven door, and the bread dough got a hiding. Then there'd be a lot of shouting and she'd go away and stay with cuzzies for a while. Once there was a black eye none of us talked about. She just got up in the morning, stared at us with one eye half closed like she was daring us to say something. Didn't even make an excuse, like it was a cupboard door or something. I still don't know what it was about.

He didn't use to drink like this. I remember the strike when I was nine, he didn't drink then, least if he did, I didn't know. He used to pour himself one glass of Leo's cat's piss and just hang on to it and it was Leo who drank the rest. Then there was a strike when I was thirteen and that's when it started; that's when the black eye happened. I hated it. Tonight the bread was getting a massage but it could change any time because the Old Man'd get started on the coalmines. Right on cue, he was banging the table and making the empties dance.

"The British coal miners would've won, even against that bitch Thatcher. If they'd stuck together, not been seduced by that sweet, soft voice of management."

"Solidarity, mate—comrade, I mean."

"We all need to be one voice. One voice, the voice of the working man. You know they're looking at each of us to find the weak link, don't you? Looking for the one they can cull out and brainwash into their way of thinking."

"Not me, mate. Not you," mumbled Leo.

Mum banged the oven door shut. One brown bottle rolled to the edge of the table and hung there, dripping home brew onto the lino. Leo'd got his head in his arms, spread out on our kitchen table. I think he'd had more of the homebrew than the Old Man and he'd passed out. Like I said, not the first time.

I took my tea into the sitting room. I'd heard the Old Man all my life and didn't need to hear him banging on again. Even when things weren't good at school, he'd tell me we had to get yourselves organised, no kids to teach meant no jobs for the teachers. I don't think it works like that. If we all went on strike and refused to go to school, it'd be us that got into trouble, not the teachers.

That bloody song was still going through my head, all about some lovestruck dude wondering what 'she' might be doing. Course 'she' didn't mean me. He'd have his floppy hair curling between his eyes. What colour were they? Blue? Grey, maybe? I'd have to have a jack.

Chapter Two

Ray Parlane

She was still locking up. She had a ruddy great bunch of keys and kept putting the wrong one in the lock. I had no idea why she was bothering. The little grass park outside the hall was bright with streetlights that said no one home and it looked like there had never been anyone home.

"The citadel will not succumb to the rampaging hordes, Ma'am," I said.

"Ray, you're such a find." she said, when she'd finished the last lock. "Which school did you go to? It must've had a strong musical tradition. Your voice sounds trained."

"Mill Hill School, North London, Ma'am. I sang in the choir in the third and fourth form."

"Your school did musicals like *Grease*?"

"Crikey, no. Not my school. That was choral stuff, sacred music, and the orchestra did proms. But I was part of a theatre group where my mother lives."

When I was Ziggy Stardust I was dressed in tights and silver sleeves, like a prince. A pantomime prince for one night. I was only fourteen and my voice hadn't broken. So I sang Ziggy as a soprano, just like when I was in the choir, but I was in clothes that Harry had found for me.

"Is *Grease* your favourite?" asked Miss.

"No, Ma'am. That's American. I like the English stars. I'm a Bowie fan."

"I see, well, goodnight Ray. See you tomorrow night."

But I could play Danny. I could do Badass Danny who got the girl in the end. It would be that brown girl. My grandparents weren't here, after all.

There was still no one around as I sloped off past the supermarket, just a few cars outside. A pickup parked under the streetlight had dogs chained to the back. They barked and growled at me, slunk back with their chains rattling when the owner came out and yelled at them to shut up. In fact, he told them to fuckin' shut up.

It was bloody freezing in the park and I puffed my breath out in little lost ghosts, musical ghosts who sang up into the stars. Ground Control was calling Major Tom. You up there, Major Tom, looking down on my two dads, Stan and Harry, on the other side of the world? The stars here don't look anything like theirs.

The bridge that crossed the stream wandered off into darkness. The water was very fast and slurped at the sides. I was freezing. New Zealand was supposed to be warm, a tropical island in the Pacific. That's what I'd thought I was coming to. I couldn't have been more wrong.

There must be cities in this country but I'd passed them by. I'd caught the bus straight from the airport and, after the bus got in about lunchtime, I hung about the house.

"You look like a lost soul," Mrs Hopewell said to me. "Why don't you go out and explore the town? After all, you'll be here for a while."

In other words, get out from under her feet while she got dinner ready. The brats were fighting and yelling and she was looking like the *War of the Worlds* was happening. I didn't know what to do without getting more in her way and those kids were ruddy annoying.

It was five o'clock when I walked through the park to the town. If this was London, I'd be battling the rush-hour pedestrians fighting for their inch of the pavement. I counted twenty cars at the intersection near the shopping area; rush hour is snail's pace here.

It didn't take long to explore the forty shops and they were closing. The library had already closed. There was a town hall that doubled as a picture theatre. They were showing *The Terminator* on Friday and Saturday night and *Ghostbusters* for the matinee on Saturday. It took about five minutes to find that out. I went into the hall because it was the only place with lights on and I needed to warm up and I wound up with a star role in some school musical with that girl, that brown girl. She was a dusky Māori maiden, with wild hair and a fantastic voice. I just couldn't help myself, joining in like that.

I pulled my jacket collar up. It really was bloody cold. Not one soul did I meet, just empty streets and a ginger cat that I stopped to stroke but it got a fright and changed its mind about this alien. I found the house. It looked sort of American, all spread out and no upstairs, like all those houses you see on TV, suburban LA. I wished Mrs Hopewell would hurry up with the spare key she'd promised, so that I could come and go under my own steam. I knocked and waited. There was a shuffling and clicking noise and something being dragged. I tucked my hands up under my armpits and stamped my feet. Someone was taking forever to open the door. When it did open, there was no one there, just an open door and a long hallway then something came out from behind the door. A wheelchair.

"Hi, can I help you?"

"Oh hell, I'm in the wrong house."

"This is the Duncan household."

"I think I'm meant to be next door."

He was about my age. All I could see was the wheelchair and his wasted legs. I wanted to ask what had happened and how he felt about not being able to walk and how he managed to go to the toilet. I wanted to say I was glad it wasn't me.

"Car accident," he said.

He was staring at me, and my face was getting hot. A man asked who is it from down the hallway then came to see for himself. It had to be the cripple's father, they looked so alike. They were both frowning and the crease in each forehead was in exactly the same place.

"You are?" the father asked.

"I'm so sorry, sir," I said. "I'm staying with the Hopewells and I've just arrived. I got the wrong house."

"Easily done," he said. "I'm Mr Duncan. I see you've met my son Paul."

I shook Mr Duncan's hand. Mine was very cold. When I put my hand down to shake the cripple's, I mean Paul's, hand. He nodded at me and kept both of them on the big silver wheels.

"We may see some more of you," Mr Duncan said. "I'm sure Paul would like that. Yes?"

Paul narrowed his eyes at me as if to say it was the last thing on his mind.

"Well, I'm terribly sorry to disturb you, Sir," I said. "I'll be off then."

Not a mistake I wanted to repeat.

Next door Mr Hopewell's car was in the driveway so I was hoping I wasn't late for dinner. It was the suburban symphony; him yelling, the kids crying and Mrs Hopewell banging pots. I bypassed the kitchen for my room. At least it was down the end, furthest away from the brats.

It was open on my desk, the lid up, waiting for me. I pressed the on switch and the green digits flickered, flipped into order and settled. The thing I've always liked about computers is their predictability. They always do the exact same thing. No matter what the phase of the moon or the ruling planet, they only do what you tell them to do and this one was an absolute darling. She was a Compaq Portable, not many about. I brought it with me, carrying it on the plane as hand luggage. It had graphics as well as the usual word processing and spreadsheets. I watched the bee flashing around the bright green flowers on the screen with some super strange electronic music trying to play. I was hoping it might drive out that boy in the wheelchair, with his *leave me alone* vibe. That it might bring back our love song and that girl.

There was a knock on my door and I turned the excuse for music off. It was Mr Hopewell. He's older than Mrs Hopewell and he must have an important job at the mill because he gets to work seriously long hours. He was holding an old coat.

"How're you settling, young man?" he asked. "Thought you might be feeling the cold. Here, I wore this in Dunedin when I was a student. Everyone had a duffle coat then."

Everyone was wearing these at University College London (UCL to us insiders). I was very grateful.

"The ankle biters are having stories. We can sit and have a beer with dinner," he said.

The food wasn't great, not compared to Stan's lasagna with crusty French bread or pork belly and redcurrant jelly. Stan was the best cook. This was like boarding school food and I made short shrift of the mutton neck chops.

"I didn't mean to, but I went next door," I said.

"Oh really?" he said. "There was someone there?"

"Yes, a boy in a wheelchair and a man who looked like his father."

"Ah, they've arrived then," he said.

I was about to ask who "they" were but he detoured the fork from its way to his mouth and stabbed it at me. The gravy dripped on Mrs Hopewell's embroidered centerpiece, leaving brown smears. My grandmother would have been furious if it had been hers.

"We need to get you started, young man," he said.

"Well sir, I've got a part in a musical, it appears."

"Ah, yes, very good. Means you'll get out and meet some young people."

There's that boy next door, he's my age. The one who can't walk. I suppose I could say I've met him and I've certainly met that Miriam girl, the one who nearly knocked me over trying to kiss me.

"So you're interested in computers. Right, well, let me see what I can do. Give me a few days to sort it out. I'll get you linked up with the computer department staff. I'm sure they won't mind you there in the mornings for the next little while."

So it was all arranged. The following week I was to go with Mr Hopewell (Sir) to work. It'd keep me out of the way of the brats and get me started on what I came here for. At least one part of it. Liz hadn't given me many clues for the other part. Just said the cosmos would line up when it was ready. The way she always does.

Chapter Three

Ima Williams

Typical. The house was in darkness and my car clock was telling me ten past eleven. It didn't look as if the curtains had been drawn. She couldn't have been home all night and I had no idea how to get in. I didn't visit my sister very often; you could say there was an understanding between us that we wouldn't crowd each other. She'd come and visit me in the city sometimes, when she had a conference or a training to attend, but I hadn't been here much. This one time I did make the effort, she wasn't even home.

What to do? I could sit in the car, but I didn't know how long I'd have to wait, so I reached for my bag from the passenger seat and got out. It was a cold, clear night, with that sharp, taut smell of a frost threatening. Notta always said that was one thing she liked about living in this part of the country; it didn't rain as much as Auckland but it was bloody freezing in winter.

So there I was, standing with the door of my car open wondering if I should get back in to get warm again, when there was a squeal of bike brakes behind me. It was Notta, all in black, the luminous vest glowing iridescent green in the street light, so it looked like only part of her was present. The balaclava covering her face muffled her voice. Her glasses glinted at me.

"Oh, it's you," she said.

"You were expecting me, weren't you?"

"Yep. Just had some business to attend to. Come in."

Her driveway wasn't even concreted and I nearly turned my

ankle in the potholes. By the time I got around the corner of the house, Notta was scrambling under a gumboot.

"That's where you hide your key?"

"Only when I bother to lock the door. This isn't the city, you know. How was the drive? You're late, thought you'd be here before dinner."

"No, Notta, I said I'd be late. And the drive was fine. Good thing about a car like mine is that it's fast. I have locked it, you know. The car, I mean."

She didn't take her balaclava off until we were in the kitchen. It was like a fridge; it had to be minus ten degrees. My coat was staying on. The kitchen looked so barren: no curtains, nothing on the benches except the electric jug and an ancient toaster, no reminders stuck to the fridge with fancy magnets, nothing on the walls except that stupid clock she's had since she was fifteen. It had always been permanently stuck on twelve o'clock and it still ticked and the hands jerked but nothing moved. God knows why she kept it. When I asked her she said it told the correct time twice a day, which meant you had to make up the rest.

You can tell a lot about a woman from her kitchen but there wasn't much anyone could tell about Notta, not from her kitchen.

"How's the library?" I asked.

"Fine. I'm the acting head librarian for the next six months. The other librarian's on maternity leave. I'm enjoying it, being in sole charge and making all the decisions."

"Really, Notta? You, in charge?"

"Yes, me in charge. Is that so strange? Do you want a cup of tea? There's no milk."

"Sorry, didn't mean to sound, well, you know. I just meant that's great, a big step, well done."

As she filled the kettle at the sink, I looked at our reflections in the kitchen window. We're twins. Not identical: sororal, dizygotic, just an ovum accident that led to half an hour between our births, and we couldn't look more different. We never claimed to be twins, ever. When we were small we had some silent agreement that we'd sometimes call ourselves sisters. Even that was pushing things.

So there was her long face and stringy dark hair and the big nose; maybe some Jewish ancestry somewhere that she could claim. It certainly hadn't reached me. She was even six inches shorter than me and the black tights did nothing for her fat bum.

"Why're you here?" she asked. "You just said you wanted to stay for a couple of weeks. What're you doing away from the Big Smoke?"

"I'm between jobs at the moment. Thought I'd try a little freelancing."

Luckily she was plugging the kettle in. My voice was steady enough, but I could feel my face fighting the smile I was trying to fix.

"Freelancing? What's there to write about here?"

"Well, strikes of course. Or maybe women's work. How women manage in a town where the biggest employer only takes men, unless you make the tea or type of course. That's one angle I could take, I suppose."

There was a silence in the cold fluorescent light that bounced off the white painted walls. She was still wearing her fingerless gloves. She was probably warmer than me, but none of that warmth was coming my way. She kept it frigid and silent while she made the tea then she plonked the mugs on the table and sat down opposite, so she could glare at me. Her glasses steamed up as she narrowed her eyes over the edge of her mug and it sort of spoiled the effect.

"Right," she said. "Another outsider to pull us to pieces. These are people's lives, you know, and you want to dissect them for your own glory."

"My own glory? What are you on about? Jesus, I just want to write a good representation, you know, tell a decent story."

"Oh yeah, a decent story. And whose story is the decent one? You're a reporter. You'll just take the management angle. Everyone does."

"Depends on what I find out. Depends on how people cooperate. Why are you so touchy? You're a woman, you work, even if it is in one of those predominantly female occupations, Notta. Is this how everyone's going to be?"

"You wouldn't understand. You don't live here."

She was staring down into her tea. When we were young, I used to pretend I could tell fortunes. I used to tell her she'd meet a short, fat man who'd make her miserable.

"I'll make you a bargain," she said. "There's a man I want you to meet. He's helping me set up WEA courses, you know, Workers' Education Association. He's got a handle on things around here. You tell him you're a reporter and, if he thinks you're trustworthy and if he really likes you, he might introduce you to some people."

When Notta had put my tea down on the formica table it had made a ring. I carefully placed the mug back, right on top of her ring. A man. Short and fat probably.

"Who is he?" I asked.

"Name's Leo. Leo Harris. He'll be at the library tomorrow, to talk about the courses we're going to run."

"A man. You need to ask a man if I can write a story about women in this town. I see."

"No, I don't think you do. I don't think you see anything. This is a Mill Town, with a capital M for Mill and a capital M for Management and that M controls everything."

She wouldn't tell me any more. As we filled hot water bottles and said goodnight, I remembered why I didn't see my sister much, why we tacitly allowed each other the space. It was that intense way Notta had about her. As if 'goodnight' had some kind of secret in it I wasn't privy to. We went to bed with the door unlocked and the key in the lock.

When I woke up in the morning, she'd already gone. Of course there was no coffee in the house and we hadn't discussed smoking inside so I got to huddle over the heater and watch my cigarette smoke curl up into the cold kitchen. There were three things I knew:

Point one: I needed to sell a story. I needed the money.

Point two: This was maybe going to be more difficult than
  I'd imagined.

Point three: I was sure I could find a good story here.

I could sell a piece to *Broadsheet*. "Women and Industry", I
could call it. "The Paper Ceiling Harder to Break than Glass". After
all, this was 1986 and feminism had been around a while in other
parts of the country.

When I got out to start the car there was frost on the windscreen. Scraped into it were four words. Very welcoming, they were.
FUCK OFF RICH BICH. My car, my precious car! How dare they!
Then it occurred to me that someone must have watched me arrive,
to know to call me bitch. That was not comforting. What was more,
that someone couldn't spell. It must have been one of the young
punks from around here. He'd better not come back with a coin
down my baby's glossy red paintwork.

The morning was sharp bare trees and icy lawns with the sun
sitting just above the hanging grey cloud of smoke, where the mill
sits and belches. The air was cold and putrid with a stench like
rotten cabbage. The rumble of steam gathering in pipes under-
ground made a hoarse shout as the bores released. There was the
high-pitched insistence of machinery. It had overwhelmed me the
first time I visited, its noise and its smell and it was overwhelming
still, this relentless giant that ran the town.

When I was visiting here once, Notta had come with me on
a tour of the mill. I'd watched the men hauling the logs in to be
ground up for pulp. They'd stood astride the logs, pulling them
in with a hooked gaff. One foot wrong and they'd have been pulp
themselves. I'd listened while the tour guide had told me about the
recovery boiler, where the margin of error for balancing the heat
and chemicals was narrow and an error would mean an explosion
that would take out half the mill. I'd watched the sludge that was
called pulp as it poured onto the racks where it dried, little by

little, moving at speed along the belts that turned it into paper. The blanket of noise had penetrated the earmuffs we'd had to wear. It had smelt hot, with a mixture of chemicals that had coated the back of my nose and made me feel sick.

After the tour, Notta had rambled on about how easy it would be for one of the workers to fall head-first onto the rollers and join the pulp spreading over the mesh. His body would mix into the slurry of broken wood chips and sulphur; he'd drown in the stench of it. He'd be laid out on the felts and, as he dried he'd be ironed into a flat man stretching over metres of wet paper that then welded him into its very fabric.

She could be macabre sometimes, our Notta.

"Imagine," she'd said, "if you opened your *Herald* one morning, and there was this hand emerging from the news, reaching out through the story about the old lady who'd lost her dog, or the increase in unemployment and what is the government going to do about it? Or imagine if you could see a man's ghostly face, like the face in the Turin shroud."

Of course, it wouldn't happen like that. If someone fell in, the paper machine would've just stopped and he would've been pulled off the line.

She spent too much of her lonely adolescence reading in her room, did Notta.

I decided to walk to town after all. Everything was close here and I had a leather coat and gloves and boots. There were probably about four house designs in this whole town. Mill houses. Notta's house was design one with kitchen and bedrooms facing the street, next door was design two with lounge facing the street. As I walked I played mix and match: there was a Notta design but turned the other way and with a red roof, instead of a green roof. If I lived here, I'd paint my house in some outrageous shade of purple, with an orange roof.

I've lived in cities a long time. The thing about a city is that no one is interested. You can walk anywhere and feel the freedom of no opinion because you're just one face in many. On these streets there were dogs to bark at me and it felt as if there were people watching me, noticing me. I looked behind more than once and I didn't like feeling paranoid so I nearly waved and yelled out, "Hi, I'm Ima, I'm a rich bitch, come to find out all about you!" Instead I nodded and smiled at the middle-aged woman out getting her newspaper from the letterbox and I didn't look back when I felt her eyes following me.

I walked past the Town Hall. No one was there. The supermarket had one or two people in the car park. The library was around the corner, its glass front doors still closed. Notta had to be inside somewhere because her bike was sitting in the foyer. She must have wheeled it up over the brown bottles smashed on the concrete and the empty vodka bottle sitting just in front of the door. Someone had spilt most of the vodka and the stink was enough to make me lightheaded. I banged on the door. Across the glass, over the black letters that said this was the District Library, was a scrawl of spray paint. B maybe, no, P … Pox. Couldn't have agreed more.

Notta was undoing the locks. She didn't lock her door at home, but locked herself into the library? First the top lock, then the bottom lock, then the deadlock, and finally the door swung open. All those books, secure from Pox and his mates. They had to get past the locks, then her, to remove any of her precious books.

"Morning. Had a visitor, have you?"

"Oh, that. Happens sometimes. Come in. I was just about to empty the returns trolley."

She pulled on the pair of rubber gloves she had tucked under her arm and wheeled out the trolley with its load of books. With rubber-coated thumb and forefinger she carefully lifted up a used condom. It had leaked over the pink cover of *The Devil's Darling* and the heroine's uplifted face was awash with anonymous semen.

"Happen often, does it?" I asked.

"Might get some more readers," she said. "The condom broke."

She marched past with the thin rubber flapping and I wondered where it would get stowed.

I stepped past the spilt vodka and wiped my boots on the door-mat. It was quiet in the library, and still. Without any voices, the words in the books were sleeping, holding their stories in loving arms, in strangleholds, in parentheses. The dust caught the morning sun coming in the high windows. Notta had always loved books; this had to be where she felt at home, here, amongst all this knowl-edge, all these thoughts, old friends. In that way we were similar, lovers of words. Maybe we could work together on this article.

Maybe.

But the mess on the front doorstep had to be so disshearten-ing and Notta, such a loyal soul, didn't complain. I half-heartedly offered to help her clean up but she looked at my leather coat and boots and wrinkled her nose. I didn't offer again.

While she was outside sweeping up the mess, I poked around in the back office. It was as empty as her kitchen. There was not one photo of Notta or any of us, her family; just benches with tidy piles of envelopes for holding little cards, spine-broken books waiting for repair, trays with glue and tape. Even the drawers were full of little plastic containers of paper clips and drawing pins. I was closing a drawer when I got a sense that someone was watching me. He was standing behind me at the counter and in my peripheral vision, I could see the green trousers and heavy jacket. He just stood there for a while.

"Nice coat," he finally said.

A sort of quiet descended, as if something had stopped, wait-ing for the next moment. I turned around and I was being pulled into his little kingdom. He was looking at me as if he was about to devour me, taking in my coat, my boots, my bra size; I swear he was running a tab on my very soul. It seemed to take forever. Him and me. Just him and me and a pulling between us, and it went on and on.

Notta started the clock again.

"Oh, hello Leo," she said.

He was so overpowering. All I could register was that he'd had a broken nose and he was shorter than me. There was a shudder down my back, and I gathered my exposed self together.

"Leo Harris, I presume?"

"Yes, last time I looked."

I didn't dare put out my hand to shake his.

"I'm Ima," I said. "Now please excuse me, I'm just going out for a cigarette."

When I walked past him my long coat brushed the top of his workmen's boots. I was stuck in confusion at the door, pushing when it clearly said pull. A hand came around me and pulled it open. I mumbled something and escaped onto the now clean porch, hoping for the quiet company of Notta's bike, but no such luck. He'd followed me.

"Where are you from?" he asked.

"The Big Smoke," I said and laughed as he pulled out a lighter. I was very glad my hand wasn't shaking as he put the flame to my cigarette. "I'm here to write a story, about the town. I've got some ideas."

"Ah," he said. "We've been waiting for you. Welcome."

I had no idea what he meant.

"Objective, are you?" he asked. "Both sides of the story?"

"Of course," I said. "How else is it done?"

Then it happened again. The stopping feeling, I mean, as if there was no one else in the world but the two of us and I couldn't escape. I was trapped like a mooning heroine in one of Notta's Mills and Boon novels.

"You can be a new comrade and tell the story how it is," he said.

"Well, as you said, both sides of the story."

"You could even tell the truth."

"And whose truth would that be?"

"The one the fuckin' papers never report."

"I see."

"I'm the secretary of the union. I've got information. The union's got the history."

"I didn't quite ..."

Another voice chipped in. It was Notta.

"You two getting on OK, are you?" she asked.

I shook myself as if coming out of water. I was on the steps of the library. Notta's library and she was not happy, no, not a happy girl at all.

"Of course," said Leo. "Ima's going to write our story. We'll show her everything we've got."

"If you say so, Leo," said Notta. "Only if you say so."

"Solidarity Notta, that's what we need," Leo said.

NOTTA'S NOTES (2)
21.7.86
Day Three

You haven't met the players in this game of truth yet. They change over time but as of day three this is who they are.

In the left corner, in steel-capped boots, smelling of sulphur, we have Team Federation of Pulp and Paper Workers:
- The President, known as The Old Man
- The Secretary, Leo Harris
- 640 pulp and paper workers

In the right corner, in white shirts and ties and holding clipboards, we have Team Management:
- The CEO, Mr Stuart Duncan (newly arrived from Auckland)
- The Manager of Operations, Mr Fred Grant
- The grey shadows of the Board of Directors

And in the centre we have the excuse for it all, Sally Wihongi:
- Who wants a job in the mill
- Who doesn't have a job in the mill—yet
- Who is not union
- Who is a woman

You need to know there have been preliminary skirmishes, in fact, two 24-hour stoppages. You also need to know that a strike has been declared and that Team Pulp and Paper Workers has been suspended. Do you want to play this game? Who will you back? Want to lay bets?

Chapter Four

Ray Parlane

"These are the ones," Mr Hopewell said.

"The what?"

"The strikers. The pulp and paper workers. Pinko militants. They have to report for work every morning, now they've been locked out." They were coming in small groups, a right bottleneck at the gate. All dressed in green: green pants, green coats, like the tube staff in London. It had to be some kind of uniform. One of them was shouting at the man on the gate, waving his arms. I couldn't hear what he was yelling because the windows were all up in the car. I tried not to stare but it looked promising because he took a swing at the bloke on the gate and it looked like it might be a real barney. The other blokes in green pulled him back and order descended again. Shame, it would've made the morning more exciting to have had the Old Bill here and people dragged off, like in the photos in the *Daily Mirror* of the miners in Yorkshire, bobbies with truncheons and miners in cloth caps. There was one photo that looked as if a policeman was running up the leg of the miner. That strike was high drama; this one looked a bit tame in comparison.

Mr Hopewell inched in past them all, keeping his eyes straight ahead to avoid the stares. He was driving very slowly when someone thumped his car bonnet. I think he might have sworn if I hadn't been in the car. There was a man in another kind of uniform waving us on and pushing open the metal arm.

I sneaked a glance at Mr Hopewell. His mouth and eyes were all pinched in and his driving was slow and careful. Mind you, it was a beauty, that old Rover of his with its polished surfaces and it was smooth, so smooth. It glided into a parking place.

"Right, that's us," he said. "I'll take you up to Ben Crossley, he's the computer man. He knows you're coming."

"Sir, I'd just like to thank you for arranging this. I really appreciate it."

"No problem, young man, no problem."

The building looked kind of temporary, like all the buildings here. Wood and tin, like the army put them up for a wartime hospital or something. It was supposed to be a big company, earning lots of export dollars and growing, according to Mr Hopewell.

Inside and up the stairs there were double doors for us to get through, with security punch pads on them. They liked locks in this town, keeping out the rampaging hordes. Mr Hopewell punched in numbers to both sets of doors and we were in a long room with computers lining the walls and workstations in the middle with blokes hunkered down, five of them, staring at screens. It had that smell, dry and cool, the smell of machines thinking. I could tell at a glance that they were top of the line. IBM, not GEC and so, so much more advanced than anything I'd worked with. I nearly broke out into it, my favourite song. If you sing it with a straight face, people don't know if you're for real or if you're being a complete git. It was running through my head: *IBM happy men, smiling all the way, in our service to mankind, that's why we are so gay ...* Me and Stan and Harry loved it, it was catchy, it was memorable, everyone knew the tune. I nearly shouted, "All together now—to the tune of Jingle Bells ..."

"Young man?"

There was a man in a white coat and he was holding out his hand. He must have had it out for a while because he was looking over his glasses at me in a psychiatrist kind of way.

"Sorry, sorry sir, I'm a bit overwhelmed. This is epic. All these ..."

I shut up before I actually broke out in song. I was shaking his hand and my eyes were everywhere else.

"Ah, meet our IBM 3084. We've had it for two years. Hope you can learn something while you're here with us. Leave him with me, Hopewell, we'll get along just fine."

So by morning tea I knew about the forty-eight channels on offer and the single system imaging that was dead efficient. They were installing a new programme to help with scheduling of maintenance that I so wanted to help with. This was Heaven.

At morning tea we went down to the cafeteria. It was full of people in office type clothes so I guess the angry mobs at the gate didn't ever get a look in here. Mr Crossley was shepherding me over to a table with three other men in white coats. He said he'd get me one, it was part of the uniform.

It was the new programme for maintenance scheduling that we all talked about. There'd been long strikes here before and if this was another one the paper machines might have to be closed down for some time. Everyone was excited at the possibilities for the new software. Then someone came in and the teacups all got put back on their saucers and there was a hush.

"Mr Grant," whispered my neighbour. "Head of Operations."

He was standing up near the tea urn and seemed about to give some kind of speech. He was a big man, standing about six foot three, and he was like my old headmaster. When he cleared his throat, you shut up.

"I've had no news from the pulp and paper workers. I gather they met yesterday. You know as well as I do what the cost of this strike mentality is. We lost twenty-five million last year from strikes by the very selfsame union."

I looked around at the hundred or so people in the cafeteria. Some were looking down at the table or into their teacups. One girl who didn't look much older than me was filing her nails. Mr Crossley was pulling at the loose skin on his neck and wrinkling his nose to keep his glasses on. He looked a bit like a short-sighted plucked chicken. I coughed so that I wouldn't laugh and get a bollocking.

This was serious business.

"We can't have a continuation of this strike syndrome," the big man continued. "The CEO, Mr Duncan, has arrived. You can rest assured we will be taking a stand on this."

There was a buzz of agreement. Mr Grant was accepting a cup of tea from the tea lady so it seemed he was finished. We went back to our critical paths and dyadic configuration conversation.

At one o'clock my time was finished and I walked out with my head full of logic and pathways. When I got back to the Hopewell house there were the three kids in the kitchen, mixing something in a bowl, with flour spilt all over the floor. Mrs Hopewell was nowhere to be seen.

"Mummy's having a lie down," said the eldest one. "She's got a headache. Do you want to help us make fairy pies?"

"Only if you chop the fairies up very very small," I said and backed out of the kitchen. The youngest one pushed the bowl over and everyone started yelling. More action here than at the gate of the mill, and I was bailing.

By five I was back for the rehearsal. That teacher everyone calls Miss offered me a cigarette. I was about to ask if she had another name when Miriama arrived with a whole crowd of mates. She'd got more than enough and the teacher was stoked.

"Right," she said. "Let's get the singing parts done first. We need a young woman who can pretend to be cheap. She's not really, but others think she is. Doesn't mean she is, just has to act it."

"You mean someone like Julie, Miss?" asked May.

"She needs to be able to sing," Miss continued.

Julie got pushed out of the crowd. She did look a bit of a slag, like she could be a Betty Rizzo. But she didn't look as if she liked it.

"Piss off."

"Language, Julie," said Miss.

"But you're saying I'm cheap, Miss."

"Yeah," said one of the boys. "You saying my cuz is only worth fifty cents?"

"It's true though," said one of the other boys and everyone laughed except Julie. She crossed her arms tight over her chest.

"No, Julie. You just have to act it. Now, here's the song."

She pressed the button on the ghetto blaster and Julie listened. Not too many plays and she was over her sulks and joining in, singing about not smoking, or drinking. Just as well she couldn't see the boys behind her. Just as well the teacher couldn't too.

Then the teacher got us to go back to the script. Back to the beginning with me and Miriama meeting on the beach. I had to hold Miriama's hand, pretending she and I were, well, getting it together. When I put my arm around her everyone started laughing and Miriama lost it.

"Shut up, shut up arseholes, bloody shut up!"

The teacher suggested she just worked with us two and everyone else grumbled as they picked up school bags and drifted out. The taller one, Jason, couldn't resist a last shot.

"Don't let him put his tongue in your mouth, you'll catch his Pommy accent, or something worse," he yelled.

The teacher said she needed a cigarette so me and Miriama were left sitting on the hard seats and staring straight ahead.

"Have you got a boyfriend?" I asked.

"Me? Course. Got lots of them. What do you think I am, a lezzie?"

"Sorry? Oh, a lesbian. So if you're not, why don't you pretend I'm one of your boyfriends then?"

"What, and you pretend I'm one of your girlfriends? Or do you have boyfriends?"

I should've got all upset and made noises in some kind of defence, but she wouldn't understand anyway.

A man in the green clothes that were "the thing" in the town clomped into the room. He was wearing those heavy boots too. He was short and sort of ugly.

"Oh, shit. It's Leo," Miriama muttered.

"Who?"

She jerked her thumb in the direction of the man. He came right up to me and folded his arms. There were blue marks on the knuckles that looked like do-it-yourself tattoos. He looked me up and down.

"So, young man," he said, "you making out with our Miriama, are you?"

"I suppose I'm pretending to, sir."

"Sir? Ah, you're a Pom," he said. "Posh, too, by the sound of it. You just be careful with Miriama."

"With all due respect, sir, are you her father?"

He sort of made a ducking move with his head, like someone was taking a swing at him. With a crooked nose like that, I suppose someone had, more than once. He narrowed his eyes at me, his head on one side, and the gold ring in his fat ear lobe shifting slightly. He looked like an escapee from Wormwood Scrubs.

"Like a father," he said. "I'm like a father to her."

"Like I need two dads," said Miriama. "My real father's the president of the union, everyone calls him the Old Man."

"The union? The one that's driving this strike?" I asked.

"Yeah, the one your cousin and his mates hate so much."

She picked up her bag and nearly bowled the teacher over at the door. Maybe it was something I'd said.

"Miriama! Miriama stop, we need to do this …"

She'd gone. The teacher shrugged and came over to me and the short man.

"Just the man I want to see. We need an older man in the production, to play the coach. Just up your alley, Leo."

"And you'd expect me to come to rehearsals? I'm a working man, remember?"

"Yes, you are a working man but not just now, from what I gather."

The man called Leo sighed. He said he'd think about it, he said maybe it would give him a chance to keep an eye on me and Miriama. Doing what, I had no idea. Fuck, this place is confusing.

Chapter Five
Miriama McLay

Jessica was five feet ten inches. I reckoned she weighed half of me, she was so skinny she could stand behind a power pole and you wouldn't see her. I was always trying to feed her up on mum's boil-up, but she only ate yoghurt. She was always talking about going to live in the city, and that our lovely town was a dump.

"What if I want a job?" she asked.

"You wanna work with smelly chemicals? Get real, Jessica. Thought you wanted to be a model."

"Yeah, but what if I did want a job? Your old man wouldn't let me, would he, him and his union mates."

"Can't see you in a hard hat and boots, ruin your nail polish hauling round the stuff in Chem. Prep."

We were outside the music room waiting to go in to senior assembly. Bunches of mates were trading smokes and more besides. Best way to do it, in a big crowd 'cos teachers couldn't see what was happening.

My cuz Selwyn was standing by the door. Mum sometimes went and stayed with Selwyn's whānau when the Old Man got too much. That was where she went with the black eye that we didn't talk about. Selwyn was the captain of the rugby team and I was real glad he was my cousin because it meant he was on my side.

"Hey, Miriama," he yelled. "You fullas OK? Things are heating up, eh? With the strike I mean."

"You should tell your old man to pull his head in," said the fulla next to him. Brian was his name and he was a big mouth, that fulla, just like his father. Selwyn gave him the evils.

"Shut up, eh," he said.

"Why should I?" Brian said. "Her old man's pulling everyone out of work. Happened before, we all know, happening again."

"You just shut your mouth," I said. "Your father wasn't too staunch last time. Noticed he went back to work just a little earlier than anyone else."

"You calling my father a scab?" he said.

"You said it," I said.

"Your father must be a homo. He just doesn't like women in his work place. That woman is my dad's relation."

Then it was all on. Everyone was shouting and Selwyn had Brian by the collar and was holding him up with one hand. Brian looked like he was trying to run to get away but his feet wouldn't touch the ground. We cleared a circle to watch and fullas were cheering for my cuzzy.

"You fight for the union, Selwyn. Union's choice."

"You show him. U-nion! U-nion!"

"Fuckin' bosses don't fuckin' know …"

Selwyn put Brian down and the two of them were doing that stand-off thing, like in a dogfight, 'cept Selwyn looked like one of Dave's pig hunting dogs and Brian looked like a runty little poodle or something. Not everyone was rooting for my cuzzy, there were mumblings in the circle too, not that I wanted to hear it.

"Stop bullying him, Selwyn. You're just like Miriama's old man."

"Strike means no friggin' money, you prick."

"What the fuck? We're just going to Australia anyway!"

There was a real loud blast of a whistle. I put my hands over my ears, they hurt. Then there was another one and it nearly blasted my head off. Miss was standing on the steps of the hall and she just kept blowing that fucking whistle till we all shut up. Man, could she blow.

"Enough!" she roared at us.

We were hanging our heads and shuffling our feet. It was serious when Miss got this racked up. In five minutes we were in the assembly hall and we were stuck there for two hours. She made us listen to some stink music from some creep called Beethoven. No one could even go out to go to the toilet. Crap, that's what it was, crap.

The day just got worse. Miss got the Grease cast together at lunchtime. She didn't mention anything about that morning, or about the strike, just gave us a long lecture on the importance of working together. What she wasn't saying was that most of the kids in the cast had fathers who were pulp and paper workers. She should know that, I got most of them to come.

But the worse thing was that after the meeting they gave me a bad time about him, that Pommy fulla, Ray. They kept calling him Dunny and reckoned him and I wouldn't be able to get it together for the show because he was a homo. I told them maybe one of them could put on girls' clothes and be Sandy. We could do the Gay Grease. That shut them up.

By the time school was finished I was real hōhā. I rode my bike so fast up to the library that I nearly burnt the rubber off the tyres. At least there'd be peace and quiet up there.

There was a big tangle of bikes all over the steps when I got there. Bloody kids in this town got no respect. By the time I'd moved three of them so I could get in the door, I knew the peace and quiet wouldn't be there. It'd be a whole lot of kids talking their heads off instead of doing their homework. Just what I needed.

But what did I see when I walked in? Six kids sitting at the back table, quiet as. Just two of them were talking and that was in a whisper. Miss Williams was strict; she wouldn't let them in the library unless they were quiet.

Then he walked in. That fulla, that Ray fulla. He was tall and skinny and he was wearing a coat this time, without the shiny buttons. He had a thing in a carry case, it looked like a sewing machine, and he started talking to Miss Williams. What was he gonna do, offer to sew her clothes? Fulla had to be gay. I pretended I didn't see him, grabbed the trolley of books for shelving and slid away to the far corner of the library. He was getting something out of the case and him and Miss Williams were putting it together. She didn't make him whisper.

"Here it is," he said. "You know, this is a serious breakthrough in computing for everyman, this Compaq."

Miss Williams had got her arms folded. She wasn't looking down at whatever it was that Pākehā homo was fiddling around with, she was looking at him.

"Brought it with me from London, carried it on as hand baggage. I can set it up and use it anywhere, including here. We could set up a catalogue system for the library. I did it at my old school."

"Has anyone said you look like David Bowie, Ray?" Miss Williams asked.

She looked all sort of sort of moon-eyed at him. It was disgusting. He took no notice, just sat down and started poking at the machine and Miss Williams gave up staring at him and the two of them stared at the screen instead.

I pushed the trolley over to the romance section. It had a squeak on the back wheel. Mills and Boons, lots of them, and *The Devil's Darling* that I was holding was a bit damp; someone must've been reading it in the bath. I hated Mills and Boon. Should be Balls and Moon, and it was always the girls with the moony look on their faces.

Not me. Wouldn't ever be me.

Miss was calling me to come over and look at the computer and I pretended I didn't hear her. Then one of the kids said Miss Williams wanted me and I had to go over, show them that Miss Williams was to be respected. Role model and all that.

I had a jack over her shoulder at the thing on the desk. It just looked like lots of green lines to me. She made me stand real close to that Ray and he didn't even look up, not that I wanted him to notice me. He was talking at the screen but it seemed like I was meant to be listening so I had to bend down to hear him. I kept my arms crossed real hard and tried not to touch any part of him. Man that was a tiny TV screen to look at.

"Get in closer, Miriama," said Miss Williams. "He won't bite you."

"And over in this column you put the publisher," he was saying. "Then you can sort the spread sheet by publisher if you want to."

I had to lean over him to look at the tiny writing he was putting in and I lost my balance.

"Mind out," he said. He turned round and caught me and I was nearly on top of him on the chair. I pushed him away and the chair went flying on its little wheels and crashed into the counter.

"Piss off," I said.

"Sor-ry," he said.

"Hey, hey, enough," Miss Williams said. "Calm down. Aren't you two meant to be, you know, in the show?"

"Yeah, but I don't do it with homos."

"What do you mean, Miriama?" Miss Williams asked. "You don't 'do it with homos?' Do you think Ray is gay?"

He was frowning at me with that long bit of hair dangling on his face. His eyes were grey, not blue, they were grey. My face was red, and hot.

"What if I am?" he said.

"I have to pretend to pash you, that's what."

"I don't mind. You don't act like a girl anyway. Thought you were a lesbian."

"You calling me a lezzie?"

"Lesbian, actually."

Then we were doing the evils' competition, staring each other down. I've never lost one of those. I could stare down a pig hunting dog and get it to back up and I wasn't about to lose this one. I could feel the kids all listening. I was just settling into it, clenching my jaw, when Miss Williams busted out laughing. She was cracking up like we were the best show she'd seen.

We stopped giving each other the evils and turned it on her. Man, she made me feel so hōhā. Then I couldn't help it, and both me and him, we got the giggles too.

"That's better," she said. "Now, where were we?"

Chapter Six

Stuart Duncan

"Mr Grant suggested you come, Paul," I said.

"What for?" he asked.

"It's one way to get to meet young people your age."

"What for?"

I gave up. He wasn't actively fighting me, so I just wheeled him out to the car and stood there with the door open.

"Wish you didn't have this stupid car," he said.

He said that every time and I always laughed. I didn't say I'd got it because it was as far away as possible from the car we used to have, or that the adjustment on the seat meant it was the best car for his posture, once he was in it. And he didn't say how hard he found it to transfer from the height of his wheelchair to the car.

"I'll just join in the rugby game, will I?" he said.

"No, Paul. Look, you don't even need to get out of the car if you don't want to. It's just a chance to see something of the town."

"So why are you taking the wheelchair?" he asked.

"Just in case."

The wheelchair didn't fit, I had to admit that. It was all very well on a fine day like today when I could put the hood down, but we were going to have a problem when it rained. Perhaps I would need to arrange a disability van for those days, if Paul would let me.

Paul must've had a bad night; his face was pinched. He put his head down. I didn't know if it was because he was too tired, or if he was just refusing to look, and it was a pleasant enough little town with trees along the creek side. Willows, mostly. There was a swimming pool steaming away—it was heated, which would be good for Paul because he relaxed in hot water. There were only three cars going into the shopping area but when we got down to the rugby field that was a different story. I hadn't been down here before but Fred Grant told me I'd be able to drive right in and park. He was right, except for the number of other cars doing the same thing.

The only park I could see was near the entrance so that was where I stopped, next to an old ute that looked like it'd seen better days.

"You warm enough?" I asked.

"I'm not putting a blanket over my knees if that's what you mean," he replied.

There was a scrum in front of us, just in from the twenty-two metre line. They were juniors, lots of big, brawny Māori youngsters. They were all around Paul's age. The halfback was dancing round, a weedy little fellow who looked about half the size of the other players. He was yelling with a high-pitched voice and looked like he'd got a sock on his head. Who knows what kind of local custom that was. I couldn't see Fred Grant anywhere, although he said he liked to come down, to be seen to be part of the town life.

I wasn't sure what to do. If I stayed in the car with Paul no one would come over but if I left him here they might. The best solution would be to get him into his wheelchair.

"I'm just going to walk around a bit, see if I can find Mr Grant," I said. "Want to come?"

There was no reply.

As I got out of the car, the skinny halfback got in under the heave of bodies pushing back and forth and grabbed the ball. The sock came off and there was a mass of black hair flying as he dodged out and away.

"Break! Break, you fullas," he yelled. He didn't bellow like a halfback should.

"Ha, Paul. The halfback's a girl," I said.

The whistle went for full time. If anyone was going to talk to Paul it'd be now, so I wandered off towards the clubrooms. No doubt word had got out: that I was living back in town, that someone from head office was down to stop the strike from escalating, just like last time. No doubt there'd be some who were rubbing their hands, thinking we'd just roll over, like management had done before.

I used to play halfback. Being of slight build, I wasn't much use shoving in a scrum. I was quick, like that young girl. I was the one who got in between the heaving bodies and broke the scrum by picking up the ball. The trick is you have to have someone to pass to and that someone has to be rock solid. He has to be someone who knows the game plan. Of course, it's better still if you've got several passing options.

I was looking around for Fred again. The last time we'd talked he'd been cautious.

"It won't be easy, Stuart, you know that," he'd said.

"Well, the board is adamant," I'd said.

"I know, but the union's had a stranglehold here for a long time."

"Times have changed, Fred. It's different this time. That stranglehold needs to be broken."

Everyone needs a Fred who's rock solid, to pass the ball to.

I could hear water, loud and insistent. Behind the clubrooms was the river. It was a powerful body of water, with rapids so fast that there were national kayaking competitions held here. It was also the reason the mill was built here in the first place. Paper mills need water, lots of it.

I was looking for some decent places to run, so I could stay sane. Over the river there were tracks that went up into the foothills. I remembered that one went up on the shoulder of the mountain, heading round past the new pine plantings. That was the track they used for the King of the Mountain each October. Anything could have happened here by October.

It was a sunny day, frost melting like butter on hot toast, river smelling cold and clean and my feet, well, they tingled. I wanted my legs pumping and my lungs pulling in the bright air. Maybe later in the afternoon, before I had to shift my attention to the business at hand.

And if Paul was all right.

When I got back to the other side of the clubrooms, there was a knot of youngsters around my car. I walked over slowly.

The car was empty. No Paul, no wheelchair. My gut pulled tight.

"Your car, Mister?" asked one of them.

I nodded.

"Cool," said another one of them. "I'm gonna have a BMW when I'm rich and successful."

"In your dreams," said his friend.

They wandered off. One of them ran a hand over the black paintwork. I almost stopped him.

If Paul wasn't in the car, someone had helped him out. I pushed my hands down into my trouser pockets. He should have been easy enough to spot. The juniors' game had finished and there were knots of older men gathering in the middle of the pitch. A thin line of supporters was spread round the perimeter but there was no sign of a wheelchair. The youngsters who had been looking at my car were heading to the other end of the clubrooms, to the door. I followed them over.

Inside it was dim. Apart from the ranch slider doors to get in, there was just a narrow band of windows along the top of the con-crete block walls. The end near the doors had a bar, with a mesh screen pulled across it. The noise was coming from down the back.

"I'll hold you."

"Come on Selwyn, you be the anchor man on that side."

"You can do it."

His wheelchair was pushed up against the pool table at the end of the room. He was being hauled up by the girl who played halfback and the big Māori boy who said he'd have a BMW when he was rich and famous. There was one on each side, pulling Paul up to stand. He couldn't stand. His early attempts to hold himself upright had just led to ferocious tantrums, then a deep black hole.

His back was to me. I couldn't see his face. I couldn't tell if he wanted this to happen or if they were giving him a hard time; tease the cripple; get him to stand up so that he can collapse in a heap and we can all laugh.

My mouth was acid. I was about to shout leave him alone, leave the poor kid alone you cruel bastards, when there was a hand on my shoulder.

"Wait, Stuart, you may be pleasantly surprised."

I went to push it away but it was Fred Grant. Hold on, he was saying, keep your nerve. He nodded at the pool table to indicate I should keep watching.

The girl and the big Māori boy had got Paul wedged between them and he was jammed in against the table. There was a sudden quiet. One of the others passed Paul a cue. There must have been half a dozen youngsters round that table and I swear they were doing what I was doing, holding their collective breath. Paul leaned over the table. I couldn't see what he was aiming for, his body was obscuring the balls on the table, but I knew he was lining up the cue for a shot.

"You used to play pool with him when he was younger, didn't you, Stuart?"

"Yes, I taught him. He was quite good. We had a table in the basement."

"I remember."

The cheer drowned out Fred's words. It seemed that Paul had sunk something; it seemed he was a great success. I blinked back that prickling behind my eyes and reached for my handkerchief.

"He'll be all right," said Fred. "They'll look after him."

I just nodded.

"Anyway, welcome. Good to have you back, Stuart. Thanks for coming down. How're you settling in?"

"Okay," I said. "Okay."

"There's things for you to attend to, Stuart. If we want to get on top of this. I'll see you in the office on Monday, but how about you and Paul come round for dinner? Cynthia would love to see you both again. How about one night next week?"

I nodded and Fred was off out the door, leaving me to watch Paul being pulled back into his wheelchair by the same two youngsters and the rest of them slapping him on the back. The girl with the mess of black hair picked up the cue. Paul was so engrossed that he pushed himself up on the arms of his chair. He took one hand off to wave it enthusiastically and crashed back down on the seat. No one offered to help. No one made any comment. He laughed.

I went out and sat in the car.

Chapter Seven

Leo Harris

It's fuckin' chuckin' it down. Man, when it rains here, it bloody rains. The mountain's disappeared, which means it'll go on all bloody day. But the smell's not around. Strange to have a wet day without the smell, usually makes it thicker and heavier, gets right in your lungs. It might make your stomach heave but it's the smell of money in this town and right now, it's not here. The air's as sweet as a toke at bedtime. Men are all turning up, yellow or green, that's us. Yellow wet weather gear, courtesy of the company thank you very much, green swannies, also courtesy. Dressed by the company. What a fashion statement we are. Everyone's in work gear for a bloody reason. We all had to go to the security gate this morning and present ourselves for work so we could be told we can't. Bloody lockout. All of us. Locked out. Every single bloody one of us. It's not a good sign, a lockout. They fuckin' did that to the Watersiders in '51, we all remember that. I could get worried. The wanker on the gate was contract labour, not union. He had the good grace to look shamefaced and some stupid bastard took a swing at him. Bet that stupid wanker's not getting double time, or dirt money.

So we're meeting in the Town Hall—five hundred and eighty-five of us. A good turnout; as far as I can see, all union. We'd know if there was someone not union, but I can't read minds, can't tell if someone's a turncoat, reporting back to management. Fuckin' good turnout, though. The Old Man'll be rapt.

Inside it smells like a wool shed, wet wool and daggy socks. Men are scraping back the chairs, plonking their safety-booted feet on some of them. That's how many chairs there are, more than enough for everyone, except they line up along the edge, all the ones who aren't so sure with their arms crossed as if to say, give us a good reason then. None of them saying a word. I make my way up to the front with the rest of the exec, next to the Old Man. All of us are in work greens, all of us in this together. The Old Man stops shuffling papers and stands up. He waits, he's good at that, just stands there quietly and waits for the shuffling and coughing to stop. When he does speak, everyone's listening.

He starts where he always starts.

Solidarity, mate. Dignity of the working man.

He says we have to stick together, says we'll win if we stick together, says we've done it before.

Fuckin' amazing he is, the way he keeps the faith, keeps the blokes in line.

Remember the last time, he says, and the time before that. Stick to our guns. We'll go back to work, all right, but on our conditions, not theirs. Our conditions. They need us. No paper's made without the papermakers and the pulpmakers. We're essential.

There's some arses shifting on chairs with that one, and a grumble of agreement.

The Old Man's reading from one of the bits of paper from his stack.

This is what the managing director's been saying, just to let you know what we're up against. He told a whole conference of management wallahs, said if we don't change our labour market institutions and attitudes, the country'll go to the dogs. Said us unions are causing the highest level of disputes in the world, mind, in the world. Said us unions have got vested interest. Said we'd all do better if the laws were changed. He's the managing director of the company that's locking us out. Remember that.

There's a silence. Then a voice comes from someone on the

sideline, one of the blokes standing with his arms crossed and his fuck-me-first attitude.

What about the woman? he asks.

I peer over the heads of the blokes sitting down. I still can't recognise the bloke who asks. Dave's taking minutes and when he asks for the fulla's name, he just gets a mumble, like he doesn't want anyone to know. He's got another question.

Does she keep her job?

A bloke in the front row's muttering something to his neighbour, about his old lady complaining that he's on night shift with a woman all night.

Dunno what his old lady thinks they'll get up to. Pretty bloody uncomfortable in the smoko rooms of the Chem. Prep. The stink of sulphur and chlorine gets in everything, probably makes her you-know-what taste like pulp. Bugger that.

The Old Man waits again till the muttering stops.

Following procedures, comrade, that's what it's about, following procedures, he says. If they follow the agreed procedures and she wins the job, yes, she keeps it.

Not your fuckin' comrade, the bloke says.

There's a heap of noise then, chairs pushed around and muttering like a wave, a wave of what? Disapproval, I reckon. I bang on the table.

We keep the language clean, I say.

He leaves, whoever he is, pushes his way out past all the yellow coats and the crossed arms. No one tries to stop him, it's a free world and he doesn't have to be here. He doesn't get to hear the Old Man saying we won't let them dictate the conditions and he doesn't see us all nodding when the Old Man says we'll end this strike on our terms. He doesn't stay for the vote or even sign up for a paper. I ask around and no one seems to know who he is.

Then someone from D shift says he's a new bloke, just odd gang, doesn't know any better.

Another bloke says what're you on about, just odd gang? Doesn't matter what he is. He's been locked out like the rest of us.

It looks like a fight could start, there's a few fists being clenched and one fulla in the third row's pushing his chair back like he's ready to launch into it. Then Dave stands up. He's a good man, Dave, worth his weight in gold he is, he could stop a fight between two stags in full roar.

Hey, he says, hey, listen. Have a heart. He's got kids. Like all of you, he's got kids who need food on the table.

They're quieter now and Dave can talk through the muttering.

That bloke, he's just started here and he's pissed off about being on strike because he needs the money. He's got four kids, he says, and a mortgage to pay. He's all right, just needs the money.

Tell him we're all in this together, I say. Tell him we'll be back in a couple of weeks if we hold tight. Just a couple of weeks, that's all.

There's a lot of shuffling. Last time it was six weeks and the time before that. Six weeks is a long time with no pay packet. Solidarity, that's what we need, solidarity.

Then the Old Man's on his feet again.

We all know it's not about this one job, the old man says. This lassie. It's not about her. There was absolutely no mention of her in the letter you got. You all got that letter, a personal letter, addressed just to you, in your home letterbox. With the company demands. Personalised propaganda, I call it. We all know what the bosses want. They're trying to wear us down, putting the screws on, he says. Our stand is clear, he says, a job created is a job kept.

Yep, they're putting the screws on all right. To them it means more profit, to us it means fewer jobs—around two hundred, which means about a third of the blokes here today. Whatever the company says, it means fewer jobs. Solidarity. That's what we fuckin' need.

No votes to go back. Not one. Not even the blokes lined up against the wall. Solidarity. Next week there'll be no more pulp and no work for those still there. The company'll be stuffed then. If we hold out, we'll win, I know we'll win.

Some blokes are going fishing out at the coast and they don't look too unhappy about a bit of time off. They're the young fullas though. Other blokes are getting jobs done around the house, so there's lots of happy missuses in town right now, those who aren't in a snitch about a sheila on night shift.

After the meeting, when the blokes are all gone, the exec does its debrief. No cracks here. We're tight.

I ask the Old Man how the family is, whether they're getting a hard time, 'specially Miriama. He says it's not like last time, not yet. The musical's helping, what with rehearsals most nights, and it's pulling the kids together. I might join in, so I can keep an eye on the girl.

I don't let on about the reporter, the woman, not yet. I'm still checking her out. Great tits though.

Dave's the last one out. We walk over to the ute together 'cos I have to take him home, his missus dropped him off and took the car. He says she was going round to see that fulla's family, the fulla who walked out. She's taking some stuff round for the kids—clothes and old toys.

The mountain's still hiding under the cloud, but at least it's stopped bloody raining.

For the Old Man, I prescribe he reads *Atlas Shrugged* by Ayn Rand. He may not know it, but its working title was *The Strike*.

For the CEO, I prescribe he reads *Germinal* by Émile Zola. Come to think of it, so should the Old Man.

Chapter Eight

Stuart Duncan

Paul wheeled himself over to the window. The sun was catching the chrome on his right wheel. The white shirt I'd made him put on was clean and ironed but he hadn't buttoned the cuffs. He was squinting out at the cars in the car park.

"I think we need another line of attack," said Fred.

Fred was sprawled across the table. That man has to be at least six foot four; he towers over me. His hands are nearly half as big again as mine and when he slaps me on the back, I have to brace myself so he doesn't bowl me over. He'd brought along that insignificant little man who was supposed to be in charge of public relations.

"Helliwell, how would you gauge the effect of the open line?" I asked.

"Hopewell, Stan Hopewell's my name," he said. "You mean the company hotline? Well, I manned the phones last week, for a morning anyway. We got three calls."

"Only three?" I asked.

"We're averaging five or six a day," Stan said.

"That's not bad for a small community, Stuart," said Fred. "You have to remember this isn't the big city."

I nodded. Paul snorted. Maybe he was listening after all, not that I had any expectations.

"I'm assuming that if you're manning the phones, you aim to take charge of the calls?" Fred asked.

"That's the purpose, isn't it?" I said, "Maybe you'd better tell me, Stan. What do you see as the purpose of the hotline?"

"It's to answer people's questions, isn't it?"

"Look, Stan," Fred said. "We need to be getting the company perspective out, strongly. Don't you agree, Stuart? Whoever's on the phones needs to be taking charge of the call, as soon as it comes in."

I took in a breath, puffed out my cheeks. I wished I could use that breath to blow this fat, ineffectual little man out the door. The pause got longer. Fred leaned into my field of vision, talking softly.

"What about your boy, Stuart," he said. "What about a job for him?"

Paul kept looking out the window. Either he hadn't heard, or he was pretending he hadn't.

"Paul, what do you think?" I asked. "What about a couple of mornings answering the hotline?"

No answer. If I'd been at home I'd have made him answer, but I couldn't do that here. I looked back at Fred and shrugged my shoulders.

"Look, I think we need to intensify the message," I said. "The one about the effect of this strike on the whole town. I don't think the majority will tolerate another long stoppage."

Stan was just sitting there looking constipated. Fred, good old Fred, picked up the pass.

"Well, we've tried a personal letter," he said. "Maybe we need to make it more public by using the media more. How about an open letter in the local rag to the pulp and paper workers from the management?"

"Could fall flat. It might look too manipulative."

"No, not if it's done in the right framework."

Three years ago we set the agenda, after the last strike, when the same bloody union didn't buckle and the company nearly went to the wire. We had to keep on the same track, because if production didn't stabilise, the company would go bankrupt. That's what the reports said, all of them. At the last board meeting I'd attended before Paul's accident, we'd gone over the strategy again. The importance of open communication, being clear to the workers about where the company stood. We were heading back into trouble again and we had to keep steady and be as honest about the situation as possible. Fred had taken on board that same approach. We were on the same page.

"I need to go to the toilet," said Paul.

It was as if he'd pressed the pause button. Suddenly we were all looking at him.

"The toilet," he said. "Where is it?"

"Down the hall, young man," said Fred. "You might have to use the women's, there's more room. Not set up for, well, wheelchairs, but you should manage."

"I'm used to it," he said.

He wheeled himself over to the door. I couldn't read his face. He had that set look, the one he'd worn ever since we arrived, ever since the accident, actually. You know, it was that fat little Hopewell who was up off his chair, opening the door and it was the same little man who offered the first thing that had excited Paul all morning.

"I have a young nephew here at the moment, Paul," he said. "He's up in the computer suite, doing some work experience. How would you like him to show you round up there?"

"Computer suite?" Paul asked.

"Yes, most advanced in the Southern Hemisphere. I'm sure Crossley won't mind."

He shut the door behind himself and Paul. Fait accompli. I wasn't sure what to think.

"You may be pleasantly surprised," said Fred. My throat tightened. Fred pulled a pad of paper towards himself and put his head down.

"Right," I said. "The first concept we need to get across is that this is real, this is the last straw."

"Desperate," said Fred. "That's the word we need, desperate situation. It's the truth; we can't keep bleeding money, showing another loss when the wages here are almost twice the national average. Ridiculous."

"Right," I said. "Use words that will make it seem that we're all in it together."

"We. Our," said Fred. "Together we must protect our future. We must protect jobs of those working for us and those who depend on us."

"Yes, that's it," I said. "Those union renegades need to understand it's all of us. What management does, it does for the workers. Can you throw something together?"

Fred turned the page on the memo pad. I wondered where Paul was. I was about to suggest I just go and see when Fred was on to the next thing.

"Them," he said. "There's us and them. We, the workers and the company. Them, the union."

"Yes, yes," I said. "That'll do fine. Is that it, Fred? Are we finished?"

"Did you know they've completely rejected the job creation initiative we set up? My brainchild. Company put a considerable amount of money into it. Might have been when you were on leave, I think, Stuart."

Those grey days when I didn't leave Paul's bedside. Yes, it might have been then.

"None of them have come to any meetings to set up the new industrial park," said Fred. "Enterprises they could get work in when we do have to make them redundant. In fact, there are a number of things we could list that would emphasise the union as 'them' in relation to the company."

My stomach clenched. It seemed extreme to me to make one union feel so much like outsiders, to make them into pariahs. I've never liked divide-and-rule tactics.

"Is that what we want to do?" I asked.

"That's what they're doing. You know as well as I do that the Pulp and Paper Workers' Union is isolated in this mill. Other unions don't support them. They don't come to the joint meetings. Their president says he won't come to brainwashing sessions."

"Nothing's changed, has it?"

"They've dug their heels in even more. They're totally unreasonable."

Honesty and openness. That was the commitment of this management. I suppose I could think of it another way. If the pulp and paper workers wanted to act like truculent teenagers and isolate themselves, they could suffer the consequences. The company just had to be honest, open, and clear.

"I want it made very clear that the company is playing fair here," I said. "These words, Fred, weave them in: stability, efficiency, and ongoing production. That's what we're committed to. Without these the mill will die and there'll be no jobs. That's what's at risk."

And I wanted to know where my son was.

"You go," said Fred. "I'll stay here and finish this off. Stuart, you've got other pressures this time round. You're like an open book when it comes to that boy."

He got a lopsided smile before I was out the door and up the stairs.

There was a double door with touchpad locks. I stood outside and wondered what to do. I was peering through the glass; it was that bubbly safety glass with wire through it, so all I could see was a dark shape looming. I could hear a door clicking open, and the dark shape came closer. The second door clicked open and Stan was peering at me.

"Mr Grant rang, said you were coming," he said.

"Thanks, Hopewell. Good of you to bring Paul upstairs like this. Tell me, how did you get him up the stairs?"

"That was a bundle of laughs," he said. "Got a great sense of humour, has Paul. At one stage young Ray and I nearly let go of the wheelchair, we were laughing so much."

I should've been happy. I should've been pleased that he was laughing.

"So, he's had a good time?" I asked.

"Having. Any reason why he can't stay? He and Ray are getting on like a house on fire and Crossley's in his element. Not that I can follow what he's saying. It's all Greek to me."

"No, no reason why he has to leave. I'll just get back to work then. You'll let me know if he becomes a problem?"

But he had turned back into the room. The door clicked shut in my face.

Chapter Nine
Ray Parlane

Good Lord, that girl could sing, and since that bit of a giggle in the library, she didn't seem to mind it was me, the homo, she was meant to be in love with, apart from hissing at me that I was a dick if I thought she meant it. Miss Whatever-Her-Name-Is told Miriama to think about yearning for something, wanting something very, very badly, then put that longing into her role as Sandy. She sang those lines so well, the ones about being a fool sitting around waiting. Not a dry eye, as they say. Then when she got to the end of the song Miss Whatsit made her sing directly at me, looking into my eyes, the whole love scene/boy and girl falling in love. When she sang about hopeless devotion, she had her eyes all wide and brown and her lip was trembling. Honestly, she looked as if she really, really meant it. We were so engrossed that the spectators in the cheap seats hushed their giggling and actually clapped when we finished.

"Sandy," I said. "What a star."

"Oh, gee, thanks," she said.

"I'm walking you home," I said. "So you can practise being hopeless."

"Don't let it go to your head, Mister. Try anything on and I'm outta here."

"You're the one meant to be devoted, remember?"

She narrowed her eyes at me. If she brushed her hair sometimes, wore something other than a track suit and stopped screwing up her face as if she was trying to squint me out of existence …

"Come on then," she said.

We left the teacher with her bunch of keys and walked around past the library. There was no one in the town centre, not one person, just a cat getting into the rubbish bin. It chomped into a chicken bone and took no notice at all as we went past. Then we walked past the hotel which was a concrete pile built on a corner and next to it, what looked like a shed. There seemed to be people in there and shouting and I could hear a guitar.

"You know that song?" asked Miriama. "Don't suppose they sing it in Pommyland. It's famous here. 'Specially for the old fullas."

"Really? What's it called?"

"'Ten Guitars'. Mum said it was the first thing I heard when I was born. One of my cuzzies was playing it in the waiting room."

I could hear a few voices, very ragged, and very drunk. It certainly didn't sound like a song to welcome a newborn babe to me, but then, each to their own. In the corner of the bar, nearest the door, was someone I recognised. He was sitting by himself, and staring into his beer. Everyone was keeping a very wide berth. It was that plonker Miriama calls her second dad. I think his name was Leo.

The drain we went past was steaming. It made me think of Gotham City where Batman keeps the peace. It smelled foul, as if he'd left a villain in there to rot. Miriama saw me screw up my nose.

"It's just the geothermal," she said. "Town's built on it. Makes the swimming pool hot and it makes your silver jewellery go black."

"I left my silver spoon in London," I said, but she just looked at me as if I was very strange.

She pointed out the sports centre that looked like a big plane hangar sitting on steaming white sand and over further, she said, was a marae. For everyone, she said, even super Pākehā like me. I hadn't a clue what she was talking about but it felt like things had changed, and maybe there was some possibility …

We were headed down a street lined with houses, all with gardens, all small cottages, all of them separate from each other. This town was young but it also looked so temporary. The houses were all wooden and only one storey, with tin roofs that made them look more like sheds. There was a feeling of here today and gone tomorrow. Just up ahead there were lights spilling out from one of the houses and several cars pulled up on the lawn in front.

"How long've you lived here?" I asked.

"All my life," she said. "I was born here. In the maternity home, before it closed. It's just …"

Someone came out of the house up ahead, shouting.

"Don't you fucking …"

Before I knew it, Miriama was running, not away from the person yelling and waving something big and heavy, but towards him. I didn't know what to do, run after her or run the other way. I was frozen, staring at a man yelling and swinging what seemed to be a baseball bat. It was the bat hitting the windscreen of one of the cars that unfroze me. The noise. Like an explosion. And glass arching up in the light from the front door. Then the bat was raised again and smashed down on the car roof over and over. Each time it came back up into the air to get more lethal and down to break and dent and destroy. Miriama was almost in range of it. My feet did it before my brain was engaged, carried me forward to get to that space between her and the bat, to dive in and pull her down to the ground out of its reach. We went head over heels but she wouldn't stay there, not pinned down by me. Hard as I hung on, it was like trying to hold down a rabid dog and she was up again, scrambling to her feet and throwing herself forward, right in line with the destruction. Next time I dived on her, I got two in one. She'd tackled the berserker and all three of us were rolling round on the ground. I grabbed the bat out of his hand.

"Fuck off, fuck off."

He was sobbing and the fight had gone out of him.

By the time the police car arrived, he was sitting with his head in his hands on the doorstep. Miriama had her arm around him and it was me who sent the policeman into the house. I could hear them inside. There was a little nipper wailing as if it would never stop and a woman trying to talk through her sobbing. The police-man knew what to do; he disappeared into the heart of the house and, bit by bit, calmed the residents down.

I still had the baseball bat. It was heavy and the wood was splintered on one side. I tossed it from one hand to the other, not sure where I should be and what I should be doing. Miriama finally looked up from her huddle with the crumpled man on the step.

"Put the bloody thing down," she said.

She patted the step next to her. I put the bloody thing down, except, thank God, it wasn't bloody and it so easily could have been. I couldn't sit down next to her; I was too stirred up. I left her talking and walked out to the road and back again, then I leant on the car until some more glass fell out of the windscreen and I had to brush it off my coat.

Finally the police officer came out again.

"Thanks, you two," he said. "It's under control. Get yourselves home."

He took the man by the arm and pulled him inside. Miriama looked as if she wanted to follow them, but decided better of it and turned back to me.

We didn't say anything, either of us. There was just the sound of our feet crunching on the glass. She was up ahead of me, stepping back onto the footpath. I followed her. She stood in a circle of light from a street lamp and the light caught the bits of glass tangled in her hair. Just outside of the orange glare there was a bench. Miriama collapsed on it, pulled up her knees and hugged them. Her head was down and her hair was a messy curtain that drooped over her shoulders and face. She was right in the middle of the seat so I didn't have any option but to sit down close to her.

The police car turned on the road in front of us. There was just the driver; he'd taken no prisoners. His headlights caught someone standing against the hedge. He was hard to see because he was wearing black. He put one hand up to shield his eyes and pushed his body further into the hedge. Just for a second I thought he might be a spy all in black, but he was probably just someone walking home who didn't want to get involved.

As the sound of the exhaust faded, I could hear it. She was crying. I moved up closer and put an arm around her, just gently, but she lashed out, one arm shoving me sideways.

"Fuck off," she yelled. "Just fuck off."

I could. I could just fuck off and leave her here huddled up on the seat by herself with a man hiding in the hedge over the road. I could be a total git and just piss off. But I didn't. I knew what to do with a sobbing woman; I had Liz for a mother. You just sit by her and say nothing. You don't say "It'll be all right," or "Don't cry," not in these trousers you don't. You just shut up and after a while you sit a bit closer and she'll lean on your shoulder and you hope your shoulder won't get too much snot on it. Then you stroke the hair away and find a handkerchief to lend. That's what you do.

When I got through the mess of hair she didn't see the handkerchief, but used her sleeve.

"You all right?" I asked.

"Nearly," she said.

I offered the handkerchief again and she used it.

"Ae," she said. "Look at all that hūpē. How do we make so much snot?"

"Do you want to talk?"

Silence. Then …

"He's just new here, that fulla. He and his missus came here from up the coast. Bought a house, he said. Thought he'd make good money for him and his missus and for his kids, four of them. Three little girls and a new baby, a boy. Her mother's staying with them to help with the new baby."

She took a big shuddery breath and blew her nose again.

"His mother-in-law. It was her who was going on about him not working. Called him lazy. Not his fault he's on strike. Got no money for groceries any more. Can't pay the mortgage on the house. He just lost it."

"Do you know him?"

"Nah, just know he's union. Works on the paper machine. Odd gang."

"You don't even know him but you ran to get the bat, to stop him. Why didn't you just call the police?"

"Why shouldn't I stop him? I care about this town. You don't know. You've only been here five minutes. This is a good town. Us kids all learnt to swim in the river. You been to the river? It's deep, and cold, and green. Green like pounamu. We swim in it all summer, piles of us kids. And the mountain, we run up the mountain every year, you must've seen that one. The mountain, it looks after us. If you keep very still, right now, you'll feel its wairua."

"Its what?"

"Its wairua. Its spirit. You know."

I didn't. But I didn't know what else to ask.

"Is that what you were thinking about? When you sang to me in the rehearsal?"

"What? Yeah. About how I wish they'd stop all the raroraro. With the strikes, I mean, all the arguments. It's hard for us here. You don't know about them either. Last time there was a big strike, our phone, every time you picked it up, it went click. It's doing that now. Going click."

"So? What do you mean?"

"Someone's tapping it, listening in. Listening to my mum ring up to ask her friend to come round for a cuppa. Listening to me talk to my mates. We give them lots of swear words to listen to. And last time? There was people ringing Mum up saying they'd followed me and knew where I went, and that they'd keep watching."

There seemed to be someone watching now, over the other side of the road. He was squashing himself into the hedge, or maybe he was just walking home and he had stopped for some reason. Seemed daft to me, to think he was watching me and a crying Miriama.

"What for? Why do they want to watch you?"

"Don't you get it, dumb-arse? My old man's the president of the Pulp and Paper Workers' Union. He gets called "pinko" and "militant". Some people in this town hate him."

"But the strike will be over soon, won't it?"

"You don't know my old man and you don't know Leo. They're staunch. They won't give in."

I remembered a conversation with Mr Hopewell. He used those words, pinko and militant, exactly the same words when he was telling me about the strike. The big boss man who stood up in the cafeteria, he called it a strike syndrome. The people I had morning tea with this morning would think I was consorting with the enemy. Miriama seemed to have had enough talking anyway. She pulled her hair back from her face.

"Do you want your snot rag?" she asked.

"No, you keep it."

I had to start somewhere. I had to do what I really came here for, and Miriama said she'd lived here all her life. It was maybe not the best timing so I tried to sound like it didn't really matter.

"Miriama," I said. "I'm looking for someone who might have lived here a long time. It's a man. He was here before you were born and he's still here."

"That's a lot of fullas," she said.

"Yes, the other thing I know about him is that he's got a nickname. He used to be called Kiwi Keith when he was young, when he lived in the States."

"What's he done, this fulla? Stole your silver spoon?"

I knew I would tell her, but just then, at that moment, I stood up and held out my hand. She took it straight away and she didn't let go, all the way down the dark road.

Chapter Ten
Ima Williams

I was sitting in the library turning the half-a-dozen pages of the local paper, trying not to keep looking at the door. Why that man held such an attraction for me, I had no idea and why I should think he might come in the library just because I was there made no sense. It was familiar, horribly familiar. I had to think about something else. That was when I saw the article about a meeting at the local marae. Women were getting together "to discuss how they could best cope with family friction arising from lack of money, food shortages and strike stress". The item was on the front page, and the expectation was that the strike would go on for a long time. If I could get into that meeting, it certainly would help in my research.

So I was waiting by a sort of gate, stamping my feet, pulling my collar up to my ears. Notta had told me to stop wearing the leather coat and high-heeled boots, to try and blend in more, which was what I was trying to do, except my track pants and top were matching royal blue velveteen and I hadn't left my coat behind either. It was far too cold. The air held a stink that reminded me of cooked egg yolk or sewage or leaking drains.

There were only the two of us, me and a young woman who looked about sixteen. Her track pants were muddy.

"What's that smell?" I asked.

"What smell? Oh, you mean Sulphur Hill, over there," she said, pointing.

"Does it always smell like that?"

"Yup. Are you waiting for someone?"

"For the meeting. Is it OK for me to come to your meeting?"

"Dunno, I'm waiting for my mum. Who are you?"

"Ima Williams."

"If you're a Williams, does that mean you're related to Miss Williams who's our librarian?"

"Yes, she's my sister. I'm staying with her."

"Well, you can come to our meeting. Your sister's my boss at the library."

I pulled out a cigarette and wondered if I should offer one to the girl or if I would get into trouble with her mother.

It was just on dark. There was a house with some carvings on it inside the gate and several other buildings in a sort of semi-circle. One of them looked like a school prefab and it was the lights from this building that were spilling out towards us. People inside were setting up chairs. Somehow it looked warmer in there. I hoped so.

I was about to light my cigarette when a battered utility stopped on the other side of the car park. He was driving. I knew it before I saw him; he was sending out a magnetic field that pulled me in. The blood rushed round in me like it was trying to find a way out. I was about to walk over, my feet seemed to think I needed to anyway, when a woman got out of the passenger seat and, as she walked towards us, the old ute drove off. He couldn't have seen me; he'd have indicated if he had, waved out at least. That girl, the one I'd been standing next to, said something to the woman coming towards us. I didn't catch it, but then she was talking to me and the woman was right there in front of us and I had to stop staring after the tail pipe. The woman looked like an older version of the girl, and her tracksuit pants were muddy too. Fashion was not a primary concern for the women in this town.

"This is my mum," said the girl.

"Kia ora," said the woman, and shook my hand.

"She wants to come to the meeting, Mum."

"She's the cat's aunty. Where's your manners, Mirlama?"

"Oh, sorry," I said. "Ima Williams. My sister is your librarian."

"I'm a McLay. My name's Stella, pleased to meet you. Why do you want to come to our meeting?"

"I mean my name is Ima, Ima Williams and I'm a journalist. I want to write about the strike and how the women cope with it."

"Ah, we'll ask," she said.

The circle of chairs was mostly full. It was a mix of ages, and they were all Māori except me. Stella patted a chair for me to sit down, then she and Miriama took up positions either side of me. Maybe so that they could march me out if the meeting said no. Notta had been pretty upset that I was a stranger coming into the town to write something for my own glory, as she so tactfully put it. I hoped they wouldn't think the same. There must have been about thirty women sitting in the room and it was gold for me, pure gold.

The chairwoman was an older woman. She was dressed in black, with a black woolen hat pulled down so that her curly grey hair stuck out at the sides.

"Kia ora," she said. "The wāhine of the town, good to see so many of you."

She nodded around the room. Everyone seemed to be waiting for her to say something else.

"We have a visitor. Kia ora, my name is Freda. We always start with karakia. That means a prayer, dear."

I bowed my head with everyone else and let the words wash over me. It was in Māori and I didn't understand it anyway. I let my eyes slide sideways to take in the room. There was a big artwork done with spray cans, with a monster coiled up and coming out of the paper at me. On the wall nearest me there was some scrappy writing on a piece of paper pinned up:

> *Hōhā*—feeling bad being bad or bored like in Maths when you
> can't do it you feel hōhā and when you cheek the teacher
> you're being hōhā

Whakamā—shamed, too shy means you gone white
Pukuriri—mad in your belly like Dad when I'm being hōhā
Raroraro—argument like when you're yelling and your
    brother's yelling and maybe you hit each other
Whānau—family. All those aunties and uncles and cuzzies
    and Mum and Dad
Whakawhānaungatanga—what Nan keeps trying to do, make
    us stop fighting and get along like we're a real whānau
Karakia—prayers that go on and on and on and on

Someone had left their Māori language homework behind.

The interminable prayers had finished. I was first on the agenda. Stella asked the meeting whether I could listen and write about what I heard and, to my surprise, they welcomed me. I pulled out my notebook.

Yes, they said, they wanted their story told, about how hard it was for families to support a strike, how they had to stretch the budget and how the kids got sick of not being able to do things because there was no money. And how people moved away because they couldn't be sure there wouldn't be another strike.

"I'd also like to talk to the woman who was the catalyst for this strike," I said.

"That bitch," came a voice from the other side of the circle.

"Hey, hold your tongue, Mere," said Freda.

"But she is, she just wants to get her claws into our men."

"Be careful, rubbish mouth," another woman said. "She's my whānau, that woman."

"Well, tell her to keep her dirty hands off our men. Why else would she want to work shift? No one in their right mind wants to work shift."

"Might be she likes the money, like the fullas in your whānau."

It looked promising, a split between the wives of the town over a woman working with their men, a real human interest side to the story. A grumbling passed around the room, some of it in Māori,

66

none of it approving. The woman over the other side of the circle from me crossed her arms. The old woman sitting next to Miriama banged her stick on the floor.

"Taihoa," said Stella. "Stop your fighting. We need to stick together, support each other. It's not about this one or that one, it's about everyone."

Another murmur went around the room.

"So how can we do that?" asked Freda. And the ideas come in from the women.

"Food."

"Send those useless men out hunting."

"And fishing."

"Yeah, send those useless men out fishing to catch some fish, not just sink a few beers together."

"And anyone with stuff in their gardens."

"Bugger all at the moment, just got silverbeet myself."

The woman Mere, who was called rubbish mouth, got excited. She might be rubbish mouth, she had no teeth.

"Hey, make my famous boil-up," she said. "You know, silverbeet if you got it, pūhā's better and there's lots up in the empty paddock by the dog pound, get some watercress from down by Ward Street, put in the pork bones, maybe carrot and spuds. Put in the dough-boys, fills the kids up, the doughboys."

"Have to boil it a long time for you to eat it."

The laughter took a while to die down. These women knew how to stick together.

"So we know how to do it then," said Freda. "Anything else?"

There was a pause. They were capable and they had prior experience of doing this. I could maybe include a section on recipes in the article, "How to Feed a Family on Not Very Much". The ideas started again.

"Would help if we knew what was going on."

"Yeah, my old man won't tell me what happens in the meetings."

"Nah, me either. He says it's union business."

"Mine is just hōhā about the whole thing. Says he doesn't want to talk about it."

So the meeting decided to encourage their men to tell them what's going on. And the women whose men would talk would tell the others. It seemed to me the men didn't have a chance; these women would make sure they didn't keep their male club exclusive. Another headline popped into my head—"Women Break Down the Male Bastion Called Union".

Gold, pure gold.

The meeting came to a close with another prayer and an agreement to hold more, at which I was welcome. Best of all, I got a phone number for Sally Wihongi, the woman who started it all.

I could smell it again as I came out of the meeting. Pungent. What was it? Not sewage, not drains, not egg yolk. No, it was the smell when you first light a match, before the flame takes. It was the smell of brimstone.

She did it again, came home on her old bike, all dressed in black. Her squeaky brakes brought her up the drive and she still had her balaclava on when she came inside.

"Business to attend to again, Notta?" I asked.

No reply. She was puffing a bit as she pulled off her jacket. At least I'd had the heater on and the kitchen was warm.

"How was your meeting?" she said.

"At the marae? Very interesting. They want me to tell their story. The women, I mean. About how hard it is when your man is on strike and there's no money coming in."

"Good. Very good."

"And I've got a phone number for Sally Wihongi. The woman who started it all."

"It's not about her. Haven't you worked it out yet? It's got nothing to do with her."

"Well, she was the start of it."

"Anything could have been. Don't you get it? They were looking for an excuse. I gather our Leo hasn't made good on his promise of helping you with the story?"

Notta was looking at me over her glasses. When I didn't answer, she sucked her breath in through her front teeth and sighed, as if she was carrying some big secret that I didn't have a handle on. I didn't want to jump to her bait and let her get the upper hand; it was so irritating when she tried to be superior. I lit a cigarette and kept my voice casual.

"Haven't seen him."

"Not surprised. Haven't seen this either, I suppose."

She pulled a slim newspaper out of her jacket pocket. It was so slim I wouldn't really call it a newspaper. It was the local rag. She opened it up and there was a full-page spread. "An Open Letter to Pulp and Paper Workers". I skimmed it. It said the dispute could have been settled using the correct procedures instead of triggering a full stoppage. That was my understanding; I couldn't see a problem with that. But I also understood that the dispute was about the new appointee, one Sally Wihongi.

"Read on, Ima," Notta said, pointing one semi-naked finger at the page. The fingerless gloves were scruffy, and her fingernails bitten. "See 'new technology, reduction in costs', and especially this one 'correction of serious overmanning'."

"Well, that doesn't seem to have much to do with employing a woman, I suppose. Sounds to me that all they want is modernisation," I said. "Technology. What's wrong with that? Reduction in costs."

"By getting rid of jobs," said Notta. "That's what this is about. Jobs, Ima, jobs that are held by people."

"And this is different to any other company? They all want to make money. They have to, to pay the people who have the jobs."

"Yes, they want to make money, to pay the shareholders more, not the workers. And to cover the losses from making their tinpot corporation. You have put that bit of the puzzle together, haven't you? They're expanding the interests they've got, buying up other companies, lots of them. They need the money for expansion, not to pay the workers."

I hated it when she caught me out like this. She was right, that was the problem. I hadn't done the background research on the company and I couldn't see how I could do it now. I'd lost all credibility with my old journo mates so I couldn't ask them and I'd lose too much face if I went to the library to do it.

She was pointing to an advertisement in the local rag.

"Did you know they've set up a hotline? The company I mean? Try ringing it in the morning. Those workers built this company. Try listening to what the company is telling them now."

"Dispute hotline? That's what you mean?"

"Yes. Manned by company clones. Give it a go, Ima. You might learn something."

She was out of the room, probably while she had the upper hand. I could hear her in the bathroom as I stared down at the paper in front of me.

"Dispute Hotline: this hotline will be manned from 8am to 5pm weekdays."

I decided to try it the next day and to ask about the woman. The one who couldn't get a job.

"Good morning, this is the Dispute Hotline. How can I help you?"

"I'm a reporter," I said. "I'm researching an article about the strike. I want to ask a few questions about the reasons for the current dispute. I understand it's about the employment of a woman, one Sally Wihongi."

The heroine of my piece for *Broadsheet*. The staunch feminist who stood up to the patriarchy.

And Notta was right. The answer, delivered in a pleasant, friendly voice, was that this appointment was the trigger for the walkout, but not the cause. And that this was the twenty-third in a year. Twenty-three walkouts in a year. No wonder the company was putting its foot down.

"And the corrections in overmanning. Isn't this just putting people, men I mean, out of work?"

"It is envisaged by management that some people will move away, some will retire, and the company will offer retraining for those interested. No one will miss out. You do know that all of the unions have agreed to this proposal, except the pulp and paper workers."

The pulp and paper workers. They were the fly in the ointment, the spanner in the works, the horseshoe nail that could lose the kingdom.

I was reassured that the mill would not close. Neither management nor the government would let it, but it had to be a reliable supplier. Without strikes.

In other words: we, the company, will not be moved.

Ironic. I knew a song by that name, and it seemed to me the union was singing it loud and strong, too. It was just that the management and the union were not singing from the same song sheet.

The BMW had been sitting in the driveway for several days. I moved it from the road, fearing for its safety, fearing that young punk might come back with a coin and tear its beautiful red shiny coat. I slammed the door shut. I'd go for a drive, a fast drive, so I could think.

At the intersection near the supermarket there seemed to be a disagreement going on. I slowed down to see because a reporter never misses an opportunity for getting a story. There was a ring of people and somewhere in the middle was a fight. As far as I could tell it was still mostly verbal; there certainly seemed to be a lot of shouting. I wound down the window and leaned across the passenger seat to try and work out what was happening, but there was just a muddle of noise and that smell, the sulphur smell that was a signature for this town. I was about to get out when someone broke away from the fracas. It was Leo and he elbowed his way out of the circle and headed over to me. Before I could respond, he had the passenger door open and was in the car.

"Get me out of here," he ordered.

"Yes sir, certainly sir, anything you say, sir."

I piled on the sarcasm. There didn't seem to be an angry mob chasing him, just one man trying and the others holding him back. Leo was staring out the window. I wasn't even sure he'd registered who I was. His eyes were wild and his hair, usually tied back in a ponytail, was hanging like a curtain over his broken nose, which had a faint track of blood coming from it. He wiped one hand past his bleeding nose.

"Well, come on. What are you waiting for?"

"Ever heard of please?"

"Ever heard of mob lynching?"

The adrenaline must have been catching. I flattened my foot and we roared away from the kerb. We were heading out along the straight that leaves the town. I didn't have any directions from my passenger so I was just keeping to my initial plan, driving fast on the long straight roads that stretched my car and my mind. He was a tense black mass in the seat next to me.

"Put your safety belt on," I said.

We were passing the mill, one tall chimney leaking smoke, the others sitting against the clouds like broken teeth with nothing to chew. The big heap of golden wood chips, food for the ravenous digester, just sat there, inert and rotting, not even a trickle of new chips adding to its bulk. I put my foot down and the speedo sneaked up and up.

"Jesus, woman! Slow down!" he yelled. "You'll bloody kill us!"

I took no notice. We were coming to the railway crossing anyway so I had to slow down, but not because he said so.

"Turn off here. This is where I live."

"Glad the taxi could be of service, sir."

The gate sat open and a bumpy drive took my low-slung red baby lurching up past an old hedge, so overgrown that I couldn't see any buildings until the driveway took us into its shelter, an old farmhouse, with peeling paint and a decrepit sofa on its verandah.

"Come in," he said as he got out of the car.

He was halfway up the steps to the front door before I could answer, so I did as he'd ordered. He not only didn't lock his door, he didn't bother to close it. I couldn't see him by the time I got up the steps to the verandah. One of the boards creaked as if it was going to collapse under my weight. I waited at the front door, unsure what to do next.

"Don't just stand there," he called. "I said come in."

"Certainly, sir," I muttered.

The voice came from a room at the end of the passageway so I went on in. He was at the sink, rinsing some glasses. An ancient sink, deep and square and cracked: original, I would think. The kitchen cupboards were in that shade of mouldy green that was used in old farmhouses. The only chairs were at the kitchen table and I startled a cat from its sleep when I pulled one out. The cat took one look at my long black coat and sprinted for the hallway.

"Don't mind her," he said. "She's called Homehelp. Keeps the rats and mice down. You'll have a whiskey, won't you?"

Before I could reply there was a glass in front of me and he was pouring whiskey into it. Good whiskey—even if it was Irish.

"Your heritage?" I asked.

"What? The whiskey you mean? Once. On my mother's side. Don't know how you say it in Irish, but good health."

We clinked glasses and he took a very large gulp of his. I usually have a bit of water with mine but somehow that seemed weak so I took a sizeable sip myself. He was calm now, and he smiled.

"I need you," he said.

I was back there again, in that place where the bloody cells in my body were straining towards him. What a cliché, I had the banging heart and, if my palms weren't so sweaty, I would've reached out and grabbed his hand with the calloused, thick fingers. I wanted to grab more than his hand. I wanted to feel the muscles of his back tense and his breath hot and his stringy hair in my mouth. Jesus, what was the matter with me?

But he'd torn his eyes away. Or, at least, he'd looked down at his whiskey. The heat settled.

"I mean, I need you to tell our story. Why we're holding the line, keeping the faith, as it were. We need a champion in the press. Will you be it?"

With the heat of the whiskey in my belly (no, not the heat of the whiskey, the heat of lust) I was likely to say yes, rapidly. My hormones talking, certainly not my head. My head was having a hard time. "Never prostitute your vocation!" I could hear it. The bald bloke with big glasses who taught us ethics in journalism school. "Your job is to find out the facts, and report them. Not to take sides!"

No, not to take sides. But I was tempted, so tempted.

"I'll do my best to be fair," I said. "To be balanced. To tell all sides of the story ..."

He had that look again, the one that felt as if it was removing every stitch of clothing I was wearing. I took a long sip of the whiskey, just so I could have the glass between him and me.

"Fuck," he said. "Suppose that's all I can ask."

Fuck, I want one, is what I heard. What I said was, "So tell me what was going on by the supermarket, before you threw yourself at my mercy."

"That? That was personal. Nothing to do with the strike. Old stuff. He thinks I was the reason his old lady left him. Had nothing to do with me."

He leaned over to refill my glass and his own. The table was not very wide and he stayed leaning on his elbows.

"I need you," he said, and I knew he didn't mean my profession. It wasn't until later that I wondered if this was what prostituting my vocation meant.

Chapter Eleven

Leo Harris

She's a great lay. Tits like that, you can bury your head. Christ, we were at it for hours. I told her in no uncertain terms: no hooks, no ties, no promises. I don't do promises.

I've got that ache in the balls, a satisfied ache, and a sore dick. And Dave must've had boil-up for tea last night, that's what you get for marrying a Māori sheila, stink farts. This must be the fiftieth time we've had to wind the windows down. At least I don't have to drive. This crappy old Cortina's not a patch on her BMW. Roars off when you put your boot down, just like her.

Pat tells us to take the next turnoff and Dave, who drives like an old lady, puts his blinker on, checks his rear vision mirror and grumbles about how much he hates driving in the Big Smoke. Pat says it's a piece of cake when you get your head around it. Poor bastard has to come up all the time, he's got kids at boarding school up here. I hate it. Place just has bad karma for me. Some places are like that, for certain reasons you just don't ever want to go back there.

Dave's getting all anxious about where to park and when I say somewhere far away from your arse, he gets all hōhā because he reckons I'm distracting him. And it was him who wanted us to bring a few to sink in the car. Reckon we'd've wound up in Wellington if he'd had a beer or five in him, or else we'd be upside down in a ditch. Lucky the Old Man put his foot down, said we needed to play this one straight.

I remind them what the Old Man said about sticking to the same points, you know, wear them down with solidarity. Then Dave asks how come the old bastard didn't just come, is he getting too old for this caper? Hope I'm not hearing a takeover, I say. Hope you're not thinking of filling his shoes, because they're fuckin' big ones. Dave just laughs. The thought of him up there doing the big speech stuff, trying to keep order like the Old Man does, makes me laugh too.

More seriously though, the Old Man didn't come because he knows if he does, it'll get personal. He's a strategic thinker, knows when to be in the front line and when to be the back room sergeant. That's why he's the president.

We're lucky, we find a park right outside the Trade Union Hall. What a decrepit old place, looks like no one's been near it with a paintbrush for years. A good advertisement, I suppose, for the care taken of the working man in this country these days.

We're the last ones to arrive. Everyone's sitting on those hard chairs they use to keep our working-class arses calloused. All in a circle like a boy scout camp with just an empty space in the middle. If they were gonna put us in a circle, they could at least have put a red flag in the middle. Not even anything on the walls, Christ, we could've been in a corporate boardroom, except it would've been in better nick, and there would've been leather cushions on the seats.

The rest of them are looking none too shit-hot. They've all got their suits on, the ones they bring out for funerals, and long faces like they've just been to one. Of course, me and the boys are in our working greens. After all, we should be at work, if we hadn't been fuckin' locked out. It shows up those pansies in suits though, arse-lickers the lot of them. They've even sent that cocky bastard, the one who tried to take me out yesterday, before my maiden in her red BMW came to the rescue. How personal can you make it? I should thank him, actually.

I do a head count. Twenty-eight, plus us three. There's at least two from each union, and the engineers brought in extra, fair enough, they're a big union, but I don't know why the carpenters had to bring one more—maybe just so they could fit that cocky bastard in to give me a hard time.

We go round and shake hands. They'll never be able to say that the pulp and paper workers aren't civil. Cocky bastard won't look me in the eye. He's turned his chair round so he can hide behind the backrest. He dangles his hand out for a limp faggot of a handshake, pulls it back like he's scared I might kiss it. Stupid prick.

Jim creeps in. President of the Federation of Labour. He's leaning on a stick, his suit needs someone else in there with him to fill it up. He looks like he should be in a geriatric home. The exec all agreed we don't want him involved; not him, and not his sidekick, once-used-to-be-Red Ken. Jim's sitting down, getting his creaky old bones on a softer chair than we've got. Once he would've refused it, said he'd have a hard chair like us. Once Jim knew his arse had pants on it because his old man had a job and once Red Ken knew what it meant to go short when the wage packet was thin. Not anymore. Fat union cats, meddling where they're not wanted. Remember Fintan Walsh, I want to yell. We know what we're fighting for.

Jim brings the meeting to order. Not that we were hanging off the ceiling anyway. When you live with the same fullas you work with, you usually talk about work. And now, well, we don't have any, and soon they won't, not if the lockout extends to them.

The meeting starts and we say our bit; how we don't want to lose the expertise and the safety that this affords, how we don't want to lose jobs and livelihood, how the company is out to smash us. I start in on the political climate, about how the Labour Government has sold the working man down the corporate creek and how the management is hand in glove with the Business Roundtable. Christ, one or more of them are on the board of directors for the company. But I'm told to shut up. Shut up by a point of order because I'm off the subject. Fuckin' idiots. Can't they see any further than their noses?

Then the other unions have a go. Some are okay, civil, they actually recognise how much the pulp and paper workers have helped to fatten their pay packets. They say how they appreciate the strict relativity we insist on, which means every time we fight for a pay rise, it washes over on them. Solidarity. Good. Singing from the same hymn sheet, as the Old Man says.

But there are mutterings. In the right corner, we bring you some stupid bastard with a gripe, spoiling for a fight. Guess who? Yup, the weak point in the solidarity dam. Fuckin' chippies. The Carpenters' Union's not even a very big one, but once they start, they take others with them.

Last time you fullas kept your long necks stuck out, we all had to pull ours in, the head honcho of the Chippies' Union says. All of us. We could see the writing on the wall then and it hasn't changed.

You mean you fuckin' gave in, I say. Couldn't see the wall, let alone the writing the company was putting on it, could you? Didn't think further than your next pay packet.

Hey, hold on, says the chippies' second rep. You fullas kept us out for weeks. Saying you wouldn't give in to the company demands. Maybe some of us are just realistic, we know that the company will have to modernise.

Yeah, I say, and you carpenters know you can all get jobs over at the new enterprise park that just happens to have been set up after the last strike, know you can get contract work with the mill and outside contracts, build houses and stuff. Pulp and paper workers make pulp and paper and no one else wants it except a pulp and paper mill.

Then cocky bastard pipes up. Seems to me that smacks of self-interest, he says. Seems to me some people can't think past their cocks, he says. Seems to me.

I see red. There may not be a red flag anywhere in the room, but I've got one all of my own and I go for him. Stupid prick just leans back on his chair and brings it up in the air. Dave and Pat grab me and sit me down again. I have to unclench my hands, drop my shoulders, breathe and light a fag. I don't look at the bastard again.

Then we start. One hour. Two hours. Three hours. Four and a half hours of meeting. Back and forward it goes. We hold that a job created is a job kept. That's the worst thing about this whole deal, that the company has free reign with "manning", as they call it. That this means loss of jobs. And we say it over and over and fuckin' over.

What do we get by the end of the day? Fuckin' old Jim Knox will come down to talk to management. He seems to think they might be open to negotiation. Jesus, is he going senile or something? Man, we're bitchy on the way home. It's hard enough being out on a limb in the town, without having a patsy like Jim Knox thinking he's on our side.

Dave says just because we lost the battle, it doesn't mean we've lost the war.

Chapter Twelve
Miriama McLay

Ho, that night the stars were so cool, big and bright, like they wanted to jump down and land on your head, turn you into a real star. No moon, so that made the sky look like a lake of lights, all knowing where they fit, all happy with being next to each other, all shining as hard as they could. Clean, clear, no arguments, no stuff.

Just before we left the lights outside the supermarket, Ray suddenly started to walk funny. He was walking along with real tiny steps and his hips swinging, like he was wearing stilettos. He put up one hand and held it out to me like I should kiss it. I cracked up. Then he raised his eyebrows real high and made his lips look all pouty.

"Like this?" he said.

"Fuck no," I said. "You look like a super Pākehā super homo."

"Sorry," he said. "Wrong show. Forgot I was doing *Grease*, thought I was being Ziggy Stardust. What about this?"

He made his legs go all loose and his body move from side to side like he'd been riding a horse and his bum hurt. Then he slid his jacket down his shoulders a bit, pulled his collar up and pushed his hair back. Styley.

"Oh, Danny," I said. "Go Greased Lightning."

He swung me round. He was real skinny, but he was strong. He didn't push it, just put one arm round my shoulder and we walked across the road to the park.

"Such a good rehearsal," he said.

"Yeah, real good," I said. He was all right, this super Pākehā. He smelled a bit salty, from the sweat from dancing. He was good. He wasn't all whakamā like the other stupid pricks. They just sort of shuffled around, but Ray was all over the place, swinging his hips around and doing a real workout. He didn't even care when they looked at him as if he was funny, funny peculiar I mean, not funny haha. But he was so good they even clapped, after I'd given them the evils, that is. Ray said he danced a lot in the shows he done in London.

"How come you got called Raymond?" I asked.

He didn't answer for a while.

"Can I tell you a secret?" he asked. "You're not allowed to laugh. Do you promise?"

"I promise."

"Cross your heart?"

"Cross my heart."

"It's not Raymond. It's Rainbow."

"Yeah, well. I got a cousin called Ūenuku. Means Rainbow. You can guess what the weather was when he was born. How come you got called that?"

"My mother was living in the United States. I was born in California and she was a hippie. Still is, actually."

"You were born in the States? Choice. You don't sound like a yank. You been to Disneyland?"

"No. Just music festivals and things called happenings apparently, but I can't remember."

"Too stoned, eh?"

He'd gone quiet. Maybe he was a bit hōhā.

"What about your dad?"

I could feel him get a bit stiff, like I'd said something I shouldn't. He took his arm away from my shoulder, put his hands in his pockets and kicked a stone from the path.

"You don't have to tell me," I said.

"I never knew him because Liz, well, she always maintained I don't need to know."

"You call your mother Liz?"

"Yes, I do. She's a hippie and she's never liked me calling her mum."

I've seen hippies. Long hair and don't wash much. They come down this way to grow dope in the bush. Me and my mates had our suppliers but there were some too stoned to bother with. Leo was a kind of hippie but he kept going on at me not to smoke, even if he did. But he was like that. Ray didn't seem like a hippie. No way. Maybe he's like his father.

"You got to know your whakapapa," I said. "You got to know who your ancestors are, otherwise how do you know who you are?"

"Well, Stan and Harry have been like fathers to me."

"Like Leo is to me? Whāngai? Like a family, but you're not related?"

We started walking again, but this time he didn't put his arm back. I missed it.

"I suppose so. Liz moved back to England when I was about seven because of some poser who said he'd look after her. We lived in a squat, abandoned houses that people just took over. Most of them were hippies like Liz. Then my grandparents paid for me to go to boarding school because they didn't want me round those Bonnington Square types or round Liz too much. They especially didn't like Stan and Harry, they're Liz's neighbours."

"Why didn't they like, what was their names? Stan and Harry."

"Because, Miss Miriama, they're gay."

It was not cool to be gay. In this town you got called an arse-prodder and a shirt-lifter. We had a gay teacher once but he was only here for one term, because one of the parents said he was giving his son the wrong idea and anyway he might just, you know. I was only ten, so I didn't know. The teacher left. Even if Ray acted like a homo, doing that kind of funny walk and the flappy hands, he was still cool. Maybe he really was one but I hoped not.

"So you lived in a boarding school?" I asked.

"Only during the week. I caught the train to Liz's most weekends, and to my grandparents' other weekends and one night during the week."

So that was why he was so Pommy and why he did stuff like try and shake my hand. He was from a boarding school and he had rich grandparents. That would be so cool.

"That night, when that fulla was bashing his car? You asked me about a man who lived in this town."

"Yes. That's the only clue Liz would give me. My father lived here, maybe still does. And he was called Kiwi Keith when he was in California."

"So that's why you're here?"

"Yes, Miss Sherlock, that's why I'm here."

"I'll help you," I said.

I looked at him and he was blinking a lot, like he got tears. I don't mind tears. That's a Pākehā thing, not wanting to cry, not a Māori thing. I squeezed his hand and we walked along for a while not saying anything. We were nearly at his house.

When I said I didn't want to go home until later, he didn't ask me why. Don't know what I'd've said anyway; I don't want to go home because Mum's probably banging the cupboards, because the Old Man's been hitting the home brew more and more and he's even got the whisky out, because I'm scared what else he'll hit? He said we could go to his house and listen to some music. I just hoped the Old Man or Leo didn't find out where I was going.

When we turned up the street where he lived, it was one of those big boss houses, the ones that are about three times bigger than our house and there were piles of cars parked outside.

We were going past the neighbours' house when that boy in the wheelchair come down the driveway. He was coming to have a nosey.

"Got a party at your place?" he asked.

"Paul," said Ray. "How are you? Do you plan to come in again tomorrow? We're working on the next critical pathway."

"Miriama," he said to me.

"You know her?" asked Ray.

"Yeah, we met," I said.

I didn't let on that me and Selwyn propped Paul up so he could play pool at the rugby club. His body felt so weird. He was all strong on top and then from the waist down he was floppy as a rag doll. Must be hard.

"Crikey, I forgot about the meeting," said Ray. "It's some kind of female-y thing. Mrs Hopewell says it's the Ladies' Business Round-table or something."

"There's the two Miss Williams going in," I said.

"We can just go in quietly round the back," said Ray. "They won't even know we're here."

Ray started walking up the drive and I was left with the boy in the wheelchair. I didn't know if I should just ask him to go home, like he was a little brother you didn't want tagging along, or if I should say that me and Ray had a date. I wasn't sure we actually had a date, we were just gonna hang out for a while. So I just started pushing the wheelchair.

Ray held the back door open and we squeezed the chair in, just. My fingers got pinched against the doorframe, it was so tight. The hallway was no problem, it was wide as and so long you could play touch in it. Ray was doing his stupid Danny walk and I poked Paul to stop him laughing, but I doubted they'd hear us anyway, there were too many women babbling. Ray opened one of the doors and went in. He poked one hand out and did a big come here kind of move with it, so I hurried up along the hall in case someone saw me. Paul was wheeling himself along behind me. Lucky he didn't have a squeaky wheel like the returns trolley in the library.

The room was about twice as big as mine. There was a double bed, all neatly made, and a long desk against one wall. Ray'd got his computer set up there, the one he had in the library, that day I nearly sat on his knee and Miss Williams busted out laughing at us. I didn't know where to sit. I'd never been in a boy's bedroom before, not without a whole lot of other mates, so I just stood there. It was so neat and tidy, no piles of clothes or books and paper like my room. He'd even got his pencils all lined up next to the computer and his shoes were sitting under the desk, next to each other. He had to be a neat freak. I should've taken my dirty shoes off.

Ray and Paul were over at the computer. They'd got it open and were staring at those little green lines, forgetting I was even there. Maybe if I took off my clothes and danced in front of them? Only if I was covered in little green writing. Instead I just sat on the edge of the bed and when I looked down, there was a letter. It was addressed to *Raymond, The Thin White Duke*, and it was from London, England. I tapped him on the shoulder. He looked at the address and his face got all worried. He opened the envelope and pulled out the paper in it. Then he dropped it on his desk and he looked so sad that I couldn't help it. I just pulled him away from the computer and hugged him. He was crying for real now.

"It's Harry," he said. "He's got AIDS."

Chapter Thirteen
Ima Williams

"Hello, Notta, nice to see you. This must be the sister you told me about."

There was a woman with shoulder pads so wide she looked like a box on legs. Shoulder pads and pleated skirt with flat shoes: it looked almost as bad as poor Notta in her one long skirt that she seemed to wear to everything.

"You must be the journalist," Mrs Shoulder Pads said to me. "I'm Shirley Hopewell. Welcome. Please help yourselves to a glass of wine. We'll start in a moment."

She slid her eyes quickly up and down my dark suit. I'd been told this was a business meeting so I'd dressed accordingly.

The room was large, with big windows that reflected the group of women gathered on the, my God, purple shagpile carpet. Who in their right mind would have purple shagpile carpet? It's so 1960s. Some of the women had stiletto heels on and they kept snagging. Imagine what you'd say at the hospital: "My broken leg? No, not a skiing accident. I tripped on a shagpile carpet and what's more, it was purple." I wished I could share the joke with Notta, not that she'd get it. She was looking as if she was about to bolt out the door. This was not her idea of a night out, not by any stretch of the imagination.

There was no red wine. Just a chardonnay that tasted far too sweet to me, but then, it would help the evening go by. I took a sip and looked around at the women. They were the wives of the

"Management" (with the capital M, as Notta keeps telling me). I don't think "wives" ever has a capital W. They all seemed to know each other. Except for Mrs Shoulder Pads, the others didn't look too bad. They could be at any charity function in the city. They had that look, with permed hair, too much makeup, and a kind of desperation that was, I would guess, the result of boring lives. I could imagine it: service the husband, take the children to after-school activities, go out of town for a shopping trip or maybe a round of golf, or even tennis. Some of them looked quite fit. I was there to look for a way in so, purple shagpile or not, I put on my bright smile.

"Let's get started, shall we?" said another of the women. She was the one with the sleek haircut and the pencil skirt. Tennis would be her game.

We perched on the assortment of sofas and hardback chairs that were set up around a fireplace. Above it was a set of flying ducks, except that one of them, the leader, had drooped and was leading the ducks, kamikaze-style, down into the fireplace.

We did a round of names. The one with the sleek haircut was Cynthia Grant and her husband was head of operations. She was the president of the Ladies' Business Roundtable.

I introduced myself and told them I was interested in the women's story behind the strike and that I'd like to just listen to their meeting, to get to know a little about them and their association. I got appreciative murmurs.

"And I'm here to ask if you would be prepared to support the new initiative at the library."

Notta was clutching her wine glass as if someone was going to take it off her. Her voice was surprisingly steady. Just for a moment I wanted to put a hand out to touch her, reassure her.

"We're starting a branch of the Workers' Education Association in the town, and basing it in the library," she said. "We want to offer adult literacy programmes, among other things, but we need support to get it going."

"Really?" said one of the women. "Literacy? You mean some of the workers can't read and write?"

"Some people have basic skills," said Notta. "They could do with literacy improvement."

"Is it just literacy or will it include hobby classes?" asked another woman.

"It'll be literacy and it'll also be education on strategic analysis. It'll help workers learn how to maintain their rights," said Notta.

Once, when Notta was about seventeen and she'd finally got herself a boyfriend, she'd sat at the dinner table and declared that she was on the pill. Dad had blown his top, spouting some parental nonsense about girls keeping their legs crossed. Notta had calmly said that she had the right to control her own fertility. Guts? Lots. Tact? None.

"I see," said Cynthia of the sleek haircut. "You don't think the workers here know enough about their rights?"

"We want to run courses about how power blocks work in society and about the history of the union movement in New Zealand," Notta ploughed on, oblivious. "Leo Harris has got a particular interest in that area."

"Leo Harris?" said Shirley Hopewell. "Isn't he the secretary of the Pulp and Paper Workers' Union?"

"They're a federation," said Notta. "They're not a union. They deregistered."

Most of the women were looking intently at the purple shagpile. Cynthia crossed her legs the other way. Good legs, great calves, definitely tennis. She leaned forward with her glass of chardonnay pointing and her eyes glued to Notta. My poor sister looked like someone pretending their library book isn't ten years overdue.

"You want some support from us to get Mr Harris to run courses in workers' rights?"

"And literacy programmes," Notta said.

"You know Mr Harris, do you?"

Notta nodded.

"You know his background, where he comes from, who he is?"

Notta looked uncertain. I was all ears. I hoped I hadn't blushed when his name came up because my blood was certainly dancing to the memory of him ramming us home.

"Let me give you a little history lesson then," said Cynthia. "He comes from a long line of militant unionists. His father was a supporter of Jock Barnes in the 1951 Waterfront Strike."

"Lockout," Notta muttered, but only I heard it.

"His father didn't work after the strike. No one would employ him. He was a communist. Mr Harris was fed on militant unionism from a baby. The other one, the president, what's his name? The one everyone calls the Old Man. He's a Scotsman from the shipbuilding yards of Glasgow and the two of them are as thick as thieves. Wouldn't be surprised if both of them were card-carrying communists. Anyway, what do you think your man's going to teach our workers?"

"I told you, workers' rights and the history of the union movement in New Zealand. Workers are entitled to know the history of their unions, aren't they?"

"How do we know that Mr Harris won't corrupt people?" said a woman sitting in the corner. "How do we know he won't bring his communist leanings into our town?"

There was a murmur of assent from the other women. He'd certainly corrupt them but not with his politics. It was ridiculous. Leo wasn't exactly a single-handed communist takeover, but my sister must have been dreaming when she hatched this plan. They'd never agree to it.

"Perhaps the committee could consider it," said Shirley. "The literacy and the history programmes, I mean."

"Yes," said Cynthia. "We should consider it very carefully."

Notta might be known for her lack of tact but she did have the good sense to shut up. I could tell by the set of her chin that she wasn't going to give up but at least she wasn't going to dig a deeper hole for herself. I was dying to find out more about Leo. Somehow,

I didn't think this was the time or the place.

"I'm interested in some background here," I said. "I'm interested in what the company is wanting to achieve for the town."

"Would you buy shares in this company?" asked Cynthia.

I'd never bought shares in my life. My BMW was my only asset. I bought it when I had a job and I thought I was going to get a promotion. Freelancing doesn't exactly give you extra cash to invest, you have to survive between selling stories.

"I haven't considered it," I said. "Why, would it be a good idea?"

"This company is part of a much bigger group of companies. You know that, don't you?"

Notta had said something like that, something about the company "expanding its holdings." I've never been a business reporter but I nodded as if I knew what she was on about.

"There are goals for that corporation. It's the biggest in New Zealand and it must be able to continue to compete internationally."

"And what does that have to do with this company?" I asked.

"This company is one of the larger shareholdings of the corporation but it's bleeding money."

"Yes," chipped in another of the wives. "There are losses, big ones, because of strikes. You've read the papers, haven't you? This town's known as strike town and easy money for workers because the company rolls over and gives in every time the union calls a strike."

"You know, my husband worked in a factory in his school holidays," said Shirley Hopewell. "He tried to get on side with that man, the president of the Paper Workers' Union, but every time they see each other, he just gets told he's a traitor to the working class."

"Old thinking," said Cynthia. "Us and them. There's already a cyclical pattern to profit from paper manufacture and it's made worse by the strikes."

"Tell me," I said. "Do you have shares in this company?"

A murmur of assent and a wave of nodding went around the circle, small town equivalents of *The Stepford Wives*.

"So you want this strike to end?" I asked.

"We want this business to be viable," said Cynthia. "The company has been trying to make the workers understand the economics of pulp and paper production and why it's in their interests to ensure continuity of production. You know there's a profit-sharing scheme, don't you?"

I shook my head. Notta hadn't mentioned that.

"The workers get a share of profits but they must make them first."

"So the incident that started this whole thing, you know, Sally Wihongi who didn't get a job, that was all a ruse?"

"Call it a tipping point," said Cynthia. "The truth is there are too many people employed. The company needs to be made efficient. It's put capital and support behind the business enterprise park, the one that's just opened. People can set up business there and contract back to the company. It's a win-win situation."

She was good, this woman, knew her stuff. I almost felt like clapping. She was definitely a wife with a capital W. In fact, a capital C as well; Company Wife.

Notta stood up. She was carefully putting her glass on the table when Cynthia drove the dagger in deeper.

"If you want to run courses at the library, Notta, you might want to run some on the economics of papermaking. Management would love to come in and take some classes. Or maybe the archaic nature of this country's labour laws. I could get someone from the Business Roundtable as a guest speaker if you like."

Notta didn't even look up. She carefully navigated the purple shagpile and was out of the door.

"Now, if you don't mind, Ima," said Cynthia. "The committee needs to meet without outsiders."

I was summarily dismissed. Keep all possible sources sweet, my old journalism lecturer used to say. Just as I swallowed hard and smiled, she had an afterthought.

"If you'd like to give me your card," she said, "We could talk some more." I pulled one out of my coat pocket. There was a big black stripe where I'd blocked out the name of my previous employer. It didn't look very professional. She pocketed it with a smile that was not a smile and I took my leave. I couldn't resist tipping my glass on its side at the edge of the table so the rest of my chardonnay dripped on the shagpile.

We headed for the BMW without saying anything. As I gunned the engine, Notta stared out the window.

"Bet she's a peroxide blonde," I said.

But Notta didn't even turn her head.

Chapter Fourteen

Stuart Duncan

It was a long drive for one meeting but a summons from the chairman of the board meant no choice. He was adamant, a phone call wouldn't do.

At least it was a beautiful morning. The mist had almost gone off the lake; there was just a tiny pocket of white lurking on the far shore. The sun made an exclamation mark over a perfectly still surface. There was nothing to disturb it: no disputes, no disagreements, not even undercurrents. I'd done this drive so often, not so much in the last year with so much time off, but the year before that, and I'd always loved the lakefront. So long as I didn't get stuck behind a logging truck or a woodchip truck rattling along and dropping bits of pine all over the road but there was no chance of that at the moment.

It was nice to be away from the heavy silences. I could only keep up a one-sided conversation for so long.

That polite young man had waved me goodbye when I left. No sign of Paul, of course, but leaving him with Ray was the best I could do.

"No problem, Mr Duncan," he'd said. "We've got some computing stuff to do."

"There's food in the fridge and help yourself to a beer, young man. Paul likes the odd beer. He can manage the toilet himself, you know."

He'd looked a bit embarrassed when I'd mentioned toileting.

Sometimes I forgot. He saw Paul as a mate with interests in common, thank goodness, but, as his father, I had to see to his needs. Paul certainly didn't. I wasn't sure how long the situation could continue. It needed to be addressed some time, and better plans made. When the strike was over. When.

The call from Sir Ron had only come in the day before and I'd had to make the arrangements in a hurry. Anyway, Paul really just needed someone there for safety and Fred and Cynthia said they'd pop in and check up on the two boys. It was Fred's idea to ask Ray. As he said, you may be pleasantly surprised. I have been. Thank goodness for someone at your back, someone to catch the ball.

I eased my foot down a little and the BMW responded. A whisper more speed, just a whisper. She was so good on these winding roads, cornering so precisely, responding to my every move. I emptied my mind and felt the joy of complete control.

The boardroom was upstairs with a view over suburban rooftops. It was one of those modern glass buildings with tinted floor-to-ceiling windows that always made me feel like a specimen in a jar. The pine table in the centre of the room was big enough to seat sixteen. The chairs were in disarray and there were piles of paper strewn everywhere. It seemed to be functioning as some kind of planning space as evidenced by three large whiteboards covered in writing. Sir Ron was at the head of the table, bending over something in a big folder. He stood up with a hand extended.

"Stuart, welcome. Good to see you," he said.

"Sir Ron," I said.

We shook hands and he indicated the chair next to him. He hadn't said what this meeting was about but I'd seen the headlines in the *Herald* yesterday.

"How was the drive up? You're living down country now, aren't you?"

"Yes, been there a week or so."

"Right. How are things going? You and Fred on top of things?

Don't tell me you're not. You know how crucial this is to us."

There was a folder sitting in front of me: *Pulp and Paper Production Cost Analysis.*

"I think I've made it quite clear, Stuart, that we can't have your company losing money the way it has been. Profit. We need to return to profit."

"Yes, sir, quite clear."

"None of this "sir" business, Stuart. Ron is perfectly adequate."

"Right. Well, we're following the board's directives. We're keeping the lines of communication open with the public and using the media."

"Yes, that was the advice from that British consultant. Successful in the UK, I gather."

"Well, yes and no. The British woman was working with the Miners' Union after the 1984 strikes, helping ease through the closures. We're not going there, at least I hope not."

"We'll see about that. Yes, we'll see. Hold a steady line, Stuart, we won't play all our cards at once."

He was nodding, the light glinting off his glasses. I found myself nodding too. I wasn't sure if I should say something about the "we'll see". I didn't want to be presiding over the closure of a huge pulp and paper mill. That wouldn't look good on my CV. I'd be known as the hatchet man. Then again, I wasn't so sure how much of it was in my control. I had no illusions about it, I was the tool to implement the board's decisions and they were not giving in this time.

The two of us sat there, nodding. I had a sudden memory of my mother's fireplace in England. She'd had two china dogs called Gog and Magog, one each side of the fender, with springs in their necks. She'd tell me stories about them, how they represented the giants who were the guardians of the city of London. I didn't feel like a giant, more like the dog's head, with someone else bouncing the spring.

"You saw yesterday's *Herald*?" he said. "The statement by David Lange?"

"Yes. For a PM he doesn't seem very well informed, if I may say so. The story that the strike was started by the company trying to employ a woman is somewhat out-of-date and was always skewed."

"You have to think more strategically, Stuart. Lange's statement won't do us any harm. It just makes the federation look out-of-date."

"I'm not sure I follow you."

"Well, I can't agree more with Lange saying managing a modern multi-national is not the same as running a branch of social welfare."

"I assume he means things like job security."

"What? Don't be soft, Stuart. He means the idea that a company looks after all the needs of its workers. All of them. Regardless of loss of profit. That's not modern management practice, went out with the ark."

"Meaning?"

"We've got the ear of Roger Douglas. As the minister of finance, he's the one who's really got the power and he's on exactly the same page as us. As Douglas said to me, we're reconceptualising the foundations of our labour laws; the employer looks for a commodity, the worker brings his labour. It's a straight-out exchange, no different from selling any other commodity. Quite a different concept to the idea the unions hold."

He seemed to be saying that workers didn't have any needs, just labour to sell. Like you would sell a surplus sofa or a car you no longer used. If the workers did have any needs, like safety or security, or consideration for their families, then the company wasn't interested. The workers could go to hell. I didn't like it.

He'd made a little steeple with his hands and was nodding over them at me. I found myself doing the same.

My mother wore glasses. I have a memory of her looking over the top of them and telling another story about her two nodding guardian dogs. In the Bible they were allies of Satan and would rise up with the end times. Was I the Gog to Sir Ron's Magog, an ally to the end of union power?

"The average working man is not onboard with our new

thinking yet," he said. "Won't do us any harm to have a smoke screen with this gender business."

He leaned over the table, looking over his glasses. I kept my face neutral.

"I'm committed to the board's directive about clear, honest communication, and ensuring that the workers know exactly where the company stands."

"Yes, keep it up. And another tip: look for cracks, Stuart, between the unions and inside them. Look for the dissidents. Divide and conquer, if you get what I mean."

Divide and conquer. Look for the cracks. My right leg had started jerking, as if it had a life of its own.

"There are plenty of ways we're ensuring that people are well informed: individual letters to each striking pulp and paper worker, mailed to their homes and the hotline is proving useful. People can ring in to hear the company point of view."

"Good man. Yes, you take care of things down there. We'll keep the other communication channels open. This country will be pulled into the modern world. A bloodless evolution, that's what Roger Douglas is calling it, evolution, not revolution, but be assured it will happen. We're at the forefront, Stuart, the forefront."

He went back to the folder in front of him. That seemed to be the end of the meeting. I was reaching for the door handle when he looked up again.

"Oh, and by the way, Stuart, we're keeping an eye on the leaders of that union. A close eye and a close ear too, if you get my drift. We've got people asking questions about the whereabouts of funds the Federation of Pulp and Paper Workers was holding in its account. They seem to have disappeared."

I had the door open when the next sentence hit me.

"We'll be reviewing your performance on this one, Stuart, in about a month's time," he said. "Keep that in mind, will you?"

I could still see him nodding at me as I closed the door behind me. I waved vaguely at the receptionist and walked back to my

BMW, each step drilling it into my brain. It was my job to implement the board's directives. I had a directive I could believe in: open and honest communication. That was my job, being open and honest, and I needed that job.

I was sitting back in the car before I realised he hadn't asked about Paul. Not once.

Chapter Fifteen

Ray Parlane

"Good shit," said Paul.

"Splendid, Miss Sandy," I said.

"Don't call me that all the time," said Miriama. "I've got my own name. Dope's grown local, you know? Good climate for it."

Paul took another deep drag. He seemed well schooled in the art and I wondered how a boy in a wheelchair got a chance. We had the place to ourselves and very comfortable it was indeed. I tried the big stereo, turning up the volume, and the notes of the Chopin piano concerto stayed crisp. If I'd only brought some Stevie Nicks or Pet Shop Boys to play. I put another log in the fireplace. It was enormous and the fire was as toasty warm as it could get. The room was huge, with big settees and a mirror over the fireplace making it look even bigger. Every time one of us moved, the reflection caught my eye. Paul was ensconced on the sofa, Miriama stretched out on the rug and I was sitting against the sofa with my feet to the fire. Very comfortable indeed.

Dear old Mr Hopewell (Sir) had nearly crapped himself in delight when he'd heard I'd been asked to keep Paul company for the night. He probably saw me as an asset in his career path.

Paul passed me the roach. I pinched it out and chewed it up. Very mellow dope, not that I got much of it. Paul got the lion's share, but then, that felt fair enough somehow.

"So, what'll we do?" asked Paul.

"Too cold to go out," I said. "It's brass monkeys out there."

Back in the lounge, Paul didn't move himself back on to the sofa. He sat in his chair in the shadow, behind me and Miriama. No one seemed to want to start the game again. It was Miriama's turn. Maybe she couldn't think of a good dare for a cripple. I could see her in the mirror. She'd pulled herself up on one elbow.

"OK, if you feel too whakamā, Paul, I can always give you a dare. My truth question is, what's the hardest thing about being in a wheelchair?"

His voice came out of the gloom. He was moving the wheelchair back and forward, just a little.

"Flat tyres," he said. "Not enough speed to get a thrill. Blisters on your hands instead of your heels."

"Must be more than that," I said, and then wished I hadn't.

"People feeling sorry for me. People thinking I'm stupid just because my legs don't work. Not being able to run or dance. Not being able to get anywhere without help. Shall I carry on?"

"Yep," said Miriama. "Be good to get it off your chest. All of it."

"Later maybe," he said. He stopped rocking the wheelchair. "If we're going to tell secrets, I've got a question for you Ray."

"Fire ahead."

"You ever, you know, done it with a girl?"

There were boys at school. We helped each other make our willies stand up tall and spit stuff. That's when I thought I might be gay, like Harry and Stan, but then there was a girl who lived at Bonnington Square for a while. We were both sixteen and we did a lot of kissing and stroking. We nearly got there. It was very different to the stuff in the boys' toilets; we liked each other, a lot.

"Yeah," I said. "She was a tall, blonde Amazon. She used to surf back in Australia and she used to yell "sheet" very loudly when she came. I was nearly seventeen when she went home. What about you?"

I could've bitten my tongue. He slumped over in his wheelchair.

"Yeah, sure. I get girls lining up to bonk the cripple. I've had them by the hundreds."

"Can you, you know, get it up?" asked Miriama. Got to give it to that girl, she didn't hold back.

"Sometimes."

"Cool," she said. "Then you'll get to have sex and have babies, little babies on wheels."

She got the giggles. Maybe it was the dope 'cos before too long we were rolling round clutching at our bellies. Paul sobered up first. He said he'd get us some food but Miriama said she needed to go home so that left just the two of us, gobbling up the cold chicken.

"Paul, I'll sleep on the sofa," I said.

"Yeah, I'd like that. We can go to your place and do stuff with the computer in the morning."

"Let's do that. Not in the morning, though. Miriama wants me to do something with her. She's on study break and I'm meeting her in the library."

"Two's company, eh?"

He sounded wistful.

"Bring them, all of them," she'd said.

So, next morning, I tucked them into a shoebox. Each one written on my birthday, starting at age six when I wrote this letter:

To My DADY I am Six today. Hapy birthday to me. Do you love me? I love you. Your son RAINBOW. XXX

"We'll show them to Miss Williams and tell her what you know about your father," she'd said.

"Why?"

"Because she's a librarian," she'd said.

That didn't make any sense to me and I felt like a real dickhead with a shoebox tucked under my arm. Since that letter had come from Stan, I'd been wanting to go home, give up this mad goose chase and just go and see Harry. Stan told me not to panic and not to come home but it was hard to stop thinking about Harry, imagining him all sick and thin with his crooked teeth sticking out from his wasted face. He always said he looked a bit like Freddy Mercury with those teeth.

"Tell me about Harry," she said.

I stopped at the bridge to watch the water swirling past us, always moving. I couldn't fix my eyes on it, it changed too quickly. Miriama leant on the rail next to me. I didn't mean to tell her so much but it just came pouring out.

"He made sure Liz didn't nut me out too much. Once when I was eight, she was learning how to read tarot cards and she needed to practise so one day she gave me a reading. She'd set up the room so it was all dark and she had candles burning and a picture of a goat head on the wall."

"What for?"

"The goat head? It was meant to be the devil, I think. Anyway, I was only small and I was terrified."

"Then what did she do?"

"She got me to pick cards out of the pack and when I picked a card with a man hanging upside down, she started howling and saying things like 'you're too young to die.'"

"She pōrangi, your mother?"

"What do you mean?"

"You know, crazy."

"She's a hippie. Anyway, Harry came in and told her off. She never tried it again."

But there were worse times; times when she was on a bad trip and Stan had to stay with her while Harry took me next door. I'm not telling Miriama about those times. When Liz was screaming at the door because it was trying to eat her and she tried to climb up the wall when I touched her. Maybe Miriama was right. She was a bit … whatever it was Miriama had said.

"These letters, why've you still got them?"

"Every time I wrote one, Liz got me to copy it out. These are all in my best handwriting, you know. We put one in a shoebox, this one actually, and she took the other one."

"What did she do with it?"

"I don't know. She wouldn't say. I always thought she was posting it to that mysterious person I called Dad. But she wouldn't tell me where he lived, just that it was somewhere in New Zealand. She got all cosmic when I said I wanted to study computers for my gap year and told me to come here to this town."

"Nothing else?"

"No, she said that the universe would align if I had the right vibes."

"Like the Old Man? He's been lining up the universe for years, shouting about how the workers get ripped off. Is that how it's done?"

"I think she means some of that other stuff, peace and love, man. You know, that hippie rubbish."

We'd reached the library and there was a crowd of children just piling out the door. We were nearly knocked over by them and one of the little kids came a cropper over my foot and sprawled on the concrete step. He was bellowing and I bent down to try and help him. Five years old, was my guess. Knuckles in his eyes, he couldn't see who I was and when I reached one arm under his armpits, he wrapped himself around my neck. I stood up with this little monkey clinging to me. Then he knocked my box of letters out from under my arm and there they all were—little squares of hope with "Daddy" carefully printed by some stranger-child. When we moved to England and I had to go to chapel at school, I used to pray to this person called Daddy who, like God, existed by faith alone.

A frazzled-looking woman took the little boy out of my arms, apologised, and ran out after the escaping prisoners, leaving Miriama and me to pick up the scattered letters.

"Loadzamoney," I said.

"Eh?"

"Harry Enfield, you know. Never mind."

"Kids have been staying at the marae. Probably got to sleep real late last night. It's not easy to sleep with fifty other kids giggling and carrying on."

"What's a whatever-you-called-it and why did the children stay there?"

"Marae? It's a big house where everyone sleeps or doesn't, depending on how many people snore. The kids are on a holiday programme put on with money from Department of Social Welfare, to help out the striking families."

She picked up a letter.

"That one must've been not long ago."

She handed it to me. The envelope said, *Father who art in where-the-fuck.*

"I think you might be right," I said. "Look, Miriama, I can't do this. I can't take these letters in and show them to someone I don't know very well. Not these letters. I can show you but not Miss Williams."

I think she blushed. She looked pleased that I trusted her, anyway.

She suggested a walk, away from the library and we headed off past the electrical shop store. There was no one inside, no one buying a new fridge or television. We headed up to the stream, where the willows dragged in the water. It was so clear and it looked very cold.

"I'll show you one of our hiding places," she said. "This is where we go to smoke."

We pushed in under a willow tree, pulling apart the weeping branches. They were still bare sticks with knobbly bits where the buds would come in spring but it was dense and dark. Miriama scrabbled around behind the twisted trunk and pulled out a piece of plastic. As she spread it out, evicting a few snails, I breathed in the damp and the clean smell of the water. We sat up against one of the horizontal branches. Miriama pulled a tin out of her track-suit pocket and took out a thin cigarette. She lit it, took a drag and handed it to me.

"This a daily habit?" I asked.

"Nah, it's a half and half," she said. "You know, half tobacco and half dope."

"A shandy, you mean."

"You talk funny."

We sat quietly for a while, the shoebox between us, passing the joint and listening to the watery murmur. I was especially mellow after last night's dope and drifting.

Every year, every birthday, before breakfast, before presents, even before anyone saying happy birthday, I would sit with a piece of blank paper in front of me and try to imagine what he looked like. Which bits of him did I inherit: my skinny toes? My love of facts that line up in logical rows to lead me into some maze of a puzzle? My fifteen percent in French? I asked him once, in one of my last letters.

Dear Dad,

Today I am twelve years old and we are still living in London. I am going to start at Mill Hill School very soon and I want to know if you are good at maths. I am very good at maths and I particularly like algebra. When are you going to come and meet me? I think I might look like you because I don't look like Liz. Do you have brown hair? Do you have a mole on your chest, just by your collarbone? Do you like the Goons? Can I come and live with you? I don't want to go to Mill Hill School. Your son, Ray

"Are you like your parents?" I asked.

"I'm like my mum. That's what people say. She's staunch, she stands up for herself."

"What about your father?"

"Him? Nah. He's old. He's much older than my mother, you know. He had another wife in Scotland before he came here but they didn't have any kids. There's just me."

"Do you think I'll know when I find him? My father I mean. Like my heart will pound, or I'll just know somehow?"

"Doubt it. Some of my cuzzies, their mum isn't sure which boyfriend did the job on her and the boyfriends are still around and the cuzzies just treat them like they're all dad."

"I think I'll know, somehow."

The joint was finished. Miriama wriggled over and put her arm through mine. We sat there for a while, just being mellow, and the water slipped smooth on the sandy bottom, on the other side of the willow wall. It was peaceful and Miriama seemed to have gone to sleep. Very gently, I eased my arm out and put it round her shoulders, one of her arms came up round my neck and we toppled slowly to the plastic. Her eyes were dark brown, like Harry's favourite velvet pants, and she was smiling. She had big, full lips. They looked vulnerable, like she was wearing her whole mouth on the outside. I couldn't help it, just a little light kiss on that smile. Just the smallest of kisses, soft. And then she was kissing me back and it was like drowning, like the stream had pulled us in, but it was warm, not cold. I tried a gentle explore with my tongue, at the supple edge of her mouth, like she was the most delicious ice cream I'd ever tasted. She giggled and pulled her head back.

"That tickles," she said.

"You like it?"

"So you're Mr Casanova, eh?"

"No, not really."

"No fullas?"

"No fellows. Not really. What about you?"

"Course, heaps."

"Oh, you're a tart then and I thought you were such a good girl, just hopelessly devoted to me."

She tried to hit me but couldn't get her arm untangled. So I kissed her again, and this time the kiss was a hoover on a mat and she sucked my tongue into her mouth. Our bodies were pushing hard one to the other and I'd got this massive hard-on that was

106

making my whole body pulse, like the mosh pit in a Cure concert. Our mouths were glued together, our breath was one breath, and I couldn't tell where I ended and she began, I just knew there was too much clothing between us.

Then there was a shout from somewhere close by. Someone was yelling, "Here boy, here boy." A sneezing and snuffling noise came really, really close, just outside our willow curtain. The dog knew we were in there.

"Keep still," I whispered in her ear.

We were wrapped around each other, the urgency seeping into the earth, as the snuffling continued. The owner called again. "Here boy, here boy." The noise stopped. The dog gave a deep woof and crashed off, splashing in the stream.

"That was close," I said. "Bit public here. What if we got caught?"

"What, are you chicken? Adds to the excitement, I reckon."

"You are a tart, Sandy, but seriously, do you want to?"

She didn't answer, just kissed me again, soft and sweet, like the first time.

"Not here, not now," I said.

We both knew we would. If not here, where? If not now, when?

If you hid in Leo's privet hedge, not that you would, but just say you did, you'd be able to see right into his kitchen. This is what you might see.

Four blokes sitting on hard-backed chairs around the old kitchen table. There's a few empty bottles, beer bottles, and there's a bottle of whisky. Two of the men are still drinking beer but two of them, Leo included, are drinking whisky without ice or water.

You'd recognise Leo; the grey hair pulled back into a ponytail, the mashed-in nose, the squat body leaning back on the chair, rocking it on two legs. You'd probably recognise the Old Man, too, his shirt tight over his belly, his double chin coming and going as he nods his head, his cigarette stabbing at the air when he talks. You wouldn't recognise the other two. They're wearing hats, old-fashioned ones, grey fedoras, pulled over their faces. They haven't taken off their coats, trench coats with epaulettes. They keep their shoulders high, both of them, so you can't see their faces. All you can see clearly are their hands as they tap the ash off their cigarettes into the ashtray that's overflowing.

But then again. This is what you might see.

Leo sitting at the kitchen table with a bottle of beer half empty in front of him. He's got his old cat, Homehelp, sitting on his knee and he's careful not to knock her off as he turns the page of his newspaper. There's a knock on the door. He leaves the room to answer it, putting the newspaper up on the bench. If you get up really close to the window you can read the paper. It says things like this:

· Even if they have to man the machines themselves, the wives of these workers will stop the mill from closing.

- *The women said:* we are afraid that if the mill closes, this town will die. With no work for the men, there will only be women and children left. It will be like a ghost town.
- *The Prime Minister said:* no large exporting company should be run like a branch of Social Welfare.

He doesn't come back. It was probably some woman or another at the door. It always is.

Chapter Sixteen

Leo Harris

He's on the phone when I get there. I can hear him being real controlled, holding on by his fingernails, I reckon.

Aye, he says, I heard you. You're all marching up to the mill tomorrow, all the wives you say? All the wives of the strikers? Pig's arse. I dinna believe you hen, you're full of shite.

The fingernails just gave way. He crashes the phone down. He's been on the whisky for a while. To get that rarked up, he has to have been, and to sound that Scotch.

He doesn't even say g'day, just slumps down on the kitchen chair, looking as if the wind's been knocked out of him. It's getting to all of us.

Last meeting, there wasn't such a good turnout, maybe four hundred, and the vote was split. We've still got a majority to hold out against the company conditions. We'll go back to work, mind, but not on their conditions. But the vote was bloody split, some are willing to do whatever the bloody company wants. Bloody management's been doing its work, chipping away bit by bit, getting at the uncertain ones, getting at the ones who can't do without the money.

I don't say anything, just open a beer and sit down at the table with him. I won't touch the whisky, not tonight, but it never pays to let a man drink alone. We just sit there, the two of us, not saying a word. There's different kinds of solidarity.

Then Stella comes home. If she'd come home before he started on the bottle, I reckon things would still be sweet, but in she sails with Miriama bringing up the rear.

You fullas can have a good long rest now, she says. Us wāhine are picking up your load. Don't want you overworking, you can really have a good holiday now.

The Old Man just sits there, staring into his whisky. I wonder what he's seeing in there? He'd left Scotland long before the big strike happened in 1984. He was here, reading about it in the *Daily Mirror*, I know, he read bits out to me about how the coal miners had nothing to burn in their fireplaces that winter because they weren't digging the coal out, about how there was nothing to eat and no furniture left in their houses because it had all been sold off or burnt to try and keep them warm. He didn't have to live through that. Not the Old Man. He didn't have to suffer for his principles, which meant he could keep them intact and he has, I have to respect him for that. Together, we've sworn never to let the bastards get us, not like the British miners. We'll be staunch.

Tomorrow, Stella says, we're going to the mill to meet Mr Grant. We've got ideas of our own to settle this.

Stella's never been like this before. All those other times, when the strikes stretched from days to weeks, she'd just grit her teeth and make it work for her and for Miriama. She wouldn't talk about it, not even with me. She'd just get on with it. But now? I'm staring at her and wondering what the hell's got into her.

I don't see it coming, the table, and the edge of it catches me a good one, right in the belly. I feel like I've been tackled by the big man Buck himself. I'm doubled over looking at the floor and heaving for breath when it happens. I can't get there in time, I'm sucking in air as fast as I can and I try, but I can't get there. He lands Stella a whack across the face you could've heard at the end of the road. I hope to hell he hasn't got the whisky bottle in his hand, I pray to every spirit ever bottled that he hasn't, but no, just the glass and that causes damage enough. But Stella, jeez, that woman, she won't be cowed by him. Not her. She just stands there, a great cut across her cheek, whisky and blood dripping off her chin. She just bloody stands there and the look she gives him would freeze a man's balls off. She pulls herself up and she's a tall woman, five nine in flat shoes, and stares him full in the face. Then, without any effort, she spits, gets him a beauty. So now he's got a dribble coming down his cheek too and they're squaring off like two bulls in a paddock.

Miriama hasn't moved from the doorway. She's standing there as if she's glued, staring.

My father's face snarling. His fist back. Coming for us, me and Mum. She grabs me and shoves me behind her and my knees hit the floor. I can't get to her, I never can. It happens again and again: after the waterfront strike, after the cop coshed him with a bloody great baton, fractured his skull, mashed his brains.

I know that look on Miriama's face. It's her I reach for.

Come on, I say, and grab her by the arm, but she won't be moved. She's watching her mum and the Old Man like she can't look away, like she's hypnotised or something. So we're all stuck, posing for a photo or something. This is what it costs, it could say on the back.

It's Stella who breaks first. I dunno what she bloody says, it's in Māori, but it sounds like some kind of curse to me. She throws these heavy words at him, as if she's heaving bricks. He's flinching. I reckon he knows what she means, even if he doesn't get every word.

Then she turns around and is down the hall, leaving me to hold on to Miriama and stare at the Old Man slumping back in his chair. He's still got the whisky bottle in his hand and he upends it.

Next thing, Stella's back. She's got a bag in each hand. She must've been thinking about leaving for a while. I reckon the bags were ready and waiting.

Haere mai Miriama, she says, haere mai e kare.

Her voice is soft now. This is no curse, she just wants her baby safe.

We're in my old ute before I realise what she means. Miriama's squashed against me in the front seat and the poor kid's shaking, no tears, just shaking, from the inside. She lurches against me as her mum shuts the door and I'm fumbling for the key. The ute coughs a bit, like it wants to spit us out, then we jerk backwards down the drive. I stop before we drive off. He's still there, sitting at the table, by the window, doesn't even look up.

He didn't mean it, I say, it's just the strain of it and him being on the turps. He'll be sorry tomorrow.

He sure as hell will be, says Stella. Tomorrow. He sure as hell will be.

We drive away, through the town, past the mill with its excuse for smoke. Past the hammerhead crane, the monster with its long arm stretching out to grab us in its bloody enormous jaws.

She's talking real soft to Miriama. I can't understand what she's saying but Miriama stops shaking. I turn on the radio, just for something to do. It's that old song about the ten guitars, the one that Miriama says is her song, the one that she says she heard when she was first born, when we were all sitting at the maternity hospital, waiting for her, and me and the Old Man made our pact.

For the first bloody time, ever, I'm not sure it was a good one.

Chapter Seventeen
Ima Williams

When Notta makes up her mind she's a force to be reckoned with. She'd made up her mind she wasn't going to work, which meant no one to open the library, which meant she wouldn't be popular with the town clerk, her boss.

"Are you sure you won't get the sack?" I asked.

"Nope."

"Don't you care?"

"Nope."

She was in the BMW next to me and we were nosing our way through the crowd: mothers in the ubiquitous track pants and children. Lots of them. Some of the kids should've been at school; their teachers would have something to say about that. There were push-chairs, a whole phalanx of them, and not a mill worker in sight.

"How many?" I asked.

"Don't know, must be around a hundred," Notta said. "Big turnout."

"Some faces I recognize from the meeting on the marae."

"Yes, the enemy within. One in every household, chipping away."

"What are you on about, Notta? These are wives. They have to keep their families fed and the mortgages paid while their men are standing on their high and mighty principles."

"Traitors to the cause," she said.

She had that set look to her jaw. The one Dad used to say really made her different from the rest of us Williams. We're all flexible people, able to see both sides of any argument, able to be a bridge between warring factions, but not our Notta. That was where she got her name, Notta. On her birth certificate it said Natasha, but she'd always been Notta. It started as a joke because she didn't look like any of us, still doesn't. She used to hate it when she was little but when she hit adolescence she started wearing it like a badge of honour. Notta Williams. It made her distinct from the rest of us.

Mum and Dad always side with you, she'd say.

Because you're always so stubborn, I'd say.

Because you're the favourite, she'd say.

Of course, my name started as a joke too. My birth certificate said Imogen but I'd always been Ima because I'd always insisted "Ima Williams and you're not."

So that was the Williams twins: Ima Williams and Notta Williams and pig-headed Notta was insisting these women were traitors to the cause. I rest my case.

It almost looked like a party. The women were chatting and laughing. Some of the littlies in their pushchairs were waving coloured flags. The older kids were running up ahead and playing some kind of complicated tag game. That's why I had to go so slow because they'd colonised the road.

A few heads leaned down to look inside as I aimed for the car park and a message went out through the women. They'd probably recognised Notta; maybe it was just as well she'd come. They parted to let me through and I finally got past the last little knot of pushchairs. The gate to the car park was hanging open. The asphalt was empty except at the rim, nearest the gate, where the cars huddled together for safety. I parked the car in the first empty space and reached into the back for my camera.

"Do you know many of them, Notta?"

"Some. The young mums come in for story time with their kids."

"Any pulp and paper workers' wives?"

"Not sure, I think there's one or two. The traitors."

"I've heard that up to five hundred are going to be suspended in the next couple of weeks."

"Then the shit will really hit the fan. They'll have to be staunch then."

"You sure you're not coming?" I asked.

Don't know why I bothered. Notta just raised her eyebrows at me.

The women had reached the entrance to the mill. The tall wire fence with its topping of barbed wire had stopped and there were two slim security arms across a driveway, one to let cars in, one to let them out. If they wanted to, they could all just duck under it and walk on in. This was where some of their husbands had to come each morning to report for work, to be told they couldn't come in. Leo said they'd been religious about it, making sure the bloke on the gate signed them as presenting for work, just to show it wasn't technically a strike. The men had voted to return, even if it was only on their conditions, not the company's, but the company was locking them out. He actually said the fucking company and that it was a fucking lockout. The way he did.

They gathered in one group and waited in the shade thrown by a big corrugated iron shed. I turned the camera up the blank wall of the building. There were no windows or doors, but halfway up was a gap and three birds were hovering.

The shadow reached right to the back of the crowd. Freda was standing there. I recognised her from the marae meeting I went to. She was dressed in a long black skirt with a red scarf over her head and she had that same calm look on her face she'd had when the woman at the marae meeting was swearing and carrying on. Freda the peacemaker.

"Kia ora," she said, holding out one hand. She pulled me in closer and I wasn't sure what she was going to do. Was she going to kiss me on the cheek or do that other thing, that pressing noses? I started out heading for her nose, at least I could divert if it was a kiss on the cheek. She had a hand on my shoulder so I couldn't escape. We got closer and closer and it was still not clear what she was doing. It was like heading into a corner with my red BMW; if I turned too soon I'd destabilise us both. But she was a good driver, was Freda, and my pointy Pākehā nose was pressing her soft Māori nose and it was all over and she let me go.

"We've asked to kōrero with Mr Grant, the big boss," she said. "He said he'd come."

"Lots of women, Freda," I said. "Wives of mill workers, are they? All of them?"

"Ae, that's right, they're all wives of mill workers. Some of them have got men who are still working, but they'll be suspended in a few days' time, lots of them. You know that, don't you?"

"What will that mean for the town, do you think, Freda?"

"See that wahine over there? That's what it means."

Freda was pointing to a young woman in a denim jacket in the middle of the crowd. The homemade patch on her back said *Keep My Town Alive*.

It did mean that. The company was the lifeblood of the town.

An old ute drove up, fast. It looked as if it was going to plough into the crowd and it was coming straight for me and Freda. I pulled at her arm to try and get her out of its path but it swerved and stopped, the side mirror missing me by an inch. Leo was driving. He looked wild. His hair was hanging loose and he was hunched over the driving wheel as if he was trying to not be seen. Fat chance. Everyone knew him.

"Shame" came from the middle of the crowd and there was a surge of energy. I was just starting to get a feeling that things could get ugly and I might have to rescue him again when the passenger door opened and out climbed Stella. She must've been crouched down under the dashboard. Calmly, with a dignity that was admirable, she straightened up, staring straight ahead over the heads of the other women, as if she was looking beyond them.

Leo pulled the door closed and backed his ute away, leaving Stella at the edge of the crowd. I was staring after his tail pipe again and it took me a moment to see what the other women saw. A long cut sliced her face, from her eye socket to the edge of her mouth. Someone had put butterfly stitches on it to hold it together, but it was going to scar. She wore it like it was some kind of war trophy but which side was she on? These women were trying to make peace. Had she? Or had she come to attack the enemy within?

"Ah," said Freda. "Her old man's done it again."

A loud voice boomed out from the gate.

Mr Fred Grant, Head of Operations, must have arrived while Leo was dropping his hot potato in our midst. I knew it was him because he'd graced the local paper so many times, and it was he who had signed the open letter addressed to the pulp and paper workers. Cunning man, that. He took every eye away from Stella.

"Lovely to see so many of you. Thank you for coming to meet with me."

He was shaking hands with one of the women. She seemed to be the spokesperson. She was reading from a piece of paper and I couldn't hear a thing but the chivalrous Mr Grant held up a hand and someone came out from behind him with a megaphone. The spokeswoman looked dwarfed next to him. He put his bulk right next to her and held the megaphone. Her voice crackled out from behind the speaker.

"And the women want a change in the disputes procedure. These long strikes don't work."

With my eye at the viewfinder on my camera, I caught a TV camera sitting on someone's shoulder, and a blonde woman with a microphone. They'd come out from behind a building and were taking the same shot as me, the one where the kind company man looked after the needs of the worker's wife. Interesting we both chose to take a shot at the same time. He was cunning, that Fred Grant, dead cunning.

"This strike started because the pulp and paper workers didn't want a woman on shift," said the megaphone. "Well, we're strong. We could do the work. We could come in and man the machines, keep the mill open while the parties sort out their dispute."

There was a cheer from the crowd. I could just see them, each with a child on hip (because no right-minded man would look after the kids) mothers and children with those yellow hard hats on and one of the kids gets fractious. The mother's distracted and the recovery boiler overheats and the mill's no longer. It was all propaganda. I wondered who'd put these women up to it. Perhaps it was that blonde with the microphone. TV news, maybe.

It was Fred Grant's turn now. He didn't need a megaphone.

"I think your points are reasonable," he said. "As our board of directors sees it, we have three options: number one, the federation could agree to our six conditions and return to work: number two, a new union could be formed and that could take on the work: number three, we close the mill."

That little speech caused a stir. It had been named. The mill could close. The town could die.

The megaphone was passed to another woman.

"We're planning further action after this meeting," she said. "There's a union meeting on Thursday. We'll be there. We've tried to talk to the federation but they won't talk to us women."

There were nods on this. I glanced up at Stella but her face was impassive. The cut on her cheek was stark in the morning sun. I got a feeling she wouldn't be reporting this back to the Old Man but she had arrived with Leo. What would she tell him?

"The situation has to change," Mr Grant said. "We won't call in a third party; the company and the union need to come to an agreement. The company can't operate within the constraints of the union demands. We'll go broke. You, good women that you are, you can influence your men. You can make it known what you want them to decide. It's in your hands."

He turned and left, the TV camera in hot pursuit. High up on a walkway within the mill stood around twenty men, the ones who were still working. They cheered and clapped as the mothers sorted children and the women turned to go home.

Chapter Eighteen
Miriama McLay

My mum was pōrangi. She had to be. She must've gone crazy. She was staunch, my mum. She stood by her man or, at least, she used to. She'd bullied Leo into bringing her and they'd argued all the way here.

"Think about what it means, Stella."

Silence.

"You're the wife of the president of the federation."

Still silence.

"If you stand there with all those women, it means you're against the strike."

Nothing.

"It means the whole town knows you're against the strike."

"That's what I want them to think," she said.

I was staying where I was. If I got out of the ute, I'd be like a scab, well sort of. All that work I did getting those wankers to come and be part of our musical, it would all go up in smoke. That would be the end of it. No Sandy. No Danny. No way for me to meet with Rainbow any more. I liked his name, Rainbow, I liked the way he got all whakamā about it.

Once Mum got out of the car Leo turned around real fast. I didn't know what to do. If I went back home with him it would be so, so boring. He wouldn't go round home and get my stuff, said the Old Man would be too angry. Besides I kind of wanted to stay and see what happened with all these women. Then I saw that reporter

120

lady's car over in the car park and Miss Williams was standing next to it. I had to tell her what had happened 'cos it'd be real hard to get to work from Leo's place.

Leo stopped again and I got out. It was weird, him being so scared of a bunch of women.

Miss Williams and me stood next to that flash red car and watched. There was a TV camera up near the gate and it was sweeping over the crowd. Some of the little kids were jumping around in front of it, trying to be on TV that night. There was Jimmy, the little fulla who lived next door with his nan. He came over sometimes when his nan was at bingo. He was doing a sort of Michael Jackson dance. He could moonwalk, that kid, and he was only four. Mum was at the back, standing next to the reporter lady, the one who owned this flash car.

"You worried about your mum?" asked Miss Williams.

"Nah, not really," I said. "Not here."

I knew she could stand up for herself. She had a lot of mana in this town, my mum, and not just because of the Old Man.

There was a big man standing up the front, like a giant he was. I'd heard my old man say he only pretended to be a gentle giant. There was that fulla Brian's mother talking into the megaphone. She was as bad as her husband, skinny and scabby. She was saying the women would run the mill. Stupid cow, that was how the whole thing started, wasn't it?

That big man held the megaphone for her, like she couldn't do it for herself. She was loving it, going on and on. I reckoned everyone just cheered to shut her up.

"Good show, don't you think, Miriama?" said Miss Williams.

"What do you mean?"

"Don't you think it's interesting that the TV cameras turn up today, when the women have decided to take a stand?"

Then it was all over and the prams were being pushed away and the boss man went back inside the gate. I felt like clapping. Miss Williams was right, it was such a good show.

Miss Williams said her sister was going back into town if I wanted to go, so we hopped in, me all scrunched up in the back. Stupid car didn't have a real back seat, unless you were a dwarf. The reporter lady had long legs too, so I was even more scrunched up. She wasn't shy. I suppose reporters can ask lots of questions and she got stuck in, even before we left the car park.

"Your mum, Miriama, what's she doing here?" and "What happened to her face?" and "What will your dad think?" and "What was Leo doing here?"

They all came out like a big log train, one after the other. I didn't fill in the spaces she left. I thought I'd get in a few questions myself.

"Are you shagging Leo?" I asked.

"Miriama!" said Miss Williams.

"It's not your business," said the reporter lady.

"Why do you think my life is your business then?" I asked.

That got her. She put the car in gear and we went backwards so fast we nearly hit the fence. She must've been hōhā with me.

We were halfway down the straight going to town when she said the next thing.

"Why do you want to know?"

"I don't," I said. "Just wanted to stop you asking me all those questions. You need to watch out for him. He shags anything in a skirt, that's what my old man used to say about him."

Her face looked all closed up, like I'd said something she didn't want to hear. I could see it in her rear vision mirror. She was getting red lipstick on her teeth 'cos she was biting her bottom lip real hard. No idea why she cared about Leo. He's ugly.

"What's happening with you and your mum?" asked Miss Williams. I didn't mind telling her. She wasn't just being nosy, she cared about me.

"The Old Man was drunk last night when we got home. Him and Leo were into the whisky and that's bad. Mum said she was going on the march today and the Old Man lost it. That's how she got the cut on her cheek. That's how come we're staying at Leo's."

"You're staying at Leo's?" asked the reporter lady.

"For now. Mum keeps saying something about not wanting to live a lie any more. I think she's gone a bit pōrangi."

Just then we drove past her. She was walking with the old lady from the marae. I forgot her name but she was always sticking up for us kids when we got in trouble for not helping do the dishes after a big meeting on the marae. She wore a hat or a scarf all the time, even when she was bossing us kids in the kitchen. She wanted to teach me to karanga, call the visitors on to the marae. She was all right. She'd look after Mum.

Back at the library, I helped Miss Williams open up and settled down in the back with the shelving trolley. I liked the quiet in the library. Peaceful, no arguments. I'd been reading all the books in general fiction since last year, starting at A and I got as far as F. Someone else had been doing another game, reading a book from each letter. There were all the letters of the alphabet on the trolley today, they'd even got Z for Zola.

Miss Williams made me jump when she came up behind me. Must be one of the things they teach you at library school, how to sneak around quietly 'cos she was real good at it. She had a whole lot of those Balls and Moon books to put away and she was turning one over and over in her hand. Maybe they leak, those books, can't think why else she asked.

"You and Ray, how are you getting along?"

"We're gonna be the stars of the show. Sandy and Danny forever, just like in those books."

"And apart from the show? Something going on between you?"

"Yeah, well."

What was it about the Williams? Both of them were real nosy. I wasn't sure what to say so I just moved the books around on the trolley. Miss Williams just stood there, waiting.

"Yeah, well, what?" she said.

"He's different," I said. "Like he doesn't know all about my life.

Like he's just meeting me and not all that stuff from my family."

"He doesn't know your history."

"No, and he wants to know me."

"That's refreshing. You both have histories though. They'll come out sometime, you know, Miriama."

I started telling her all about Ray wanting to find his father and the letters and his mum being all secretive and just giving him hints. She was real quiet, must be another librarian thing, she could listen.

"Kiwi Keith," she said. "Interesting. Maybe he could start by looking for all the people called Keith in the town. And asking. Someone's bound to know."

An old lady came in wanting her at the counter. Before she went she told me to be careful, me and Ray she meant. Just like my mum would say. Then I was back doing the alphabet in my head and getting stuck on K.

Chapter Nineteen

Stuart Duncan

"So then the wife of the head of the Sparkies' Union started. What's her name? Can't remember, anyway, she's an upright member of the community, does basketball coaching if I remember rightly."

Fred paused to drink his wine. His big hand almost engulfed the fine crystal glass. He always looked like some kind of enormous bear next to Cynthia. I could hear her talking to someone as she shut the oven door in the kitchen. It was Paul.

"How many women do you estimate were there, Fred?" I asked.

"At least a hundred, I'd say, and piles of kids. That's the best part, all those little kids. It'll look very good on the telly, all those mothers and children who need their men to go back to work."

"It was Jennifer Price who came down, wasn't it?"

"Yes. It paid off, Stuart, your connection with Jennifer. Not only did she come to film this, she's definitely coming back."

"So we might get a half-hour feature, do you think?"

"Definitely," said Fred.

He poured some more red wine into my glass. It wasn't the best wine. I'd have preferred a beer but I didn't want to deny his and Cynthia's hospitality and Fred seemed to think we should be having something of a celebration, especially since Jennifer said she was definitely coming back. Of course, it wasn't a foregone conclusion. I'd not spoken to her, she was a big shot presenter, but her associate would have passed my name on. It had been difficult enough making the intitial phone call, but when Fred had told me she might come back and I'd probably have to talk to her face-to-face, I'd had trouble hiding my trepidation.

I'd watched the demonstration from the staff canteen window. I'd seen her there, her coat collar pulled up and her hair bright in the shadow.

Paul had been here since five, helping Cynthia make pizza. Fred had organised it. He'd taken my tension temperature and told me to go for a run and to come on over when I'd run enough. It'd been just what I'd needed. I'd headed upriver from the bridge, and there'd been no one on the track apart from some youngsters behind the soccer field. They were throwing sticks at the willows on the other side, trying to lodge them in its branches. Each step on the pumice track had jarred me back to this place, this now, my feet pounding, the rhythm of my breath. By the time I'd got up to the rugby field, the shadow was inching up the haunches of the mountain. I'd have liked to have followed the line up, one foot in sun, one in shadow, running to stay in the sun, both sides of the line, but it was getting too late so I'd left it for another day. Timing was everything.

When I'd got to Fred and Cynthia's I was still carrying the last glow of that sunset. Paul's eyes had slid past mine and he'd kept silent when Cynthia had insisted her two little girls come out from the TV room to say hello. They'd stood shyly peeking at his wheelchair. I'd had a brief fantasy that he'd offer them a ride sitting on his lap, wheeling round the dining room table, laughing, but he'd turned back to the kitchen as quickly as he could. I'd clung hard to the gold of that sunset.

"Shall I take the plates now?" Paul's voice came from the kitchen.

"You bring the plates and salad, Paul, I'll bring the pizza."

"Knives and forks?"

"No, they're on the table."

They emerged in a procession, Cynthia with oven gloves on her hands, balancing two trays, stepping carefully after Paul's wheelchair. He was intent on the stack on his lap. He stopped just inside the archway from the kitchen, reversed a little, shifting his weight so he

was balancing on his back wheels. His face was screwed up with con
centration. Cynthia almost tripped over him. The plates rattled and
clashed on his lap as his front wheels hit the carpet again. He was
smiling.

"Well done!" said Fred, his big hands applauding. "We'll have
you in the para-basketball league yet, won't we, Stuart?"

I nodded, bit my lip and nodded. Cynthia was dishing pizza on
to plates, piling on salad.

"I'm not going to try and get the girls in here, Fred," said Cynthia. "They're watching that movie *The Neverending Story* for the
hundredth time. They can eat in front of the TV. Can you take
theirs in please, Paul?"

He could only do it one at a time. If I'd asked him, I'd have just
got a withering look but off he trundled with a plate on his lap.

"So, tell me what you see as the benefits of today, Stuart?" asked
Cynthia. "As well as the media coverage, I mean."

"Well, I think your husband's a marvel," I said. "He's showed up
again as being on the side of the townspeople."

"It was you who sent me out, Stuart, to meet them," Fred said.

"It's breaking down the perception of management being aloof,"
I said.

"Shows the cracks in the unions, doesn't it?" asked Cynthia. "I
heard that Stella McLay was there."

"Stella, who's she?" I asked.

"Wife of the president, the one they call the Old Man," said
Cynthia. "I heard she turned up with a great cut along her face. I
can understand her changing sides if he did that to her."

"Oh, but Cynthia," said Fred. "It gets stranger and stranger. It
was Leo Harris who dropped her off, in that decrepit ute of his."

Paul had come back for another plate. He stacked one on top
of the other. Seemed he preferred the TV to us.

"The inner circle falling apart?" I asked.

"Won't do our cause any harm," said Fred. "See what else you
can find out, Cynthia."

"I will," said Cynthia. "What do you think of getting wives of the management to join some of those protesting women when Jennifer Price comes back? We could stage a feminine insurrection."

"Very funny, Cynthia," said Fred. "You'd look very chic in a hard hat."

"Maybe not. Anyway, it's got possibilities. Just think about it," said Cynthia. "Stuart, I'm curious about how you know Jennifer."

"Old friends, Cynthia, that's all," I said.

I concentrated on getting the stringy cheese on my fork, hoping she wouldn't ask again. Jennifer had been a friend of Paul's mother, Carol, my late wife.

You're having an affair, aren't you, she'd accused. How could you? She's my best friend. I could see Paul through the open door. I'd smiled, hoping against hope that he hadn't heard. I don't think I'd said anything incriminating. Neither acknowedged nor denied.

"I haven't seen her for a long time," I said. "It's great she came. Lovely pizza, thanks very much for this."

"I believe we've lost Paul to *The Neverending Story*. He's in there with the girls," said Fred.

The television was flickering in the corner of my eye. The Nothing was eating away at the Empress's kingdom, making it smaller and smaller and she was stuck in a tower that had no foundation. Someone had to rescue her.

There was no one to rescue me. Jennifer was coming back. She was coming back and she was going to want to interview me, the CEO. Me, whose world had shrunk since I last saw her. Me, whose only commitment was to Paul, and, of course, to open and honest communication.

Chapter Twenty
Ima Williams

"And the old man carved the little puppet's face very, very carefully. He made the face look like his own face might have looked when he was a little boy. A laughing mouth, and a little turned-up nose. When he made the nose, the old man found a tear running down his own. How he wished he had a little boy like this one. A little boy to love him and play with him."

There were five little turned up noses and ten big brown eyes looking up at Notta. She was in her element. She told me this was the best thing about being a librarian: story time with the little kids, because they still believed in things.

"The old man was feeling very sad and very tired because it was late. So, blowing his nose on his big spotty handkerchief, he blew out his candle, put the shutters up at the windows and went to bed. That night while he was asleep a wonderful thing happened. The moon peeped out from behind a cloud and sent a moonbeam down through the window. It touched the little puppet with the laughing mouth. In the moonbeam, silvery and beautiful, was a fairy. Her job was to make wishes come true."

"Has she got a lightsaber, Miss? You know, like in *Star Wars*?"

"Well, she's got a wand, a magic wand. I guess it's a bit like a lightsaber. Anyway, she waves her magic wand over the puppet and guess what happens?"

"He turns into a transformer, Miss, and he goes boom, boom and the whole house gets blown up."

"No, Hoani, that's not what happens. The puppet comes alive."

"Like a vampire, Miss?"

"No, like you, like a real boy. He becomes a real boy and it's because his father wished so hard."

I could see that Hoani was thinking about this. I admired Notta's patience but I knew it wouldn't last with this onslaught. There was another arm waving around, a little girl's.

"Like when I wished for a new bike for my birthday, Miss? And I got my sister's old one with a pakaru wheel. Wishes don't work."

"Ah, Prudence, sometimes wishes and magic spells are tricky. This magic spell has another bit to it. This real boy has to always tell the truth because if he tells lies, something happens."

"He gets a hiding, Miss?"

"No Prudence, he doesn't. His nose grows very long and it stays long until he tells the truth again."

"That's a stink story, Miss. He should become a werewolf and eat up that old man and the fairy."

Notta was losing the patience she'd been practising so hard. She had these kids for another half hour. Their mums were outside smoking. She was going to have to hold it together.

"Hoani, you watch too many of your big brother's videos! This is what happens, he grows up and the old man loves him very, very much. When he's big, he leaves home and he makes bad friends, very bad friends. They make a gang and call themselves the Business Roundtable. They have patches and special handshakes and they hijack the government and they all become very rich."

"And he gets to buy a big car and have a TV that works all the time and he can pay the grocery bill, Miss?"

It was one of the mothers. She'd wandered in without Notta seeing her but Notta was full steam ahead now and she just carried straight on.

"This wooden puppet, let's call him Pinocchio (although he doesn't like the name because he prefers to be called Grant), he becomes a head of operations. He tells so many lies that his nose grows and grows until he can't move anymore and he turns back into a wooden puppet, with no feelings at all! Then the union workers come and tip him into the ground wood and he gets made into pulp. The end."

With that, Notta stood up and left five little faces and a mother in confusion.

"Well done, sister mine," I said.

I just got a "humph" and she disappeared into the back office.

"Do you want to come to the meeting on the marae, Notta? It starts in fifteen minutes and you could close the library for lunch time."

There was no answer. I just left it. Stella would be waiting for me. It was she who had asked if I wanted to come and I was meeting her at the gate over with the smell of rotten eggs, or was it brimstone?

There was a crowd of people inside the gate but I couldn't see any sign of Stella. She'd told me to wait. I was the only not-brown one and I wasn't sure if I should join them or not. I was dragging my feet, trying to look as if I could just be going past when that ute pulled up behind me. Leo leaned out the window. I could feel the pull of him, it was as if his body was a magnet. What was it with that man? Digging my heels in, I stared at his hand resting on the window frame. Those callouses had scratched me.

"What're you doing here?" he asked.

I pretended the sun was in my eyes and put my arm up as a shield so he couldn't see the blush going up my throat.

"Might ask the same of you," I said. "Thought this was for Māori only."

"Just dropping this one off," he said.

"Miriama?" I said. "You coming to the meeting?"

"He's got me under arrest, Miss. I haven't been read my rights. Can you tell your sister to get me a lawyer?"

"Miriama!" he said. "You just go and meet up with your mum and I'll come back for you later."

"Fuck off," she said.

"Don't you talk to me like that, young lady," he said.

She got out of the ute and slammed the door so hard that the toolbox on the back tray jumped. If looks could kill, she'd need a lawyer all right. Leo was off with his back tyres kicking up more dust and I was left with a sixteen-year-old wrapping her arms around herself and glowering at me so hard that I couldn't watch that tail pipe disappearing.

"Nice day," I said. "Where's your mum?"

She almost snarled back at me and I was wondering what to do if she told me to fuck off too when Stella came across the grass to the gate. The first thing I noticed was that slash down her cheek. The skin was knitting into a puckered line. The next thing I noticed was that she wore a skirt, as did every other woman, even Miriama. I was in trousers. Dress code wasn't the only mystery. Stella came straight up to Miriama, put her hands on her daughter's shoulders and started talking to her in Māori. Her voice was soft and reasonable but the staunch teenager wasn't thawing, not one little bit.

A woman's voice sang out from the crowd over at the carved house. The call rose high and drifted. The hair on the back of my neck rose with it. It was as if the sound was pulling us in and the crowd at the gate began to stir. Stella kissed her reluctant daughter on the top of the head, and moved towards the front of the crowd. She began the answering call, starting low and lifting her voice to weave with the other caller's voice as the women started to move on to the grass between the gate and the carved house. Miriama shoved me to the front next to her mother. The sound pulled us in as the threads of the voices linked and knotted together. The crowd had rearranged itself. There were six men behind us and I caught a glimpse of two clerical collars. Stella told me that today was a chance for people to talk about support for each other. I hoped this didn't translate into a church service, with everyone bowing their heads down as they walked, it certainly had a feel of it.

Then we were sitting outside the carved house, facing a few of the crowd who were sitting opposite us, and the sun was warm on our backs. It was almost spring. There were speeches, first from the other side, then ours. Stella led a song after each of our two speakers. She was at home here, strong, a woman with a place. Maybe I could bring that theme in: women and their place in a town where men fronted everything, including this.

A fair crowd stood behind the seated speakers. Stella whispered in my ear that this meeting was for pulp and paper workers and their wives, to give them a chance to talk in a place where they felt comfortable. The Māori bishop had come to help out. All of the faces were brown.

"Suppose you don't know how to do a hongi line?" whispered Miriama.

"A what?" I asked.

"Go and greet everyone. You can just shake hands and kiss people on the cheek. Even you can do that."

So I followed her and shook and kissed and shook and kissed. And people said something in Māori and I did my best and said kia ora, which was about all I knew. No one asked me why I was here with my white face and my leather coat. Maybe they just thought I was the bishop's fancy woman and were too polite to ask.

We were finally all inside the carved house, without our shoes. The two men in clerical collars sat behind a table set up at the front and a local man sat with them. I'd seen him around but not in a suit like this with his hair all slicked down and his bald patch shining with hair oil.

"He's the chairman of the marae committee," said Stella.

"Is he a pulp and paper worker?" I asked.

"All of them are," she said. "Except the bishop and his assistant, of course."

As the prayers droned on, I counted the people at the meeting. Forty men, so they must have been the pulp and paper workers, and forty-seven women, which meant one wife for each worker and a few extra.

At last the bishop sat down and the chairman made an announcement.

"This meeting's for us to talk about how the strike is affecting us all, not to paddle the canoe of any one cause."

After a long pause, an older man got up and cleared his throat. He didn't look up from the floor so it was hard to hear him.

"It's hard to talk at the meetings," he said. "I feel too whakamā. I don't want to look like, I don't know, to look stupid."

He sat down and there was a murmur of agreement.

"They don't listen to us anyway," said a voice from the back.

"Come on man, stand up," said the chairman. "Let's see who you are."

A long string bean of a man got to his feet.

"They don't listen to us," he said. "The union exec, they don't want to know what we think. Even if we get up the courage to talk, they don't want to know."

"Even if they don't want to hear," said another man, jumping to his feet, "you need to keep telling them. You can use your vote, man."

It went on for another hour. None of the women spoke. None of the men were happy with the union's conduct.

Afterwards we were balancing cups of tea and scones in the other building and subdued conversation was going on around me.

"Thanks for inviting me, Stella," I said.

"Did you get some good stuff for your article?" she said.

"I think so. Things aren't so solid, are they?"

"You could say that."

"Would you say people seem to be turning on the leadership, on your husband and Leo?"

"I'd say they're sick of being out of work."

I was itching to ask about her and Leo and what her staying with him meant but I thought I'd better stick to my knitting, as my grandma used to say, so I tried to leave Leo out of it.

"As a union wife, where are your loyalties, Stella? It's interesting that you went on the march against the strike. Where do you stand with the federation?"

"We have a saying, where I come from. 'Mate atu he tētēkura, whakaete mai he tetēkura.' It means, 'When a leader falls, another rises.'"

"So you're pulling your support from your husband and putting it behind Leo?"

"That man, he's not my husband."

"And Leo?"

"Let's just say it's complicated. Come on Miriama, we have to go."

She threw a last comment over her shoulder at me.

"What makes you think every leader is a man?"

Not the best interview I'd run. If she was referring to the skinny woman with the megaphone leading the mother brigade she was dreaming. She must have been talking about herself. I didn't get a chance to find out.

Chapter Twenty-one

Ray Parlane

The conversation with my mother—with Liz, I mean—in a public phone booth must have sounded stark raving bonkers to anyone who could hear it. It went like this:

Me: *Liz? It's me. No, me. Rainbow, your son. I'm ringing from New Zealand.*

Liz: *Darling, I was waiting for your call. I dreamt last night, you know, that you were lost in a green, green forest. Lost in your heart chakra, if you know what I mean.*

Me: *Yes, it is. It's very green. I don't know about the chakra bit.*

Liz: *I'm sure you're doing some deep work. That's what the heart chakra is about, forgiveness and love, you know.*

Me: *Right, well, if you say so. I'm trying to find out how Harry is. Can I talk to him?*

Liz: *I don't think so, Rainbow. He needs to be present to his mortality right now. That takes stillness and I think you would disturb that.*

Me: *Do you mean he's dying, Liz, is that what you mean?*

Liz: *We're all dying, darling. All of us.*

Me: *I promise I won't upset him. I just want to talk to him.*

Liz: *Darling, I know you would want to put Harry's wellbeing before your own so, well, no, you can't talk to him.*

Me: *What about Stan? Can I talk to Stan?*

Liz: *He's busy meditating with Harry right now. Can I give him a message?*

That was when my coins ran out. I was none the wiser, just furious with my mother. Sometimes she was Medea incarnate. She'd cut me up and feed me to the sea, just because. She'd never wanted me to be close to Stan and Harry and she wouldn't give me any more information about my real father. Bitch.

I was supposed to be going to a rehearsal, all day since it was Saturday, but the last thing I wanted to do was sing and dance. I wanted to see Harry. I wanted to go home.

Then Miriama came roaring up on her bike and jumped off like Boadicea exiting her chariot and I didn't want to tell her about the phone call. It felt too far away from here and she was so innocent, anyway. To try and get the conversation with my mother out of my head I told her about the pep talk I'd got from Colin yesterday, about how I shouldn't be seeing her, because it'd look bad for the Hopewells. I told her that I'd said I was open-minded about the whole strike thing and that he could use the association between me, his guest, and the daughter of the president of the federation to show that this town kept talking even when things were difficult.

"What did he say?"

"He said that was wise thinking and showed how mature I am, especially if I keep an open mind about the advantages for the mill when the workers agree to the conditions."

"When the workers agree? We're staunch, man, you don't understand that, do you? We won't be giving in."

"What's the 'we', Miriama?"

We'd reached the steps of the hall before she could answer. She dumped her bike and was in the door. I had to follow her; I'd promised I'd be in this musical but most of me just wanted to piss off.

It was one of those splendid blue-sky days that never happen in England. A day with the colour so intense you just wanted to fly up into it. It wasn't so cold; the frost had been light, just passing fingers on shady grass, and there was warmth in the sun. It felt like the town was holding in a toke of cold winter, letting the smoke dribble out towards the spring that might come next week maybe, or even tomorrow.

For all that, I just wanted to go home. Autumn would be coming. Big oak leaves curdling in the gutters near the park, clouds full of rain moving in then tipping it down. The dark coming early.

"Danny," called that Miss Something. "We're waiting for you."

"Yeah, Mr Star, come and shine on us," said June.

I had to be present, in a production.

"Now I know there's some of the cast who can't come today," said Miss Something. "Yesterday's meeting has caused some problems but, all of you, this show matters to your town. There are only three weeks to opening night …"

"And the show must go on," I said.

"That's absolutely right, Ray. The show must go on."

"Miss, I'm just glad to get out of my house. All the raruraru and stuff."

"Yeah, me too. Too much of nothing to do for my dad means he falls in love with the bottle."

"And my dad, he was talking about how stink your old man is, Miriama."

Miriama was sitting against the wall with her head down. She'd closed up like a jack-in-a-box, her spring set to lethal so we started the rehearsal with Miriama glaring at me and me still in a blue funk about Harry. Miss got us started on my song to Sandy, after she'd rejected me and I'm all heartbroken. I sang about being in misery, which wasn't far from the truth. Miriama sat and glared at me. Miss made me do it over and over. Just like when Stan and Harry were putting on a show, we'd rehearse until our voices were almost gone. My voice caught and I coughed. When Miss called for us to take a break, Miriama scrunched herself up against the wall again.

"Hey," I said, hunkering down next to her.

No reply.

"We don't need to be like in the roles, you know."

No reply.

"Miriama, what is it?"

"You wouldn't understand."

"Try me."

"Nah."

If I stayed, we were bound to have a barney, so I started inching my way back up the wall, just slowly. Me pretending to leave seemed to unblock the dam.

"It's Mum. She's staunch my mum, she's always been staunch. She's union, eh. Then she goes and walks with all those other women, like she's saying the whole strike is wrong. The Old Man shouldn't've hit her, he shouldn't, but he did, so she gets all hōhā with him and goes walking with the other women. That's all right. I get that."

I was back on the floor. I leaned sideways a bit so my shoulder was touching hers. No hand, I knew she couldn't manage a hand yet.

"Then she's at the meeting on the marae, agreeing with that dick who says he feels too hōhā to talk at the union meetings because the Old Man's a bully and going along with starting a special committee of pulp and paper workers. So she's still hōhā with her husband. I get that, too."

She had both her hands cupping her face, like blinkers on an old carthorse, and she was looking straight ahead.

"But if she's so staunch about calling off the strike, what's she doing in bed fucking Leo? That's where she was, Rainbow, this afternoon she was in bed fucking the secretary of the union."

I've found my mother in bed with snake charmers, clairvoyants, shamans, and young men just passing through. It never seemed to mean anything to her. "Share the love," she'd say. Or the crack, or the dope, or the LSD.

"I don't know who she is anymore," she said.

"Maybe you're right, she's getting back at your dad. Maybe."

"Yeah. Well, why's she joining in with that committee to try and get the strike busted?"

"Maybe she's changed her mind about the strike, Miriama. People do."

"Fuck you! Fuck you, you stupid Pom! You don't know. You just don't know about being staunch, do you? Just like stupid Danny in this dumb musical. You're just a stupid prick."

I grabbed for her hand but she pulled it away and stormed out of the hall. I should've called out to her, followed her and tried to calm her down but I was stuck back in that bloody phone conversation this morning. "You must be doing deep work, darling ..."

Mothers.

By the time I got out the door, I was sure she'd be long gone. I was just about to slope off home, such as home was, but there she was huddled up next to her bike and she was sobbing. Silently. The most painful kind, when your body has to do all the work. I knew what to do. I sat down next to her and fished out my nice clean handkerchief. We'd been here before.

I sneaked it in past the tangle of hair and she snatched at it. Then I sneaked my arm around her and she shuddered and gasped and blew her nose. No one I know can cry, I mean really cry, with any elegance. Not even this staunch Māori maiden.

She was trying to say something and it was coming out in gasps but I could get the gist. This morning she went back into the bedroom she shared with her mother at Leo's house and Leo and her mother were at it. They didn't see her but she saw them and she said her mother was calling him darling. Sounded to me like another round of the fight between her mother and father. No wonder she couldn't deal with the song this morning, with Sandy feeling so cheated by Danny and Danny so miserable about it.

She leaned into me until there were just hiccups left.

"Hey," I said.

"Hey yourself," she said.

"Shit happens."

"Ae, lots of tūtae."

"Speaking of which ..."

Leo was coming over the little bit of grass up to the hall. He looked as if he'd just got out of bed, which I suppose he had, in a manner of speaking. He stood right in front of the sun so I had to squint up at him. Miriama was suddenly very interested in her feet. I tightened my arm around her and it was all very still and quiet.

"I've come to take you home, Miriama," he said.

"Not coming."

"It's time we talked. Me and you and your mother."

"Fuck off."

"Don't. Please Miriama."

"Why should I?"

"Because we know what you saw this morning, girl."

"So what's there to talk about?"

"Whakapapa, Miriama."

That word. It was the one Miriama used when she said I needed to find my father, I needed to know where I came from. What it had to do with this God only knew, but Miriama unfolded herself from the step and stood up. I was still squinting into the sun as Leo turned around and walked away with Miriama following in his wake.

Chapter Twenty-two
Miriama McLay

So I was under arrest for real. Jammed in between Mum and the ugly man who kept shoving his elbow in my ribs when he put the old ute in gear. He turned the corner and I crashed over to Mum, turned another corner and I crashed over to Leo. He swerved and swore at me.

"Slow down, e kare," said Mum.

What was she doing calling Leo e kare? That was what she called people she loved, like me. That was what I wanted to call Rainbow when he got all amorous on me. E kare.

We were heading along the straight now, past the mill, and at least I didn't have to push my feet so hard to try and keep my balance. The floor of this old ute was so rusty I could end up like the Flintstones, running with my feet through the holes.

"No more woodchips," said Mum.

"Stopped the ground wood," said Leo. "Sawmill's been down a few days."

"Fullas must be feeling hōhā about that," said Mum.

"Yeah," said Leo. "Not their fight either, just got caught up in it."

The mountain of woodchips always glowed, even when it was a cloudy day. Me and my mates had dared each other to break into the mill and climb it. Reckoned it would be harder than climbing our real mountain, Putauaki, with its ash that made you go one step up, two slides down. The only thing that put us off was when someone said their brother caught rats out there, hundreds of them.

Under the glowing top, that big heap must've been rotten.

"I want to go and stay with my mates," I said.

"You can't," said Leo.

"Not for you to say," I said.

"You can't," said Mum. "Not yet, anyway."

"Look, Miriama, we just want to have a talk to you, me and your mum."

So we sat in the ute, driving along, like some kind of happy family. Leo was even whistling. It was that song, the one my cuzzy was playing when I was born, the ten guitars one. He was such an arsehole.

Mum was out of the ute and in the house before me and Leo. He was farting around in the glove box, didn't even notice when I gave him my best evils, so I just got out and went inside. Mum had already changed out of her marae gear, back into her trackies. We liked trackies, me and Mum. She was fussing in the kitchen.

"Where's the cat?" I asked.

"Catching rats I hope. Miriama, sit down love. When Leo comes in we've got something we want to tell you."

While she was getting out cups and stuff, I had a good look at my mum. A proper look. She was good-looking, Mum. Like me, she had a face that was real strong, a warrior face that said, "don't mess around with this wahine". Somehow she looked different, softer, and she was wearing makeup. She had lipstick on. Even when she went to the marae and did the karanga like this morning, she never wore makeup. She wouldn't look at me.

Finally, Leo came in and the teapot was sitting in the middle of the table and both he and Mum were staring at it. Then they looked at each other in that way that adults sometimes do as if they've got a secret code that means they're about to launch at you with their superior knowledge but they want the other one to start. I couldn't stand it.

"Shall I ask the questions?" I said. "Like why you two were, you know, at it this afternoon?"

Mum's mouth opened like she was about to tell me off but Leo put a hand up. What did he think he was, some kind of prophet or something?

"When you were born, Miriama, I was there," said Leo.

"So was half of Mum's whānau. So what?"

"Did you ever wonder why I've had so much to do with your life, from when you were really young?"

"I just thought you were a sad old man with no children so you pretended I'm yours."

"You are mine, Miriama. You're my daughter."

He was so ugly, Leo. He had a squashed nose and a whole lot of stringy hair that he tied back. He didn't look like my father. I didn't believe him. My father was the Old Man, the fulla who banged on all the time about the evils of big companies with lots of money and the greed of shareholders. He was union. I was union. Up till he hit Mum, she used to be union too. That's who we were.

"Oh yeah," I said.

Then Mum started. She went on about how she married Dad before Leo arrived in town and she and Dad were trying to have babies and how she never got hapū and Dad got tested and he was firing blanks. Then Leo arrived and became part of their family and they decided that Leo would be the father of this special baby who everyone would love.

That meant he was screwing Mum. He screwed anything in a skirt. That was what the Old Man said about him, even though he was round our place all the time and he and the Old Man were best mates. It was disgusting.

"So you and Leo were at it right from the beginning?" I asked.

"We decided that it was better I stay with the Old Man, I mean, with my husband, and that you would be brought up by us."

"That was the contract," said Leo. "Secrecy was part of it."

"Why? Why didn't you two just get together?"

"The Old Man's a big name in union circles," said Leo. "We decided it was important to keep his reputation intact. It was our way of supporting him."

So I was lied to so that union could stay out of the gossip, like it was more important than me. It didn't make any sense and I felt like the water going down the plughole, the me I thought I was just disappearing like dirty bathwater. The real me, I was just the scummy soap mark that had someone else's skin in it.

"Were you ever going to tell me?" I asked.

Mum was squirming in her seat. She'd bitten the lipstick off her bottom lip. She reached a hand out and I snatched mine away.

My ten guitars song was going round in my head. It was the song that everyone sang at my birthday parties when the cake Mum made came out, with one more candle each year. Leo always there with a present, and a kiss, right on my forehead. Mr Union, the Old Man, at the back, just watching. The birthday parties marched through my head, the one when we gutsed on chocolate cake and I was sick all over Leo, the one when Leo organised a big treasure hunt and we were all pirates. He was Captain Hook and made my best friend cry because he was so ugly.

"We were going to tell you when you turned eighteen, e kare," said Mum.

"But things have changed," said Leo.

I couldn't look at them anymore. I was hiding under my hair and my guts were all tied up and I couldn't even look at them.

"Miriama," said Leo. "I've always loved you. You've always been my little girl."

I was out of there as fast as I could. The chair caught my foot and down it went with a crash. I made it down the hallway and out the front door before the first earthquake sob came up.

Bastard.

I was thrashing through the privet hedge to the middle part, where I could sit and cry and no one would try to make me feel better.

Jeez, I hated crying, I hated that I couldn't be staunch and just keep it all in. I hated that I got so much hupe and so much upset.

I hated it. Something soft plonked itself down beside me. It was Homehelp, Leo's old cat. I pulled her up on my knee and she purred as I wet her fur and her claws dug into my knee.

"Leo." Her claws were pushing it into me. "Leo, your father is Leo."

Fuck.

Chapter Twenty-three

Leo Harris

It feels like there's a hole in this head just lately and all I thought I was doing with my life is just falling out. I thought I'd bloody got over her. I thought we'd finished this years ago. We'd agreed it was too risky to keep fucking, to keep having the kind of thing happening like when our baby was born, that one and only time I'd felt I'd done something with my no-good life. I'd made this perfect little person, with toes and fingers and she looked at me as if I was part of her and she was part of me.

That's when I fell in love, not just with that little brown baby, but with her mother.

Fuckin' awesome she was. She sang when she gave birth. The cuzzies might have been singing "Ten Guitars" out in the waiting room but Stella was chanting something, real soft, that made my insides melt. Guess hers were too, because there was this little black circle of hair, then these eyes looking at me. While she was still being born, she was looking at me like she knew who I was, like she'd already met me. Then this slippery little body all covered in some kind of white stuff, and blood, Stella's blood. She was perfect. So perfect. She didn't even cry, just looked and looked as if to say "Yeah, I've been here before, I'm back now."

It was me who held her first.

I think that was a mistake.

Still, no one suspected. We kept the contract. We kept the pact. Union first, we said, always union first. Anyway, me? I'm not one for commitment. No ties, that's me, they just get you staying with someone when it's killing you, I mean, really killing you, like you're getting your head smashed in. That's what commitment does for you. Commitment to that fuckin' dangerous stuff called love.

Fuck. It's all gone down the tubes now. She's in my bed again after sixteen years and I still feel like we're part of each other; me, Stella and that stroppy daughter of mine. We go together like strawberries and cream. All that fuckin' stupid romantic stuff.

So I'm left with a choice. Family reunion or Union with a capital U. Yes you, you Leo Harris, you need to make the choice. What a fuckin' choice. I just can't think about it.

And then there's that big shot from TV One. She's chasing me because she can't get hold of the Old Man. She wants to make a TV programme about what's happening in the town. That means about the strike. I've already got a hole in the head and I don't need another one. I know her name, Jennifer. I've seen her on TV before. She's a good-looking wahine who sounds a bit American. Bloody hell, I need her chasing me like I need to fall in love with Stella again and I know if I don't talk to her she'll do a fuckin' one-sided thing like everyone else does. Union with a capital U. That's what I'm committed to.

She wants a tour of the mill. Not with management, but with management and union. She said she tried ringing the Old Man but got no reply. She wants shots of her walking in the deserted paper machine between management and me. Shit.

It's no use asking the Old Man if I should do this, no use at all. I think he's probably been on the turps since Stella and Miriama left. Still, a few phone calls and the rest of the exec's OK with me doing it. They back me up on it being a good chance to put the union point of view. So Miss Jennifer picks me up in her rental station wagon with all the camera stuff and two blokes in the back. Only one of them even looks at me. Miss Jennifer says he's called Gary and he stinks of Old Spice. I get a grunt then he goes back to picking his nose. The other fulla I don't even get a name for, he's rooting round in a bag and pulling out cords. At least it takes my mind off all that other stuff.

The scabs on security haven't got any instructions about the TV crew and they're real worried about me. After all, I'm locked out, not allowed inside the place because I'm one of them, the "troublesome union". We're left sitting there while they ring up old Colin Hopewell for directions so I get a few shots in. I start by complaining about how itchy old scabs are, 'specially when they been there for what is it now, fifty days, how you just want to tear at them with your fingernails. No response, just the stupid bastard looking worried, so I ask the rear vision mirror how it must be for the staunch federation members who're being true to themselves, how it must feel to have some other prick doing their job, how they must feel like throwing a brick through a window or something.

Then Mr Gary Grunt asks me if I'm threatening the prick on the gate. What a fuckin' cheek, as if it's any of his business. I say I was just speaking rhetorically, he can make of it what he wants. I can see him glaring at me in the rear vision mirror, then he gets his finger back up his snorer. The prick on the gate waves us in, except Miss Jennifer has no idea where to go. She says we're picking up a Colin Hopewell so I direct her to staff parking, just as if I go there every day.

There he is, Mr Hopewell, Assistant Public Relations Manager for the company, Assistant Master of Weasel Words. You can see his dirty fingerprints all over the press releases, starting back with that bloody letter we all got shoved in our letterboxes at the beginning. I'd shove it back up his jacksey given half the chance. We all get out of the car with Gary Grunt pulling out his camera and his shadow holding on to a long furry thing. That's for the sound, says Miss Jennifer, so we can pick up every word. I take a cue from the cameraman and grunt at Hopewell, just in case.

Another scab gives us hard hats and I say I would've brought my own if I'd known. He just looks nervous. Hopewell looks ridiculous in his office gear and a bright yellow hat. Miss Jennifer looks very sexy, I think, and I sort of tell her so, say it sets off her blonde hair a treat. She just looks at me as if I'm something the cat dragged in. The cameraman and soundman refuse to wear them. They've got big earmuff things to wear. The scab lets them away with it. Let's face it, there's no danger from a stationary paper machine.

My last shift was a midnight to eight and it was business as usual, with the cocktail of chemical smells at the wet end, where the slurp of bleached mush gets laid out on the meshes to dry. You wouldn't want to fall in, not when it's your job to check the wood pulp's not clumping up. You wouldn't come up smelling of roses, fact is you might not come up at all. Then there's the high-pitched sound of the press section where the water gets squeezed out, the paper going through roller after roller like your undies through an old fashioned wringer, would take your arm if you're not careful. Then the paper threads through felts to dry, so hot it makes your socks itch inside your boots. We left it running when we walked off and the maintenance boys swore at us as they raced in to shut it down. It's us who make the paper, it's us the company bloody needs.

I walk behind them, Hopewell puffing his fat self down the gangway, Jennifer TV sandwiched between us. Like a little trail of ducklings crossing the road, we come down on to the floor of the paper machine and we're walking around a sad, still place. The three of us walk alongside each other. I give the emergency stop button a push and it swings on its cable. There are sparrows chirping up high in the corrugated iron roofing, crapping on the last stretches of white empty paper still on the machine, threaded through and around the dryer section and disappearing into the calender stack. There's no lights on the control panel. It's a dead dalek.

Interesting what an office jockey like Hopewell thinks he knows about papermaking. Bastard is rabbiting on to Miss Jennifer like he's been the machine supervisor for twenty years. I'm not saying anything, not till we get to the end of the machine where a half-filled roll sits on the winder. It's ripped and the loose end of paper flaps gently. There's a bloody great hole in the floor here and I tell her what it's for, that this is where the odd gang pulls the paper off when there's a break, and they push it through the hole in the floor. Once a young fulla who was new here forgot the rules about the hose you use to wash the stuff down that bloody great hole. He wrapped it round his waist. It's high-pressure water and the hose pulled him in. That shut Hopewell up.

I tell her that the paper machine's a dangerous place that needs skilled workers and enough men to watch your back and keep you safe, that Management (with a capital M) haven't got any bloody idea of what it's like to work down here on the floor. I just keep talking when Hopewell starts going on about the manning ratio in Canadian paper mills. The bastard's never been near this one when the noise blasts you near off your feet. He wouldn't know what it feels like when the paper breaks at four in the morning and you're knackered because you've done a double shift and haven't slept for a coupla days and you need to be awake because otherwise you'll wind up like that young fulla, screaming as you disappear down the hole with the waste. Gone before we could get to the emergency button. Lived in this town all his life.

We use hand signals when the machine's rolling. We've got one for middle management wallahs like him. It's tongue out to lick the air, and a slap on your own arse. Jennifer TV catches me with my tongue out and gives me a strange look. She says she really wants an interview with the Old Man and would I jack it up for her.

That puts me in a bind, I can tell you.

Do you play Scrabble? You've got such control. You get to move the letters around to say anything you want. Mind you, there's a catch in that: you have to take into account the words others have said. It's not hard, though, to make new words, new meanings. You get what I'm talking about, I'm sure.

Guess which words are whose?

The final word in the matter at present is STALEMATE. There's never a place to put that word.

The newspaper's good at playing Scrabble. Watch these slippery words carefully now, so they don't just slide off the page and onto your Scrabble board.

"Get them back to work, Jim."

"The crowd were stunned, then horrified."

"Cries of anguish ..."

Count the number of words in this paragraph:

"'The mill will remain mothballed and will stay that way while the militant faction is in control of the union,' said Mr Grant, the Manager of Operations."

There's more than in this one:

"The Northern Federation of Pulp and Paper Workers has consistently argued that a job created must be retained."

I think you could say that the company gets a triple word score for "militant faction ..."

Chapter Twenty-four
Stuart Duncan

*I'm running, or at least my feet are going up and down, but
I don't seem to be moving. Maybe it's the surface, maybe it's
moving and I'm not, but I don't know what I'm running on,
or why, I just know I'm getting nowhere. For all that running,
I'm going nowhere.*

I sat up and my heart was bashing itself inside every part of me.
My feet jerked against the floor and met carpet. Maybe that was the
problem, I was trying to run on carpet. I was barefoot and there
were walls around me and I was sitting on a bed. The blood rushing round my body shut up enough to let in a bird, twittering as if
it mattered in the world. My eyes opened and they registered the
clock saying it was five twenty-two, in bright green. As I stared at
it, it moved to five twenty-three. So sure of itself.

Before I could think about it, before the dream could seduce
me back in, I took off my pyjamas and pulled on my track pants
and a sweatshirt. I had my shoes laced by the time the clock rolled
over to five twenty-eight.

I was about to open the front door when that same feeling came
back, as if I was trying to get somewhere and my feet wouldn't take
me and I didn't know where that somewhere was or why I couldn't
get there. I had to go back, listen at Paul's door, hear nothing, get
halfway to the front door, go back to Paul's door, turn the handle
and change my mind. I stood there for some fog of a time; maybe

the clock turned over another minute or another ten.

"Do something, Stuart. Stop dithering," I muttered.

It got me going. I was out the door and down the path.

It was on that edge, not quite night and not quite dawn yet. The squeaky bird was a little premature. I didn't plan my route; I turned my face to the east and my feet followed. The path took me downhill, along the creek. There was a dim orange light from the road nearby and patches of black. It was wet under the willows, and I wished I'd put on thicker socks. The creek was sliding along beside me. Every now and then it interrupted itself, as if to make some point that was completely lost on me. I took the first bridge I could and ran out onto the sports field. The grass crunched. My breath deepened.

Up ahead of me, on the horizon, was a series of chimneys, some in clumps, some standing by themselves. A thin stream of smoke came from one of them. For no reason I could fathom, that was where my feet were going. They took me across a deserted main road and down one of the streets. The houses were still asleep. Inside, there would be snoring and dreaming and maybe someone awake, worrying about money and the mortgage. Some of the men in these houses should have been up the road, making the chimneys smoke. All they needed to do was say yes. They didn't seem to believe that there was a distinct possibility those chimneys would never smoke again.

When Paul was small he would play with Lego for hours. He never followed the instructions that came in the boxes we bought for him, preferring to use his own imagination. He would spend all day making enormous buildings with towers, chimneys and secret alleys. Then he'd smash them, methodically, with an intent look on his face that would turn to pleasure when his buildings, so painstakingly built, were razed to the ground. It had crossed my mind that I should worry about it, once. In comparison, it seemed trivial. Life sent you bigger challenges.

"I think you could handle the interview, Fred."

"Won't do, Stuart, she'll be expecting to speak to the CEO. It'll have to be your face that TV viewers see."

"She can expect away. She'll get whoever she's given. Look, you've been closer to the action than me this last year. I'm a late-comer to all of the background to this dispute."

"Doesn't matter," Fred said. "You just need to hold the company line."

"Sometimes I think you're clearer on it than me."

I could feel Fred eye-balling me. I stopped shuffling paper, moving one on top of the other then to the bottom, as if chance was going to intervene and my hand would improve. He'd never make a poker player. I could see his disapproval of my elusiveness.

"Come on, Stuart, what's the matter with you? You know as well as I do that things have changed. This is a modern company; it needs to earn profits and hasn't for a number of years. You know all that."

"Yes, yes. It's overmanned, not an arm of social welfare and all that."

"And this union has held us to ransom for too long. We've talked about it often enough, known this showdown would come."

"I know all that, too."

"Look. This company is good to its workers. It always has been. You and I believe in this company, Stuart. You've been through a hard time, I grant you, and the company's supported you through it. Remember that."

He was right. All that leave I'd had to take. The company had just accepted the need for it and Fred was the one who had carried on in my place. I owed him. The problem of HER still remained.

You're having an affair with my best friend. Paul came in to the accusation hanging in the air and stood by his mother. She was

When she came into the room, I was scribbling on a memo
pad, nonsense, anything that came to mind. Blondes have more
fun. Praise the Lord and pass the ammunition. Free association,
someone would have called it. I didn't look up. The busy CEO,
conscientious, committed, that was me. She was positioning her
cameraman with a fine edge of authority in her voice. I had no
memory of that authority: but she was a junior reporter then, on
the local paper.

"I need him behind the desk," she was saying. "Deal with the
lighting issue. That's what you're paid to do."

There were mumblings and shiftings but I still didn't look up.

"I'll want some decent close-ups. Of both of us."

That made me look up. The "both of us."

"Ah, Stuart," she said. "Good to see you again. Hope we haven't
interrupted something important?"

I glanced down at the memo pad. Dear God, I'd written. I
turned it over.

"Jennifer, I'm really busy. I'm sure you can understand why. Still,
this interview is important."

She gave me one of those cool, calculated looks that I'd seen
on TV when she was considering spearing her interviewee with a
particularly barbed question.

"We'll get on with it, then, shall we?"

She started with a short introduction, facing the camera.

"This is Stuart Duncan," she said, "the chief executive of a
modern eighties-style management team, where profit is the bottom
line in an increasingly competitive world. Pitted against him is an
old-style union, protecting what it says are hard-won victories."

She finished her sentence, held still for a moment and the camera was lowered.

"Your turn now, Stuart," she said. "Something about how you see this strike, this union. Trust your inner voice, Stuart. We want something genuine."

I took a breath. I was calm. This was my professional self she was getting.

"There are two thousand jobs at risk here," I said. "That's a lot of jobs."

"You can do better than that, Stuart," she interrupted. "Come on, something with some feeling."

I rubbed my right eye, blinked.

Somewhere behind that blink is a decision, made so often that it's automatic. Red light: stop. Orange light: foot down. But my timing is out: a shriek of tyres slewing sideways, a world turning, turning and us held, still, in the middle. Then it explodes.

"I could cry," I said. "I could cry for the stupidity of this situation. A union deciding to destroy the jobs of two thousand people, the lives of this whole community. Some nights, I could go home and cry."

I stared into the camera, my face set.

She nodded, looking at me intently as if we'd been sharing this conversation for some time.

"So this is a struggle about power," she said. "Who will control the future of this country's biggest export earner, the company or the union?"

"This was a showdown waiting to happen," I said. "For too long the company has backed down to union demands. We can't afford to do that, to be bled by this union."

"And the leadership of the union? What's your opinion on that?"

"The president is sincere, I'll give him that. I have no doubt that he believes in what he's saying but this is a man who doesn't believe in the capitalist system, who thinks that profit is a dirty word. We've been good employers, everyone will tell you that, but we are not some branch of social welfare."

She nodded at me again, looking intent, then waved at the cameraman.

"Thanks, Stuart," she said. "Good interview. I'll let you know if we need anything more."

She stood up, smoothed her skirt and hesitated just a fraction as if she was going to say something.

Jennifer came to Carol's funeral. I couldn't look at her. She came to see Paul when his life was hanging on a thread and there were no words to say. The guilt between us had measured forever.

She reached over the desktop, her arm straight, offering her hand. My feet were entangled in the chair and it took me a moment to stand. It may be she had to hold it for too long because by the time I reached for it there was a tremor that I could only just detect.

A tight smile and a brief clench of our fingers, then she took her hand back, pushed the chair away and she was gone.

Chapter Twenty-five

Miriama McLay

At school, Selwyn asked how come Mum hadn't gone to stay with them again and I just said I didn't know. I wasn't telling them anything about her and Leo, it was none of their business anyway.

Jeez, I don't know how they kept it secret so long. No one knew or maybe they did and just didn't tell me. Maybe everyone'd just kept it secret from me. I didn't care what they said, Leo and Mum, I wasn't staying there, not with them at it in the next room and Leo never did go and get my stuff, it was still at the Old Man's. Anyway, I'm staunch, even if it looked like Mum'd sold out, just 'cos she was mad with the Old Man.

My bike brakes needed fixing, they jammed when I used the front ones, so I nearly went over the top of the handlebars when I saw it, the friggin' front porch. They'd been calling the Old Man a commie and they'd gone and made it real clear. Red paint, a whole lot of it, tipped on our front porch. Bastards. As if he hadn't got enough to deal with. It was sticky as. Must've only done it last night, I reckon. Prob'ly the Old Man was blotto. Prob'ly whoever did it knew he was and hoped he'd leave it there. At least it showed them all we were still staunch.

The back door was wide open and the house was freezing. I shut it behind me and there he was. He must've been sitting there in the kitchen for a while but there were no bottles, full or empty, in front of him. He looked like shit but he was sober.

"Lass," he said.

I couldn't say anything.

"What you after?" he asked.

"Just come to see how you are."

"Och, never been better. Got them on the back foot, lass. Got them running scared."

"Have you seen the front porch?"

"Aye. Last night it was. I found it this morning."

"Nice colour."

"Aye, lass, it's right bonny."

He was staring down at his cuppa, like he was stuck for the next thing to say. I knew he wanted to ask about Mum, I knew it, but it was stuck in his throat and my head was a friggin' milk shake of things I could or I should say, like, I'm still your daughter, or Mum's just mad at you, or I hate Leo too. But my mouth wouldn't work either so I just stood at the kitchen door wondering what to do next.

A car pulled up beside the house but the Old Man didn't seem to hear it, he just kept staring at his tea and he didn't even move when there was a knock on the back door.

"Come in," I yelled.

They didn't. There seemed to be more than one of them, unless someone liked talking to himself. By the time I got to the back door, I already knew who prick number one was.

"I'm staying here," I said.

"That's fine, Miriama," said Leo. "It's the Old Man I want to see."

"I don't think he wants to see you," I said.

"We'll see," he said.

There were some people behind him. The woman I saw on the march, with her TV cameraman and some other creep with a furry thing on a pole. What a cheek, and Leo'd just marched on up with them all in tow, thinking the Old Man'd cave in and talk to them.

"Wait here," I said.

They did wait. For the fifteen minutes it took for the Old Man to have a shave and put on a clean shirt. I didn't ask them in, let Leo keep them entertained out in the cold. If I'd been the Old Man,

I'd've told them to get lost. He wouldn't though. He was staunch. He was union through and through.

By the time he was ready, I had to interrupt the TV lady and her crew pointing the camera at the front porch. Leo stood on the front lawn staring at them. He looked like someone'd pulled his plug out, he was sort of deflated. Reminded me of when you take the bung out of a lilo and it goes all flat. Served him right.

"Mr Harris," called the TV lady.

"Mr Harris," I said.

"Shut it," said Leo.

They set up the camera and the TV lady in the lounge, round the Old Man, like he was the star or something. The Old Man, he'd done this kind of thing before and I was proud of the way he looked her right in the face. He was a real pro. The TV lady was into it straight away.

"Some would say," she said, "that the union has its back up against the wall."

"We're a federation, lass, not a union. Get your words right."

"Federation, then. You, as the president, have your back up against the wall."

"Pretty solid wall, lass," he said. "We still have a majority in the federation voting to reject the company's demands and, as long as our members are voting that way, I'll represent it."

"Some say that there's intimidation at the meetings, that the men are not free to express their views."

"Some say, some say, who says? Our meetings are democratic. Our voting is democratic. The company's been using terror tactics on our members for weeks now and our members aren't having a bar of it."

Leo'd gone into the kitchen. He was too shamed to stick around. Shamed because the Old Man was reminding him that union was still strong and that he was not, he'd got Mum staying with him. The Old Man was steady as a rock, not shifting. The TV lady took a breath and started in again.

"So the current management's been in charge since 1981. There's only been one year of profit for them in the last five years. They say they're wanting to bring your union into the new age of industrial relations."

"It's not my union, lass. The federation belongs to the pulp and paper workers. What's more, prior to this management, prior to Sir Ron Trotter and his management, we had a record of industrial relations as good as any company in the country, until now, until this management, so don't you go blaming the federation."

"But things have changed and, as I said, the company is wanting to bring the union into the new age of industrial relations."

"Och, hen. Dinna ya hear me? I said don't go blaming the federation. We'll be the ones to drag the management into the era of modern industrial relations."

"And what, may I ask, does that look like?"

The Old Man was just winding up. He leaned forward in his seat. She was in for a lecture, I knew it, he'd got that look about him. Off he bloody went.

"Let me tell you what the company's interest is. They want to increase the shareholders' funds at the cost of the workers, pure and simple, and they're a big company now, a multinational. We've seen the history of multinationals in the UK. We've seen what happens to jobs. We've seen what happens to whole communities when profit is the only motive. Look at the coalmining towns. Ghost towns, the lot of them. What about moral values, lass, what about them?"

"So you think that because the company has overseas interests, that will reduce the jobs here?"

The Old Man just gave her a dirty look, made his mouth a straight line and slowly nodded his head.

"You don't approve of the profit-sharing scheme the company introduced?" she asked.

"Some of those unions, not the pulp and paper workers, but some of the others agreed to it. Let me tell you, they've lost the battle, accepted their thirty pieces of silver and lost most of their membership. It's a bribe."

He sat back in his chair and rubbed his hands on his knees. It meant he thought he'd made a good point.

"You don't attend the union meetings with those other unions."

"Aye, I don't go because they're brainwashing, that's what they are. You get to listen to the company point of view, and more than that, the management's sitting there, looking for the weak links that they can work on, noting down the ones they can pick off."

She seemed to be stuck, had to think for a minute. She waved for the cameraman to turn it off and sat biting the end of her pen. The Old Man folded his arms and sat watching her. He looked like he could wait forever. Leo cleared his throat in the kitchen like he wanted to say something but the TV lady waved at the man with the camera and started again.

"You don't seem to trust the company."

"You could say that, hen, you could say why too. The company cannot trample all over its workers like this. The person employed as a cleaner is no different from Trotter and his business roundtable cronies who think they're so high and mighty. Our union members are telling Trotter to get lost."

"So you'll continue to fight, then?"

"We'll always have Ron Trotters and his ilk. Always. So long as I live and breathe, I'll stand up to power, lass, so long as I live and breathe."

That was the end of the interview, except for the thank yous and the packing up of gear. Five minutes and they were out the door, except they left Leo behind. He was still in the kitchen.

He came out with the whisky bottle in his hand and two glasses. The Old Man leaned back on his chair and shook his head.

"No more, laddie," he said. "No more."

Chapter Twenty-six

Ray Parlane

"I'm about to close up, Ray," said Miss Williams. "How much longer do you want to stay?"

"If it's not too much trouble, let me just get this link to work," I said.

It was the link that could pull up all the due dates of all the overdue books and who'd got them out. Ingenious, if I did say so myself and I nearly had it.

"What about you, Miriama?"

"Kids' books to do. About ten minutes."

The link didn't go through. All I was getting was a bloody error reading. My eyes hurt. I'd tried it about five different ways and I still couldn't crack it but then, of course, it might be the limitations of the first commands in the software I wrote. Back to the drawing board …

"Finished! That little Pākehā girl who reads all the Jill-and-her-pony books is gonna have to find a new author. She's just read the last one."

"I'm trying to get her to read *Watership Down*," said Miss Williams. "Move her on to another animal."

"Rabbits aren't quite the same as horses," I said.

I loved *Watership Down*. Read it under the blankets at school and cried in the part where the rabbits die of the white blindness, mixama-something. Had to cry really quietly otherwise I'd've been ragged by the other boys. Myxomatosis, that was it, a sort of epidemic a bit like AIDS, and there I was thinking about Harry again. All roads led to Harry just lately. Maybe I should just go home.

"How're you getting on with the work experience, Ray?" asked Miss Williams.

"Depends. I've learnt lots but all the work for closing down the mill is nearly done."

"Well, you never know," said Miss Williams. "Things might change and everyone back at work very soon."

"Nah, not us," said Miriama. "Union's not giving in, Miss."

"Who says the management won't?" said Miss Williams.

"Well, they do," I said.

I'd been getting it in the ear from Mr Hopewell about the archaic labour laws in this country and the new thinking that would sweep the country into modern times. He thought it was all just a matter of the company holding on.

"Might not have anything much to do soon," I said. "Might just go home."

"You can't do that," said Miss Williams. "We need you to finish this programme, then I'll be able to persuade the town clerk to buy the library a computer."

Miriama was leaning on the counter, scowling and biting her lip. She looked just like the four-year-old Hopewell child when she was told off. She'd probably say she was giving me the evils. We hadn't seen each other for a few days, not since she went off with Leo after that last rehearsal, after he said it was about some Māori word, the same word that Miriama said to me when I told her I was looking for my dad.

"I hear you've gone back to your dad's to live, Miriama," Miss Williams said.

"Yeah, I'm sticking with the Old Man," she said.

"What about Stella?" Miss Williams asked.

"What about her?"

"Where's she with all this?"

"She's with Leo. I'm not."

"You take care of yourself, Miriama, you hear me?" said Miss Williams.

Miss Williams was looking at Miriama in a kind of worried mother sort of way, the way Harry used to look at me sometimes when Liz was especially bad but Miriama shook her hair over her face so no one could see. It was like a hiding place for her, her hair, or a keep-out kind of fence. There was a pause, with Miss Williams standing there with the bunch of keys in her hand. I closed the lid of the computer with a clunk and Miriama did that toss of her head that made her hair fly back. Her face had a hard look.

"Leo's not gonna get what he wants," she said.

"Whatever that is," said Miss Williams.

"You still want to find your father?" Miriama asked me.

"Oh, that. S'pose so. I'm not sure any more, what with Harry getting sick."

"Might be a very big shock when you find him," said Miriama. "Might be you don't wanna know."

"Now, Miriama," said Miss Williams. "Seems to me Ray's come a long way to find out who his father is. It may be his only chance."

It had been my mission all my life, since I was six years old at least, this wanting to know the identity of my father. Every year the letter sent, who knows where to. Every year the same questions to Liz and every year the same piffling answers. It all seemed too difficult.

Miss Williams handed me a list of names. Quite a long list, two pages' worth. She said she'd been through the electoral rolls and found every Keith in town. I could've done this on the computer, with enough time to write the programme, but there it was in her neat librarian handwriting. It must've taken her some time.

"Thanks, Miss Williams," I said politely.

"I've put in the addresses. You could visit or phone if you match the names to the phone book and just ask if they've ever been to the USA."

"Yeah, ask if they ever shagged a crazy lady," said Miriama.

So I had my starting point. I'd have to stay, for a while at least.

"Come on, Mr Sherlock," said Miriama. "We've got a rehearsal."

We started at the beginning with the song that I had joined in on, the first love song. Me then Miriama, almost back in synch, almost making great music together. When she sang about being hopelessly devoted to me, I remembered what it was that made me first think she was so special. It was the way she put herself into something, like she really believed in it. I tried to sound that sincere when I was singing back to her but my heart wasn't really in it. Harry kept getting in the way.

We finished with the first run-through of the next song. Miss Whatever was trying to teach us to hand jive. We started off very slowly, putting it together, but then June poked Jason in the eye with her elbow and he rolled around on the floor like a football star, calling her a dumb cunt, and Miss clapped her hands and pretended not to hear.

"Good try, everyone," she said. "The TV programme about the strike is on tonight so I think we'll finish there. I want to watch it and you probably do too."

"Any of yous in it?" asked June.

"Nah, didn't want to break the camera," said Davey.

"The Old Man's in it," said Miriama. "He's real staunch."

"They interviewed my dad too," said Jason, one hand over his eye. "He wants to go back to work. He wouldn't tell us what else the TV lady got him to say."

"Your dad's not thinking of being a scab, is he?" asked Miriama.

"Whad'ya mean?" said Jason.

"Being a one-eyed scab, pretending the stuff's all sorted and going back to work when the union's still voting not to."

"You mean your old man's making them vote not to. My dad says his one eye's a red one."

The party was turning nasty. I grabbed Miriama's arm before she could launch herself at Jason. She was so wound up she felt as if she could snap. I wrapped my arms around her and she kicked and tried to bite me. Jason got out the door while he could and Miriama eventually shrugged me off.

"Come to my place," I said. "I've promised to meet up with Paul. Mrs Hopewell and the kids are away and Mr Hopewell's working late. We can watch the programme on their big TV."

We were halfway across the athletic field before Miriama stopped her sulking. She put her hand into mine and gave it a squeeze.

"You ever done something you really believe in that means everyone hates you?" she asked.

"Yes. Bit of a dust-up once, at school. Some boys were going on about faggots and being a bum chum. I lost my temper."

"What happened?"

"I got called a faggot for the rest of the term."

"And?"

"And I did this."

I did my Ziggy Stardust walk that made her laugh last time, the one with the limp wrists and sashay of the hips. She didn't laugh this time, just wrinkled up her forehead. I put my arm around her and tried to sound casual.

"What did Leo want the other day?"

"Whakapapa."

"You keep saying that word. What do you mean?"

We'd reached Paul's house and she wasn't going to tell me.

While I got beer from the fridge, Paul wheeled himself over to turn on the TV. It hadn't occurred to me before but Paul and Miriama's fathers were about to meet head-to-head on the telly. The music had finished so the item must have started, but Paul was in the way.

"Paul, Paul, you make a better door than a window," I said.

He didn't move. Miriama got up and pulled his wheelchair back. He was staring at the screen like a fox caught in headlights.

"You all right?" I asked, holding out his beer.

He wasn't responding, just staring. One hand came up in slow motion and he took the beer without looking away from the screen.

He was staring at the interviewer and he'd gone as white as my grandmother's knickers. I hoped he wasn't going to throw up or something. He got the beer up to his mouth at least so I sat down next to Miriama and put my arm across the back of the sofa. Mr Duncan was on. He was wearing a suit and tie and sitting behind his desk. He was every inch the boss man except for his expression; he looked like he'd lost his dog. "Sometimes I could cry," he was saying, and I believed him.

Paul made some kind of strangled noise and choked on his beer, spraying his knees.

"You all right?" I asked again, but he was engrossed in the TV.

I would never tell Miriama this, what with the way she went on about Leo, but her Old Man was no oil painting either. He was wearing a suit and a shirt with a tight collar. Maybe that was what was making his face so red, more likely it was what he was saying. He wasn't behind a desk. He was at home and he was leaning forward on the sofa and shaking a finger at the interviewer. His accent was so thick it was hard to make out what he was saying, something about multinationals and profit. Miriama pulled her feet up on the sofa. She nodded furiously and bit a long strand of her hair.

The scene changed. The interviewer was walking outside with another man. He was saying something about feeling intimidated by the union leadership, except I couldn't hear because Miriama exploded.

"That's Jason's father," she yelled. "Bloody scab, that's what he is."

I took the beer out of her hand, just in case. Maybe she got her temper from the Old Man. Wouldn't do to have her throw a bottle at the TV. Then I caught Paul's expression. He looked as if the life had drained out of him.

Chapter Twenty-seven

Leo Harris

She comes up behind me when I'm grabbing the spuds, nearly gives me a heart attack. Haven't seen much of you lately, she says, with a look from under her blonde fringe like I really should've, done more than let her see me, I mean. The spuds wrestle around in the plastic bag and I nearly drop the buggers. I put them in my trolley, take a quick shufty round, but the supermarket's almost deserted. Just as well. I reach for a paper bag and I haven't got a clue what I'll put in it. She starts. Having trouble looking me in the eye, are you, Leo? she says, like she can read my mind.

Of course I'm having trouble. She's trouble. My life's complicated enough without her. I try to keep it sociable, being the kind of man I am. How are ya, Ima? I say, keeping my eyes on the tomatoes. Never know, they might cause difficulties, being red and all that. I'm hoping she'll just disappear, hoping it'll all go away.

Then she gets down to brass tacks; about how she's not making much progress with the story, about how the help she was promised evaporated, about how she thought union kept its word, kept alongside someone when they promised to.

Fuck. From the corner of my eye I can see her boots. High-heeled boots, fuck-me-boots the boys call them. Fuck-me-boots for a bit of fun, that's all it was. Just a bit of fun. I thought I'd made that clear and now she's doing kick-arse boots.

I try doing the innocent. It usually works, needs a certain boyish charm but that's me, all charm, so I say that I thought she'd changed her mind about the story and that I thought she wanted to do it from the sheila's point of view.

Then—fucked if I know why I do it, sometimes there's a little Japanese Kamikaze sitting in my head just waiting for the very worst moment, mostly when I'm doing innocent, doing boyish charm, like now—I say that Stella's happy to talk to her, any time.

We're both staring at the tomatoes now. She's got her hands in her pockets and I'm holding on to that paper bag like grim fuckin' death. It's a long pause. I can see her biting her lip. I'm even considering saying I'm sorry for what I just said.

The interruption comes from a domestic just down the aisle. He's put something into the trolley and she's taken it out. None of that before you're working again, she says, and don't you think you're buying any smokes either. You get that no good union of yours to see sense and get yous back to work and there'll be smokes again. He's looking up and down the aisle to see who's heard. I start to move the tomatoes round and pretend I'm as deaf as a doorknob. Poor bastard. But I'm fuckin' glad he and his missus are nearby, stops me doing something else stupid, I reckon.

Then she catches my hand, tomato and all, and says my name. The domestic stops right by the onions. I can feel them listening. That poor prick's probably holding his breath to see how I get on with this mad sheila. She's still holding my hand and the tomato in it. She squeezes. Hard. The tomato juice is dripping on the supermarket lino. You're a bastard, she says, a selfish prick and a bastard.

That bloke, I can hear a bit of a snort from him. I wish I could just keep looking at the tomato, it'd make life so much more fuckin' simple if life was just a squashed tomato. But I can feel her real close, the heat of her and those tits, well, my face mashed into them, licking. I look up and there it is, no denying it. I still want her, on her back, with me deep inside. On top, riding me like we're going to Texas.

I want her.

She lets go, taking a tissue from her coat pocket, wipes the tomato off her hand and stalks off. The fulla with the pissed-off missus stands there holding a bag of onions. He shakes his head at me and puts them down again.

It's a very quiet trip up to the meeting in the car. With five of us, we're packed in like sardines. It's still dark when we leave and the dawn doesn't creep up till we're at Hamilton. At least I've got a window seat, and I watch the fog on the river, can't see what the hell it's hiding, and it sneaks in the car like it's got skinny wet fingers. We get through three packs of smokes and a dozen cans. There's no comment on staying off the piss this time round, no jokes either. At Pokeno, Pat starts a long grumbling rumble about what to say to the bank manager when you go and ask to have a break from your mortgage. Pat had to go last week and he said the bank manager just told him to get back to work. Fat lot of use that was. Then they're talking about the TV programme and how the Old Man let us down. They're saying he didn't represent our point of view. I didn't have the energy to tell them how much he'd said that hadn't make it to the programme. They know, radio and newspapers been doing the same thing for weeks. It seems no one wants to know what we're fuckin' standing for.

We're all in a foul mood by the time we hit the trades hall. It's fuckin' packed. All the unions are there, every last one of them, and they're doing that thing; standing round in groups and turning their backs on us.

Pricks.

Fred from the Seamen's Union and his mates beckon us in. There's still a few who're staunch and the good old Seamen's Union knows what it's like to have the world against you. I offer round some of those smokes and Fred, who's from somewhere in north Pommyland, says it's a bit of a do and calls us lads. When I ask if they've still got work he says there's no paper to go out at the port and the busy work's run out and there are about twelve hundred lads been locked out. Twelve fuckin' hundred. That's a lot of blokes with no work.

I look round at the crowd. I reckon this looks like a mob about to start a riot. Every time I catch an eye, there's a cold shoulder. Just a few of us staunch ones and we're all standing together.

The ones nearest the door start to move in. The same old wooden chairs with metal legs, all in rows this time, none of this boy scout stuff with chairs in a circle. There's a table up the front, must be for the Federation of Labour boys. Fred signals us to the back. Maybe he's thinking we might need a fast escape route, but it does mean we get a good view of things. In come old Jim and Ken and their henchmen. This time they're the only ones in suits. All the union boys are in casual gear and, of course, us pulp and paper workers are in our work greens. We reckon this is still work. Fuckin' hard work.

So Jim starts with the same spiel we heard when he was down home, nothing different. He goes over the six conditions that the company wants, he goes over the history of the pulp and paper workers holding out and then he gets interrupted. Some prick from the Carpenters' Union yells out that the pulp and paper workers had refused thirteen requests from the management to discuss the manning levels on the machines, like it's a magic number he's yelling. He's just read it in the fuckin' paper.

Dave's hand's on my arm, I must've started up off my chair. Yeah, I hiss at him, thirteen times they tell us the same old story, thirteen times we say we don't want to buy it.

Red Ken is chairing the meeting and he calls for silence. There's a grumbling and a shifting on chairs. He calls us all comrades, says it's a mass lockout, no more work until this is settled. Like we didn't know.

Then the Old Man walks in. He's picked up a chair from out in the foyer and he's bloody walking all the way up the aisle with it. Right up to the bloody front. He's got a way of walking, his back like a ramrod, staring straight ahead, lifting his feet up and planting them, like he's in the army or something. Me and the boys are just gobsmacked. He'd said he wasn't coming this time either, that it'd got too personal and it was better he stayed out of it and here he is, in his best fuckin' suit, the one they'll bury him in, and soon if he's not careful. He's taking the chair up to the front table and putting it next to Jim Knox.

You could hear a pin drop. All the blokes absolutely fuckin' silent. Shock, I reckon. He sits down and crosses his arms, looks up over our heads and it makes me wonder what he's looking for, divine intervention maybe. The FOL fullas look at him and keep looking at him, and he keeps looking out over our heads. Then Jim asks the Old Man if he wants to join us, the pulp and paper reps, down on the floor.

This time the Old Man turns, very slowly, his arms still crossed, and stares Jim full in the face. You don't represent us, Jim, he says. You know we're not part of the Federation of Labour. Cool as can be. Red Ken chips in, says it was the FOL called the meeting.

The Old Man doesn't even look at Red Ken. He looks back over our heads. He says the FOL has no right to call a meeting, the pulp and paper workers aren't affiliated to the likes of a body that sold the working man down the drain with this Labour Government.

Red Ken looks even redder but he's sat with so many old union radicals, he knows that losing your temper gets you nowhere. He calmly points out that the FOL is just trying to settle the dispute.

We're all sitting glued to our seats, waiting for the next move. It's like being at a movie when the sheriff's got his hand over his holster and the baddy's taking a bead with his shotgun. Every eye's on the shoot-out.

It's the Old Man's turn now. Cool as a cucumber, he is. He looks down at his fingernails, like he's considering getting a manicure or something. He takes his time, inspects each fingernail, narrows his eyes at Red Ken. You don't have a mandate from us, he says. We're our own Federation of Pulp and Paper Workers and you know that. I should be sitting up here, right enough, but not you, not the likes of you.

I'm on my feet and halfway up the aisle just as the noise starts. It's like the paper machine after a shut, it starts slow and you can hear the individual bits of machinery come on line. I can hear some mutterings from the stirrers and there's one that nearly stops me in my tracks. Some bastard yells, Who gets to keep Stella?

I've reached the front table and I don't know what to do next. It's going round in my head. Who gets to keep Stella? Who gets to have that feeling that you're whānau, that your bits were friggin' made to fit together, like a paper roll nestled into its holder, spinning and singing?

I look the Old Man in the eye along that bloody table and try to get Stella out of my head. There are other things: the decision we kept from him when he was lost to the booze, that the Federation of Pulp and Paper Workers did ask Jim and his cronies in, without conferring with the Old Man, because we knew he'd disagree.

Red Ken calls for a short break, like he wants this stoush to be private. The noise rises as chairs are scraped on the floor and blokes start gabbing, probably taking bets on who's gonna hit who.

I walk slowly along the length of the table towards him, the Old Man who's taught me everything I know, whose home brew I've drunk, whose table I've sat at. We share a daughter and, fuck it, a wife. Now he's looking at me with narrowed eyes and his mouth's all pulled in as if there's too much we haven't said to each other for too long. There's a tic in one cheek that pulls me step by step.

Mum's cowering behind me. I'm big enough now. I'm thirteen and I'm bigger than him. He takes a swing at her but I've got an arm out and his fist whams into my forearm. I'm big enough now and I grab that flailing arm and push as hard as I can. He takes a chair down with him and the breath's gone from him. He's winded. Get out, I growl down at him. Get out and leave us alone. My voice behaves, stays down so there's menace in it and I stand over him with my fists clenched. I'll hit him all right, the bastard's done it to us just one too many times. This time, I'll hit him. He's retching on the floor and there's tonight's booze thick and sour. Mum whimpers behind me, and tries to come

I'm big enough now and I step in front of the Old Man. My
voice behaves, it's steady as a friggin' stream of piss first thing in
the morning, just pours out. Enough, I say. They've had enough. He
stares at me, tries a little smile, as if I'm joking. What you bletherin'
about, he says, like he's said so many times when we've been chew-
ing the fat over a beer or five.

But I'm serious. The men, the town, everyone's had enough,
I say. The smile's gone. He's got his chin stuck out and his eyes
screwed up and he levels it at me. You turning scab, Leo? he says.
You running scared?

Scab. The worst. The worst he could call me. It's out there, on
the table, next to the other one we're not saying. Next to Stella.

I'm not backing down. I didn't say I'd had enough, I said the
men and the town, they want to go back to work. Then he's nodding
and gives a little snort. What work? he says. What bloody work?
We're standing close now and his finger comes up, marking the
points he's making. First, he says, they want to get rid of a whole
lot of jobs. Second, they want to cripple the union so we can't fight
them. What work are you talking about? It's the same stuff. It's the
same stand. Only this time there's no fuckin' rock to stand on, just
sand and that's fuckin' shifting. So I tell him that, after today, after
the meeting with the FOL, the Minister of Labour wants a meeting
and that I'm going.

The blokes are standing around at the back of the hall and outside. I can feel the bastards watching us, waiting for this standoff,
waiting for the old bull and the young bull to square off.

He folds his arms. He's got a way of looking at me so I feel like
a kid, a beginner. He's always civil, is the Old Man, even when he's

three sheets to the wind, he's civil. He picks his words, he knows words, does the Old Man. He knows his industrial law backwards. He knows every entitlement and every loophole. He knows how to negotiate without saying a word about the real issue. He asks, since when were you the president, Leo? He leaves a long pause before he says the next thing. I'll be doing that meeting, Leo, he says.

The other stuff's not said but it lies there, like the fog on the river this morning. We've reached an unspoken agreement, without talks, without negotiation. I get to keep Stella; he keeps leadership of the union.

I walk back to the knot of men at the back of the hall. I feel like friggin' Moses, they part before me, like the friggin' Red Sea, but no one's following me.

The meeting's called to order again. The Old Man stays just where he is, on his chair, with one leg crossed over his knee and one hand on the table. He's got a coin in that hand and he's moving it across his knuckles from one finger to the other and back again. You can't help watching it, willing him to drop it. It draws everyone's eye. He doesn't say a word when Jim Knox declares again that the FOL has been asked to represent the Northern Federation of Pulp and Paper Workers. His face is impassive, like they're talking about someone else. Then, one after the other, the delegates from the other eleven unions that make up the combined union stand up. You'd think they'd bloody rehearsed it. One after the other they say it. If the FOL's representing the pulp and paper workers, then it's not representing them.

The Old Man just smiles and nods, like he's expecting this. The coin keeps up its journey, across the same track on his knuckles.

On the way back in the car, we're even quieter than on the way up. It fuckin' starts to rain. I watch the windscreen wipers on the same journey, back and forwards, back and forwards, and I list where we're up to.

1. The pulp and paper workers have got the FOL,
    but everyone else has sidestepped except for the
    Boilermakers', Labourers', and Seamen's Unions.
    So we're fuckin' isolated again.
2. I've got Stella.
3. But I haven't got Miriama.

Chapter Twenty-eight
Ima Williams

I left my car around the corner just in case. I was sure someone would be watching, even though it didn't seem anyone was at home. I walked along the street with its large, long houses and trimmed gardens, all very neat and ordered. My car would be safe here, at least I could be sure of that. I wondered why she'd agreed to see me, even though she did take my card that night when Notta got so incensed and I left my chardonnay to drip on the shagpile carpet. I pressed the doorbell and it chimed inside somewhere. The solid wood door opened without a sound.

"Ah, Ima," she said.

"Good morning, Cynthia. How are you?"

"I didn't hear you drive up. You could've brought your car right up the drive, you know."

"Thank you so much for agreeing to talk to me."

"Well, we'll see, shall we? We'll see how it goes, what you want to write."

We'd reached the lounge with its big picture windows and there was someone else sitting in one of the armchairs; a small woman, with dark hair, not very prepossessing. Cynthia introduced us and we shook hands. Interesting. Very interesting. She was Ms Fraser, the local MP for Labour, sitting here in the house of the operations manager. Whose side was she on? I always thought the Labour Party was on the side of the unions, but, of course, that was before what Notta calls the "neo-lib about-face." This meeting had become even more intriguing.

No cups of tea or small talk for Cynthia. She sat herself down without even ushering me to a chair so I just sank into the nearest one. Clean white leather. I was scrabbling in my handbag for notebook and pen when she started.

"Let's leave this off the record, shall we?" she said.

"The whole conversation?" I asked.

"Maybe. The beginning, at least. While we sort out where we all stand."

I left the notebook on my knee, closed. I'd go along with it to see what developed. I pulled myself out of the cushions that were threatening to swallow me and sat on the edge of the chair. I was about to ask Ms Fraser how she viewed the current strike when Cynthia started again.

"Now, Ima, I want to know if you are going to write a balanced article about what is happening here?" she asked.

"I'm a journalist. I'm interested in angles and telling a cohesive story."

"Not both sides?"

"I'm interested more in a perspective. After all, it's a feature article, not ongoing daily reporting. I want to write an in-depth article from a point of view."

"A point of view. And which one might that be?"

So, the decision point. I'd made a pact with Leo, well, half a pact, because he didn't seem to be keeping his side of it. I'd given him the idea that I'd write the union story, except he'd disappeared with another woman and I didn't feature anymore. If I said that I was going to write the story from the point of view of the unions, then I'd be very unlikely to get anything from sleek Cynthia. I could get lots if I played my cards right.

"Perspective is not taking sides. It is a window into a situation." It was that bloody voice again, my journalism lecturer who used to harp on and on about what he called "the fundamentals."

"I'm really interested in how this strike is impacting on women."

Lovely. A picture window that included her. I'd get more mileage with this than from joining the head-on collision of union and management and it was true, really. It was Sally Wihongi applying for the job that drew me here to start with. I'd been to all those meetings and even Leo had changed his tune and had gone on about me writing from the woman's perspective.

"Like you, Cynthia, as the wife of the manager of operations, and you, Ms Fraser, as a member of parliament. How do you manage in such male-dominated settings?"

"Really?" said Cynthia. "I thought, what with your sister … I'm surprised, and I must say, delighted. It is true that this strike mentality impacts heavily on all of the women of this town."

"Including you, Cynthia."

"Oh yes, it certainly does. Behind every good man, and all that."

I was warming to my task, on a roll you might say. I thought I'd landed Cynthia. Now I'd try for the MP. She was sitting back in her chair, her fingers playing with one earring. Her big glasses caught the light, reflecting it back at me.

"And Ms Fraser, as an MP, you go every second Monday to a meeting between the company and the combined unions, I understand."

"Yes. I do. All of the unions except the pulp and paper workers."

"So the pulp and paper workers aren't going to those meetings?"

"That's right, they say that management is just trying to brainwash them."

So the Old Man and Leo had excluded themselves. They really were out on a limb. I doubted I'd be able to get Leo's perspective on that one.

"And as a woman you're in a male-dominated parliament," I continued. "That's two settings. It must be something of a struggle at times."

"I'm a member of parliament. I have a job in the House. As a local MP my job is to listen and to represent my constituents, all of them."

She was taking her time with her answers, as if she was deciding what to tell me. It was now or never. If I confronted her I may get something. If I didn't, well, nothing lost. She didn't look like one for giving much away.

"And what about your position, Ms Fraser?"

"Ms Williams, I'm a Labour MP. We're built by the unions. We're also in the middle of modernising the labour laws to be in line with a globalised economy. That's what the party is doing. Not in line with the opposition, you understand, with Bill Birch and his push to make union membership voluntary, but to bring New Zealand into the globalised economy."

"And what do you think of the president of the Federation of Pulp and Paper Workers saying that globalisation means more focus on profit and less on jobs?"

She gave me that look again, the careful one.

"Economic reform is necessary, Ms Williams. The global tide of change will sweep us up. It's a matter of how we manage that reform. That's the bit that should be thought about carefully. Meanwhile, I'm a local MP and my job is to listen to and represent my constituents' views. Now, if you'll excuse me, I have another appointment."

While Cynthia saw Ms Fraser out, I scribbled frantically in my notebook. There had been an awful lot of her telling me she had to listen to and represent everyone.

Notes to self:
1. Check Labour's attitude to union membership.
2. Check Ms Fraser's contribution at the combined union meetings (if any of the staunch men will talk to me —ha, ha)
3. Whose side is she on?

My notebook was closed by the time Cynthia came back in the room and my face was neutral. Journalists are neutral.

"Ah, glad you could meet Ann," she said. "She's a good local MP, a good voice in parliament."

"I would have thought your politics were more with the National Party."

"It's not a matter of party politics, Ima, you should know that. Anyway, I have a proposition for you."

"For me? Really?"

"Yes. Our head of public relations needs a bit of assistance. It's a very big job, just at present."

I was sure it was. This was a critical time and public relations were part of the picture.

"We need someone in there assisting Colin Hopewell. He's a mediocre sort of man, not much verve or imagination. Needs spicing up. I wondered if you would be interested?"

This was such a turn-up for the books. Me, sister of activist for the working man, one-time bonk of the secretary of the Federation of Pulp and Paper Workers. Me, writing pretty script for the company, I mean Company. The question was, what was in it for me? I asked her and then wished I hadn't.

"I have some connections in the media, Ima," she said. "I heard about your last job, with the *Herald.* I heard the story from your old boss, remember him?"

Oh yes, I remembered Stephen, the promises he made: he'd leave his wife, I'd get promotion, we'd be a great team together and blah, blah, blah.

"He says there was a little difficulty, and that he agreed to keep certain things quiet if you left without a fuss?"

My face was stuck. In neutral. I couldn't seem to find first gear to open my mouth to respond. The ballpoint pen I was clutching snapped but the rest of me didn't seem to want to move. If I stayed here, in this position, I could just pretend it wasn't happening.

"Been having trouble getting work, haven't you Ima? Never mind, this would put you nicely back in the job market. If you're interested, of course."

She stood up and smoothed her blonde hair. It had to be peroxide. White-blonde hair, sleek, smooth. She moved to the door and

I was terrified that I should be doing something. It was just that my body didn't seem to want to move. Somewhere a phone was ringing.

"Excuse me, Ima. I'll just get the phone. You have a little think on my proposition, I won't be long."

She closed the lounge door behind her and I could breathe again. I leaned back and crossed my legs the other way.

Stephen.

I'd been in love. He was just having a bit on the side, a dalliance with a feisty woman. He liked that in me. Then his wife found out and suddenly it was all around the office. He turned the tables on me, saying I was a family-wrecker and, worse, a ball-breaker and I had stalked him. As if he had nothing to do with it!

More fool me, I did as he suggested. I left without a fuss, hurt, shamefaced. Not a feisty woman anymore. Never again, I swore, never again. Then Leo turned up and I fell for his line. Rebound, that must have been what it was. I owed nothing to either of them, nothing at all.

She came back into the room very quietly, Cynthia of the feline disposition. She sat down opposite me and I wasn't sure which of us was meant to go first. I put on my *I'm interested and I'm not home at the moment* face.

"Well," she said. "I'd love to be interviewed for your little article, Ima, really, and I'm sure some of the other wives would too. Now, what do you think of my proposition?"

I was just about to say that I'd think about it when she slammed me another one.

"Oh, and there's the matter of Mr Harris. I gather you have a liaison with him?"

I should've known, a small town. You get away with nothing. I was struggling to keep my face in order, wondering what would come next.

"It would be quite useful to have you able to talk to him about the company intentions and vision for the town, don't you think?"

I didn't answer. Behind my blank face I was promising myself never to talk to him again.

By the time I left I had a job offer: working with Colin, dear Colin who tried so hard, you know. If I wanted the job, I was to report to the office tomorrow, past the man on the gate telling Leo he couldn't come to work, past all the other pulp and paper workers in their work greens. She was suggesting I use my "liaison," as she called it, to be a kind of small-town Mata Hari. I wasn't taking that one on. The best part was that I would get a parking place for my little red baby. If I took the job.

It occurred to me that this job could give me some insider knowledge for my article and some insights into this whole mess. I wouldn't have to give up on that. Perhaps I could do both. I climbed into my car. The umbrella Cynthia had lent me was unwieldy, difficult to manage and I wasn't that dry by the time I got it stowed properly. I longed for a day when I could put the soft top down, flatten my foot to the boards, blat out on the open road and clear my poor cluttered mind. I wouldn't be doing that with the clouds blanketing the mountain.

I knew I had no real choice. I needed a job. Unfortunately, I would have to tell Notta what was happening before she heard from someone else. I supposed I could tell her that I was infiltrating the enemy, then she might let me stay. I had no money for the motel.

When I got to the library, Notta was up a ladder hanging a big illustrated story across the wall behind the children's section. The colours were really eye-catching.

"Great pictures, Notta. I didn't know you were an artist."

"Not just me, Miriama helped."

She was tacking up the last large painting as I started at the beginning.

"Once upon a time there was a foolish king called King Canute. He thought he was the boss of everything."

Picture: A king in a crown and long robes, his sceptre pointing at people marching in line. They're all dressed in green with boots and hard hats on.

"Every day (except Monday when he played golf) he went down to the sea to tell the tide to stop coming in."
Picture: The king with his ankles in the water, his arms extended out to sea. He looks suspiciously like Mr Grant, Head of Operations, husband of Cynthia.

"It did not work."
Picture: A crown floating on the water. People doubled up in laughter on the shore.

"So the people organised. They hatched a plan."
Picture: The king floundering in the shallows, dripping. The people huddled together.

"They worked hard. The king had no idea what they were up to."
Picture: The king sitting on his throne on the beach, scratching his head. The people carrying tools and bags of things.

"They built a sea wall, together. It took quite a long time but they helped each other and got it finished."
Picture: The people finishing the sea wall. The king on the beach, practising his golf swing.

"The king was very pleased. He told everyone that his great idea meant he could keep the tide from coming in."
Picture: The king talking animatedly to a group of other kings, pointing to the sea wall. The kings all look like Sir Ron Trotter, Chairman of the Board.

"The people were very cross that the king thought it was his idea, so they opened the secret gate they had left in the sea wall."
Picture: The sea gushing through a gap in the sea wall. The king watching his golf ball head over the hill, yelling "Fore!"

"The people united will never be defeated."
Picture: The king being swept out through the sea wall gate and the people cheering.

"Your story I assume, Notta? Interesting variant on the traditional one."

"Only on the children's version. It makes him look like a puffed-up git. The historical account says he wanted to show that the power of kings is vain and trivial."

"You didn't want to tell that one?"

She gave me a withering look. I was just wondering if the king and the people were round the wrong way. Maybe it should be the people being swept out to sea and the last caption should read: *Money speaks, more money speaks louder.*

Chapter Twenty-nine

Ray Parlane

"You knock this time," she said.

"Only if you come right up to the door with me," I said.

"Course I will, but you've got to knock."

"Sorry, I just got cold feet."

It wasn't cold feet. I was standing back at the letterbox of the last Keith for the night for a reason. I was a Londoner and I'd picked up some street sense. If you ever walked round Kennington in London, you'd know what I meant. I just caught it from the movement, something dark, something that didn't want to be seen, but I wasn't sure it was there. Not the first time. When I was with Miriama that other night, when that chap went berserk with the softball bat, I saw it then. Same thing happened this time, whoever it was just melted into the hedge. I didn't want Miriama too far away from me.

We were both watching the glass panels on the door, but I'd got half an eye out for any movement on the street.

"Your turn to talk," she said.

"No, you do it, you're much better at it than me," I said.

"Cold feet freezing your brain? Maybe freezing your balls?"

The door opened before I could think of a good riposte. The man in the hallway looked about the right age. The last two had been way too young, unless you could sire a child when you were age six. I was hopeful.

"Good evening, sir," I said.

"You Jehovah's Witness or something?"

"Not me," I said.

"Nah, me neither," said Miriama. "We just want to make sure you know about our show. It's gonna be cool."

"Sir, we want to make sure that folk know a group of students are going to put on a musical in the next fortnight or so. Do you know the musical *Grease*, sir?"

He was shaking his head. At least my "sir" had got his attention.

"It's American. Have you ever been to the States, sir?"

"Not me. No. I can't afford to gallivant round like that, not with these bloody strikes. Wouldn't want to anyway, rather go to Aussie. I might get to earn a living instead of sitting on my arse while the bloody unions scrap it out."

"You wanna job?" said Miriama. "You want good pay? You want safety at work? Who d'ya think gets those for yous?"

He shut the door. Slammed it, more like it. We trudged back to the footpath.

"Miriama, sweet and lovely young woman that you are, you'd better hold on to your temper."

"What? I was just doing a bit of education. Creep doesn't know how bad it'd be without the union sticking up for his rights."

"That's not the point. We're supposed to be finding a Keith who's been to the States, not spreading propaganda."

We were walking towards her house. We'd checked out five Keiths. That was half a page of Miss William's handwriting and not one of them had ever set foot in the U S of A. Still, there was another page and a half to go.

The clouds were clearing after it had been tipping it down all day. There was a full moon smudged behind a thinning cloud. It looked like the mistakes in my early letters, when I was only six or seven and I used to press so hard with my HB pencil that it dug into the paper. Liz helped me rub out the mistakes but they never quite disappeared. I wasn't sure about that Darth Vader poser I'd seen earlier, whether it had disappeared or had even been there in the first place.

"Come on, walk you home," I said.

"The Old Man's not home. He said some fulla was picking him up this morning and he'd be back late. We could have a smoke if you like."

"Where was he going?"

"I dunno. Why?"

"Just wondering if he might suddenly come home."

"What? You scared of my Old Man?"

I didn't reply. I just didn't want to get Miriama into hot water. The house was dark when we reached it, so it looked like we were safe so far. I'd never been to her place. It wasn't posh. People thought the Hopewell's house was posh; I'm glad they didn't ever get a gander at my grandparents'.

She sat me down in the lounge and, while she went to get the dope, I looked around and tried to identify what was missing. There was furniture to sit on, a big television in one corner but no bookshelves. Not one book. I'd always lived in houses with piles of books.

I watched her roll a joint, her fingers fast and practised, her tongue quick. She was a master of this art. This time it wasn't half tobacco and, I must say, the dope was very good. She said it was locally grown, some of the best. She put on music. I never did like reggae but I suppose it went with the mood. She was grooving around the room, singing along. I joined in and we fused the chorus together, "yeah, yeah, yeah," and we were still playing its possibilities when the song faded. She was standing in front of me and it was she who sang the last "yeah." I reached out for her and pulled her down onto the sofa. We wrapped around each other so I wasn't sure which leg was mine and which was hers. Our mouths met and her tongue was pushing into my mouth and our teeth clashed. "Yeah, yeah, yeah" was pounding between us. She wriggled one arm out and pulled off her track pants and her underwear while I scrabbled with my belt buckle and heaved my hips up to shove the clothing out of the way. Somehow we'd broken apart and my head wasn't sure but my body was on automatic. I wriggled myself so I was half-sitting, half-lying on the sofa, but it was Miriama who was astride me and it was her hand that guided me into her. She arched her back as I pushed and I could feel the mounting pressure and it was all over so fast. I wrapped her back into our cocoon and held her. She was crying.

"Miriama, I'm sorry. You wanted it too, didn't you?"

"My cuzzy said the first time would hurt, but I did want to, Rainbow, I did."

I sang her that Madonna song about a virgin and the first time and we collapsed into giggles.

When I kissed her, it was gentle. I nibbled at her bottom lip and she sighed. I could feel the heat rising again and I was hard for her. She grabbed at my arm, and this time when I entered her it was slow and I sank myself into her, deeper and deeper. I was looking into her eyes and there was that moment of fear of losing herself, before she gave in and we were flowing, one movement, one body, arching higher, higher and deeper until that shuddery moment when we smashed the world into a million ecstasies.

"I love you," I said.

"E kare," she said.

And we folded together, like a letter in an envelope.

I woke up with the birds and that stupid line from Romeo and Juliet running through my head, something about whether it was a lark or a nightingale. This one sounded more like a blackbird chinking me awake. We'd forgotten to pull the curtains and the light was stealing in. I left her asleep, with her hair all over her face and crept out the back door. If her old man had come home he would have found us, wrapped up like a welcome home parcel on his sofa, but the windows in the bedrooms just look blankly back at me. There'd been no one home except us, all night.

Chapter Thirty

Miriama McLay

"I know what you two been up to," said June. She had our fag hanging out of one corner of her mouth and she looked so stupid, wiggling that skinny little arse of hers.

"Shut up, eh?" I said.

"Nah, you been having a rehearsal, that's all, eh?" said her sister May.

"None of yous business," I said.

My face was all hot. I grabbed the fag and took a big drag and blew the smoke out to try and hide it. It was none of their business, what was happening with me and Rainbow-man. It was no use wondering how they knew. It just wasn't me or Ray who told them.

"It'll help," said June. "Means you two don't have to act, just be normal, you know, when you have to sing to him that he's got to keep you satisfied …"

"Shut your face, June," said May. "You don't even know what you're talking about."

"And you do?"

I left the two of them bickering in the toilet, finishing the fag. I was shaky, felt like I just got off a bloody big ferris wheel and my insides didn't know which way was up. I was scared of being sort of public about Ray and me, like it had become real.

That night, he didn't go till it was light, thought I was still asleep, but I was just pretending. I didn't know how to do the morning thing. Cook him breakfast? What would a posh fulla like him eat, anyway? Not the stale porridge me and the Old Man ate. Anyway, prob'ly people saw him leaving and that's how they knew. The Old Man hadn't come home till later that day. I was hoping like hell no one would tell him. He'd kill me, what with Mum off with his best mate, with that sperm donor, and now me bonking the enemy.

I felt sorry for the Old Man, his wāhine weren't behaving and the support for the strike was going down the drain. Dunno where he went the last few days, but he came back real quiet. He said we should forget about the musical, about putting on *Grease*, that we should have a wake instead because there was nothing to celebrate. Then he got the whisky bottle out again. Last night when I got home from the library, I just put a blanket over him. He was out of it on the sofa with the goodnight kiwi climbing the stairs to bed on the TV.

Rainbow-man was fiddling round with the ghetto blaster, him and Miss. He'd got a bit of hair flopping over his forehead. It was part of his David Bowie look and he said he put gel on it to make it sit like that. It was so cool. He was cool. He had these grey eyes, I'd never seen grey eyes before, and he had long fingers, they were soft and made me shiver when he touched me, made me all shaky inside. Jeez, maybe this was that Mills and Boon stuff.

Maybe he felt me looking at him, 'cos he looked up and his smile pulled me right across the floor, over to where he was. He held out his hand.

"We're well warmed up, I see," said Miss.

"Red hot, Miss," said Davey.

He winked at me, didn't even go red. Ray, I mean. My Rainbow-man, who was still holding my hand.

"Right," said Miss. "Let's get down to it. Strike while the iron's hot, so to speak."

She pressed the button on the ghetto blaster and the music was with us and we were into it. I got to tease him, tell him to shape up, tell him he was the one that I wanted and he was hilarious, falling over himself to be my man. We nailed it. Three times through and we had it and the last time? Everyone was clapping and cheering, everyone except Miss.

"That's a great climax, Ray and Miriama, fantastic."

"Yeah, great climax," said Davey and everyone was hooting and laughing at us. Ray took a bow. Me, I just went red again.

"Everyone, we need to be clear about this show," Miss carried on. "Opening night is in two weeks. We need to think about whether it'll serve the town to have us go ahead. We need to think about the timing."

"But we can't not do it, Miss," said May. "We all worked so hard."

"The strike's still not settled," said Miss.

"Will be by then," said Ray. "Pulp and paper workers can't hold out much longer."

"What are you talking about?" I said. I squinted my evil eyes at him.

That morning, when the Old Man'd woken up, he was looking very bleary eyed. He'd said, that you lass? Like he was surprised to see me there. Then he'd said, they're all jumping ship, you know that, don't you hen. The rats are jumping ship. You don't have to stay.

But I did have to stay. I'd made him some porridge, made him eat it, told him not to give up, told him even us kids could see that we needed to hang in there.

So I gave that Pommy boy with the grey eyes the evils and told him the same thing.

"We're staunch. We won't give in. Ever."

Except there was a big silence from the rest of the "we" and there weren't so many "we" as there used to be. Half the cast had stopped coming.

"The future's uncertain," said Miss. "That's what we know. There's a possibility that in three weeks' time the whole company could be closed down and everyone out of a job."

"Vast possibility of that," said Ray.

"How do you know?" said Jason. "You don't even live here. You didn't go through the last time, or the time before that. How come you know so much?"

Ray didn't answer. I reckon he'd been listening in when he went to work on the computers and he must've known something we didn't.

"Well," said Miss. "What do you all want to do? Either we carry on, maybe see this as a way to cheer the town up, or we give up now."

There was a whole babble from the "we". None of us wanted to stop. We were gonna do it, even if it was to a town with no jobs. We'd all worked too hard to stop now. Then Ray the Rainbow-man changed colours. He was looking down at the floor, then out the window like he didn't want to look at us, and it seemed he didn't want to be here.

"I don't know if I can stay for another three weeks," he said.

There was that big silence again. My ears had got indigestion. He'd said that in the library but I didn't think he' meant it. I didn't want to hear this. He couldn't mean it. He couldn't just go. Not now. Not after last night.

"I need to go home," he said. "I don't know just when but it's probably soon."

I knew what this was all about; his poofter friend with the AIDS, that man who was like a father to him. I knew about that, about men who you think of as a father 'cos the real one's a dick. He must've got some more news.

"Let's say we're going ahead, shall we?" said Miss. "Let's not waste all this wonderful talent."

"Yeah, Miss," said Jason. "We're so good, we should be on TV, not just on this piddly little stage."

"You're not that good," said May.

"Oh, but you are, darling," said Jason.

"Catching, is it?" said Miss. She was smiling again. I reckoned she'd wanted us to say we'd go for it.

So our homework was to think about our characters and see

what we could find in the way of costumes. All I had was track pants and T-shirts and a school uniform. I might have to borrow some cool clothes from Jessica, the wannabe model, if she was still talking to me.

Ray was outta there before I could say anything to him. Not that I wanted to talk to him anyway, him and his going home. He could've told me first before he made a public announcement of it. What kind of fulla tells you he loves you then just disappears to the other side of the world?

When I got on my bike, the steering was all wobbly and I nearly wound up in the garden. I had a flat tyre and no bike pump. Well, it'd just have to be a walk home.

The park bench where me and Ray sat, that night there was a domestic and we helped stop the fulla with the softball bat, that bench was all dark. The streetlight was pakaru. I sat down anyway, leant my bike against the back and pulled my feet up so I could have a think.

It was real quiet. Lights were on in all the houses except the one that had the cars beaten to death on the front lawn. That fulla, him and his family went back to the coast. It got too much for them. Wonder what he did about paying his mortgage. There were a few empty houses in the town. Some fullas had gone to find some other work, under the table work, not official because they were supposed to be on strike. Some of their kids had gone with them and told the school they were going for a holiday to see the whānau. We all knew, just didn't say anything.

There was a big hedge down one side of the empty house and something was hiding in it. It sort of looked like a black hole in the hedge but it moved a bit. When I looked right at it, it didn't move, but when I looked down and put my hair over my face, then it did, just a bit. Maybe someone was thinking about breaking in. Maybe they were just waiting for me to go then they'd try and get a window open. Except there was nothing to pinch. Maybe someone wanted a place to keep their stash, or smoke it even.

Then I remembered about my Rainbow-man disappearing from my sky and I didn't care about some creep trying to find a way to get stoned in private. I just didn't want Ray to go, except I didn't want him to know either, so I'd just have to be cool, be staunch, pretend he didn't matter. Well, he didn't really. Not really. What mattered was my Old Man, my mum coming home again, the strikers winning and the town getting back to work. Not Rainbow-man, he could fuck off back to Pommyland.

It was getting late and the Old Man'd need some tea, so I picked up my bike and got walking again. I was nearly home when my bag fell off the back of the bike and when I stopped to pick it up, there was that hole in the hedge happening again, just over the road from our place, and when I farted around with my bag, watching out from under my hair, it moved. So I dropped my bike and my bag and ran hard out towards it. There was a big commotion and something jumped the fence behind the hedge but, by the time I got there, there was no one.

Chapter Thirty-one
Leo Harris

So Dave asks me if I've got a permit. What a joke, no one'd give me one. Not that I didn't go in and apply, I'm pretty careful around hunting 'cos I had a mate who shot someone once and he got two years for manslaughter. The poor bastard lost his family and his dogs. When I went in to the office, the prick on the desk just said they'd reached quota, what with fullas getting meat for their families. He looked me right in the face and said they wouldn't need to go hunting if they had work. I felt like smashing his ugly mug in.

Dave says it wouldn't have been worth it.

We keep bumping up the track. The road up to the forest is smooth now, it needs to be for the whoring great log trucks that come down it. But I've remembered this track, not much of a one really, goes to a good spot for getting deeper in the forest. I checked on the map up on the office wall when I was deprived of my right to lawfully hunt in this forest. It said no logging's been done here yet. When I asked about permits for this section, of course the little prick behind the desk just pretended I hadn't said anything. I should have known, he's the brother of one of those scabs from the Carpenters' Union, just a chip off the old block.

Dave takes a deep drag of the joint and near pisses himself laughing when I say that, about the chip off the old block. I thought it was quite good myself. I reach out for the dope, take a toke and the ute bumps to a standstill. I'm not sure what this is doing to the shocks. Anyway, this is far enough, means we won't have to lug stuff too far if we do bag something. Then Dave's looking all sad sack, like he's lost his best friend. Poor bastard has really, he's had to farm out his dogs while the strike's going on because he can't afford to feed them.

Dave's dogs are legend. He misses them more than he'd miss that sheila of his. He's got a big part-mastiff with shoulders like a bull. When Mac gets his teeth into a pig's throat, it's curtains. Mac's got a long scar across his chest where a big boar got him and it's almost like Mac took it personally. He goes for those tuskers like he's taking revenge. Best bloody dog I've ever hunted with. We have a minute's silence to remember him.

By the time we get out of the cab and unpack the guns from their cases on the back, it's nearly four and there's already a chill in the air. I lift out my gun, caressing the long clean barrel. I spent today cleaning her up. She was pretty grotty, hadn't been used in a while. Now she's sweet as a sheila on a Saturday night. I've sharpened my knife too, it could cut paper when I'd finished with it. I strap it to my leg and pull on my swannie. I hang the torch over one shoulder and my gun over the other, tuck my pants into my socks and I'm all set.

It must've been good dope. It's playing my whole body and I've got that feeling, like my blood's reaching every bone and joint, and I'm so alive I could jump a pig and just slit its throat.

I take the lead. Dave's never hunted this block before. I can't remember who I was last here with, maybe it was two or three years ago when some of the fullas from our shift would do stuff together. It didn't matter then which bloody union you were, you just all went to work at the same time and made the paper together and your missuses were all mates so the blokes could hit the piss or go hunting or whatever. Now it's just me and Dave.

It's already getting dark under the trees. The pine needles muffle my footsteps and the only thing that gives away the fact that someone's walking on them is the smell. Sharp, a buzz almost as good as the dope we've had. As a kid I tried smoking pine needles. I'd heard it gave you a high but all I got was a coughing fit. The thing about pine forests is the silence, the birds don't like foreign trees. So there's me and Dave, quiet, moving along among the trees in our work greens.

We're heading for a clearing further in. There's a stream that comes down from the mountain. The forestry boys used to camp there when they were pruning in this block. Now it'd be a good place for the pigs to come and drink and root around in the bracken. It's not too far, I hope. The dope's done that stretchy thing with time, like it seems to take forever for my foot to come up off the ground and hang in the air, then gently dive down onto the pine carpet. I'm enjoying myself. The air's cold and clean and smells like Christmas. I've got a mission and a goal for the first time in weeks and we've got more good dope to share when we get ourselves a pig.

Dave nearly comes up my rear. He's chuntering on about what he'll do with pork chops. I put up my hand to shut him up. I heard something up ahead, like something was moving in the under-growth. We may get lucky. We know how to do this: freeze, listen, find the direction, move very, very slowly. It's not the time to get the gun off the shoulder or to put on the torch, not yet. It's the time to use your ears and your eyes and to sniff every now and then. A pig doesn't travel alone and it's the smell that gives them away, every time. It's sort of like the long drop on a cold day. I take a deep snort of air. It's still Christmas and no pork crackling. Absolutely fuckin' nothing. Not even a sound. Maybe it was a possum getting up too early and deciding to climb to another perch and go back to sleep.

We move on. This time Dave's shut up and there's just that soft noise of our feet and the branches whipping back behind us. We've not gone far when Dave hisses that he needs to take a leak. I'm waiting for him. He's got his back to me and it's so quiet I can hear his piss hit the tree. This time, I'm sure I hear something. Not the blundering of a pig, jeez, they don't know the word quiet, but a much softer noise. Dave's zipping up his fly and I mouth at him—Deer. He nods.

The trees are thick here, must've been some forest worker with very short legs. Take one step, plant a tree, must've been a very small guy, a midget. These trees would've been hell to prune, getting the ladders in and out is hard enough when there's room, but it does mean there's not much undergrowth and we can move more quietly. The light's very dim, it's hard to see further than about three trees ahead, but I'm sure there's something there, just out of my eyes' reach.

There's a sharp crack. Maybe Dave's stood on a branch. That'll be the end of any deer. I'm just about to rip into him when there's another and I can feel it like a wind past my right ear and hear the thwack in the tree behind me. Some stupid bastard's shooting at me! That fuckin' shot could've been my head!

I'm fuckin' furious and I yell hey as loud as I can. It's weird how muffled it sounds so I try again—Hey, you crazy bastard!

Nothing. I wait, listening. Not sure what I'd hear anyway, my heart's banging so bloody hard. The bush is still, just the noise of me and Dave panting like we'd run fuckin' miles. About now, someone should come out of the trees, with his gun pointing to the ground and a very scared look on his face. Nothing. Dave's right behind me, his gun up and pointing into the bushes. I push it down. I yell—You there?

The pines just drink up my voice. No echo, no answer. We strain to listen, then we hear it. Someone's moving away through the undergrowth ahead, but it's too dark to see. We're standing peering into the dark, muttering about what stupid prick wouldn't front up.

Then Dave says it. He says that maybe the prick did it on purpose. I feel sick to my gut. If he did it on purpose, he must've known we were here and he followed us. Worse than that, he must've wanted to do some damage, maybe terminal damage. It doesn't bear thinking about.

On the way back to the ute we don't say anything. There's no more treading carefully and quietly, no more wanting not to be heard. There's enough noise in my head to scare off a whole family of pigs. We lurch through the trees with the branches whipping at us and I don't know who's swearing the most, me or Dave. By the time we get back it's fully dark.

I can see the lights of a vehicle just over the rise of the track we bumped down. I yell at Dave to get in and jam the key in the ignition, rev the old lady up. Dave's still half-out the cab when I take off. His door slams as we hit a ridge and he swears as his gun barrel catches him on the nose. I hope like hell he's got the safety on and I hope like hell my gun doesn't bounce off the tray where I threw it.

The lights are dipping up and down ahead of us. It's no dunga old car he's driving, whoever he is, got to be at least a four-wheel drive. I'm spinning the steering wheel to the right, to get round a bloody great stump, then to the left to get round another one. Dave's hanging on for dear life and yelling at me. I've got no bloody idea where the track is, I'm just following the bastard with the gun. I'll beat the truth out of him if I have to. What the fuck did he think he was doing?

The ute lights are swinging from one tree to another and, up ahead, there's a bloody great ridge. No way through here. I'm broad-siding the ute to try to avoid planting the front end in the dirt when it happens. A fuckin' great boom under the truck. Dave's screaming and yelling that the bastard's shooting at us again. He's trying to get his head under the dash and his bloody gun's jabbing me in the neck. I'm screaming at him to get the gun out of my face and pushing my right foot flat to boards. The steering wheel's spinning and jerking as the ute crashes and lurches and the fuckin' gun's in my face. My arm's pushed off the steering wheel and my elbow does a great jab in Dave's direction.

Then the gun goes off and I'm fucking deaf and maybe I'm dead and the world's just trying to spit me out.

Time does that stretchy thing again but this time it's not the dope. It's Stella's voice, yelling you want that union or you want me? And it's the Old Man with a sneer that says you're not good enough.

It's my father, lying on the floor as if he won't ever get up again. The ute spins and time is elastic and it bloody goes on and on.

There's a great whack as a pine branch hits the windscreen. It shatters and suddenly we've got a tree in the cab with us. The branch jams against the back of the cab and stops the crazy spinning. Dave's yelling as hard as he can and I can't see him through the branch and the ute's engine's screaming and my face is full of pine needles and glass. I spit it out, reach forward and turn off the screaming engine.

Silence. For a long time, there's silence. I try his name. Maybe he's still alive. Maybe I'm still alive. Dave, I say. Mate. There's no fuckin' answer. Then there's a voice from down under the seat— What the fuck happened, mate?—and I just want to cry. I never thought Dave could make me cry but he's alive and that means I'm alive and I'll see Stella again. I tell Dave we hit a tree and he says the bloody thing's taken out his vitals but, when I ask if he's hurt, he says he doesn't think so.

I push at the door on my side and it creaks open. At least I can get out, or fall out, more like it. I put my hand up to my head, it's as sticky as shit. Maybe the bullet skinned me, maybe Dave managed to fuckin' shoot me. Maybe I'm just numb from the shock of it. With one hand on my head to staunch the bleeding, I pull the torch from my left shoulder and try the switch. The beam cuts into the dark. Fuckin' good, at least something's working.

I get round to Dave's side of the cab, round the back of the ute 'cos the front's stuck on a tree branch, impaled like a pig on a spit. I pull at the door on his side and when it's wrenched open he falls out too. In the torchlight his face is scratched to buggery but he stands up. He looks like he's been pulled through a bloody gorse bush backwards. Mate, I say to him, mate, you bloody shot me. I hand him the torch and he waves it round so the beam catches the gun. It's jabbed up through a hole in the ute's roof. A fuckin' great hole. I tell him I'm bleeding.

He prises my fingers off. I'm hanging on to the side of my

head in case my brains fall out. He bends my middle finger back so hard it fuckin' hurts but I let him. I need to know the worst. That much blood, it's gotta be a deep wound. Maybe even got the bullet still in there. He's poking at it, at the sticky bit and I'm sure it hurts like shit.

Next thing he's laughing. The prick's doubled up laughing and the torch beam's going in my eyes and I could kill the bastard. I ask him what's so fuckin' funny and put my hand back up to my head, protecting it. He can hardly get it out. He gasps at me—Gum, the tree bled on you.

Sometimes I get life very wrong. Sometimes this causes me a lot of trouble. Sometimes I wind up with someone like that fulla who thought it was me broke up his marriage. I just thought she was a hot sheila with a bloke who was never home and that she wouldn't tell. This time, this time I'm just bloody relieved I was so wrong, bloody glad I haven't got a head injury. I know about those.

Dave gets himself back to sanity land, we pick up the guns and head into the bush. Lucky there's a moon up. Lucky I can tell which way to go. Lucky we hit the track again—just over the left of the fucking great ridge we came to grief on, who'd believe it. Dave asks about the ute. I say they're welcome to it, the forestry company, it was on its last legs anyway and I fancy something a bit more styley. Then he reminds me we're on strike and there'll be no money for a new car for a long time.

Man, I'm stiff as an old boot. I get my feet on the floorboards and my back's telling me that getting upright's not gonna be easy. That was one long walk home. Even with the great smoke we had to help, me and Dave didn't get back till near midnight. He gave me a ride from his place and when I got home, no Stella, and she still hasn't turned up. Maybe she stayed with one of her cuzzies, she's got enough of them. Maybe she's buggered off. Maybe she's regretting coming out to stay here, now her face has healed up. But she bloody won't talk to me. Won't tell me what's going on.

It feels like we're all just holding our breath, waiting for the axe to fall or the horse to bolt or a big pile of crap to fall on our heads. Something's gotta go. I pull myself up like a fuckin' old man and wonder how I'll get into town tomorrow for the meeting. The big meeting. When the pile of crap arrives.

Jeez, it's going to be a pain without a vehicle. Maybe I could try hitching but I'm not sure I'd get a ride. Some bastard'd try and take me out more like it. There's an old bike in the shed but the brakes don't work. Still, if I get desperate. There's always good old Dave, he'll come and get me.

Anyway, the sun still came up this morning and the newspaper's probably been delivered, so I might as well get the day started. The front door jams as usual. Maybe I should use some of this time off to do a bit of house maintenance, take the door off, scrape a bit off the bottom. The bloody thing near knocks me out when it finally comes free, cops me a great whack on the forehead, right where the pine tree did me in last night. I don't know if I'll ever forgive Dave for laughing so loud.

Then I walk right into something. What the fuck! It's hanging from the front porch, and it cops me another great whack. Jesus. It's something furry and it's got a tail. Someone must've hung a fuckin' possum up in the front porch. What'd they go and do that for? It's not a possum, it's skinny and black. Fuck, it's Homehelp, the bloody cat. His teeth are sticking out over his lip and his eyes are all sunk in, he's dead as. There's a bit of wire round his neck and he's been strung up on the rafter of the porch, poor old bugger. When I pull on the wire, the string snaps and he lands with a thud at my feet. There's a bloody mess down one side of his body, like he's been hit by something, hard. One leg's all mashed, it's just about hanging on by a thread of muscle.

What prick's done this? What did poor old Homehelp ever do to anyone? Jesus.

I can't help it, it comes from somewhere in my boots, a bloody great tide of it. Next thing I know I'm sitting on the front porch, in my T-shirt and grunds, sobbing like my heart's gonna break, or my guts. There's the poor old cat, in a mashed heap next to me. There's the bullet that just missed me last night. There's my empty bed last night, no Stella, no reason why not. There's Miriama hating me, now she knows she's really my daughter. Then there's the whole fuckin' mess that this town is in.

I can't stop. It just keeps coming. The snot and the tears all mixed up, all running down my face. Lucky there's no one around, lucky no prick can laugh at me, see how much it all hurts. I just put my head down on my arms and let rip.

I don't even hear her coming up. Next thing I know there's someone sitting next to me, sitting real close with a warm arm and a warm leg against my cold bare skin. It grinds to a halt, all that heaving and crying finally leaves me alone. I wipe my nose on my singlet and, when I look up, the sun catches me right in the eyes. She grabs the hand I put up, pulls it down and puts a flower in it. A spring flower. A little trumpet of a thing and the smell's sweet. Even with a nose full of hupe I can smell it and I can smell her.

She doesn't say anything, just holds my hand and the flower in it. We sit there in the sun with a dead cat and the future looming. You came back, I say. Yeah, course I did, she says, did you think I wouldn't? I don't say anything, I don't know anything anymore, not what will happen tomorrow, not what will happen with her and me, not what will happen with our girl. It's all just hanging there, trying to find a place to land.

I don't tell her about the bullet stuck in the tree, just that the ute's wrecked, just that me and Dave walked home last night. She laughs. I don't.

Then she's all sober sides again. She tells me she's been with the cuzzies who're in the federation, the ones who stand against the wall with their arms crossed when we have a union meeting. She says they're talking about starting another union, if there's no decision to go back to work at tomorrow's meeting. The new union would agree to the company demands and go back to work, because they've had enough, because they're all broke, because they're sick of being the pariahs in the town. Worse than that, they say they've got the numbers.

I remember the Old Man telling us about the miners, how a group of scabs started another union and kept the mines open. Those who'd fought for the wages, the jobs, the working conditions, just went hungry and cold and wound up with no jobs.

I feel like poor old Homehelp. The noose has tightened. The only way to get the corpse down is to break the string. That's the end of it, of the federation, of the stand for jobs, of holding out against the big company. Tomorrow it'll be all over.

My arse is hurting and I'm cold. Spring might be on the way but I'm fuckin' freezing. When Stella says we should have a cuppa, I pull my weary bones up and nearly trip over the poor old cat. We'll need a funeral, I say. She just looks at Homehelp, like it was something that couldn't be avoided, and says yeah, a tangi, we need a tangi.

FINAL BOUT
TEAM MANAGEMENT VERSUS
TEAM PULP AND PAPER WORKERS

Do you want to change your bets? Who are you backing now? It's major entertainment in this town—in fact, it's the only game in town. Who do you think will win? The venue's the Town Hall. The whole town will be there. You won't be able to go inside, of course, but come along and support your favourite team.

Free spot prizes: jobs for those who back Team M (do you believe that?), and mystery prizes for those who back Team PPW.

All your favourite people will be there: Ima will still be chasing Leo, I expect, and Miriama will be cheering for her Old Man. Stuart won't be—he'll be pacing the floor in his office (or maybe not, he may be completely calm because he thinks he knows what will happen). Raymond will just stick around in the library with me and watch it all. It's Leo and his mates who will make the decision that will matter. And you and I won't be able to tell which side they're backing.

Chapter Thirty-two
Ima Williams

Well, even to Leo I never said I was going to be partisan; I always did maintain I'd present both sides of the story. So I've moved to the other side, for a job, with pay. My orders for that day were given to me in the first meeting I attended, by Mr Grant (call me Fred, Cynthia spoke very highly of you) and Colin (I could've done this by myself you know). Cynthia was right, dear Colin did need spicing up, but she didn't say what a creep he was. He was short, but he could've at least tried to look me in the eye when he was talking instead of mumbling into my boobs. Anyway, he didn't get the task. I did.

I was to bat my eyelashes at the reporters from the *Sentinel* and *Bulletin* and any other media who might turn up and I was to invite them to a meeting with the manager of operations, Mr Grant, for a press conference. Directly after the meeting had finished. Fred said he was confident of the outcome, which meant I was likely to keep my job; more likely than Leo.

I parked my red baby in the supermarket car park and walked over towards the Town Hall. It was a huge crowd. Interesting to see how the groups clotted. Stella was with some of the Māori who were at the last meeting on the marae. There was a bunch of kids who should be in school. Her daughter, Miriama, was with one group, and another one clotted together with their backs to her and her cohort. It seemed to be the pattern; groups coalescing, repelling other groups. I threaded my way between them. I was a satellite, a roving eye.

"Kia ora, dear," said a voice from behind me.

"Good morning Freda," I said.

I kissed her on the cheek. She was wearing her best clothes by the looks of it and a hat, with a red rose. This was an Occasion.

"What do you think will be the outcome?" I asked.

"I've been saying karakia, now it's in God's hands."

"And the hands of the pulp and paper workers, I'd say."

"Ae, but we've been praying. We've been praying for a peaceful end to the strike."

"But someone has to give way, Freda."

"Ae, there's that too. Come on over here, dear. There's Sally Wihongi, the one all this fuss was about."

Miss Sally Wihongi was dressed in track pants, like most of the women in this town. A catalyst, maybe, but not the cause, and no use to me anymore. I said I had other people to see and excused myself.

The press were hanging around near the front steps of the Town Hall. What do you call a bunch of reporters and photographers: a gossip, a vulture? Their behaviour was the same as the general crowd—clots. They looked settled in for the duration. The meeting started at ten and it was only ten-fifteen, so they must have come for the grand entrance, for the arrival of the royalty of the labour movement, old Jim Knox and Ken Douglas. The two of them must have swept up the steps and through those big doors, the ones that were now closed tight. I heard both of them were coming down from Auckland. No wonder Freda wore her hat.

My best strategy was probably to talk to each group in turn. Then I could say so-and-so was coming to the press conference, give each of them the idea they'd miss out if they didn't come.

I was up to the third group and success all the way, when a man in a peaked cap came up to us with an armful of newspapers.

"Would you like to buy the real truth?" he said.

"Can get the *Truth* at my local dairy, mate," one of the reporters said.

"Paper's called *Socialist Action*. Doesn't print gossip. Just the real truth."

"Oh yeah, whose version?"

"How the company's been out to crush the Federation of Pulp and Paper Workers."

"Yeah, well, they've succeeded, haven't they?"

"Nope. They've failed. Power to the workers."

No one wanted his paper. I took one. Made it clear it was for research purposes.

The third group of reporters had been invited and they'd accepted. Mission accomplished. I was making my way back to the car, not much point hanging round here as the press would tell us the outcome, when someone took my arm. I was led away from the crowd and we walked along the footpath that goes to the library.

"Want to have a little kōrero, wahine to wahine," she said. "You know, a little talk, woman to woman."

"Ah, and what might that be about, Stella?"

"I think you know. I think you don't know what else is going on."

"I'm sure what else is going on is none of my business."

"You've met my daughter, e hoa. You've met Miriama, that young girl at the marae, at the meetings."

"Yes. So what?"

"Do you know who her father is?"

Her father, as far as I knew, was the Old Man, as they called him, the president of the Pulp and Paper Workers' Union, the one whom Cynthia accused of being a card-carrying communist, along with Leo. I didn't see what that had to do with me and I told her so.

"Things are not always what they seem, Ima. Her real father is a man who has trouble keeping his dick to himself. He needs to learn about that so he can be a good father."

"Her real father?"

"I think you know who I mean. I suggest you remember there's more than one person being affected here, Ima. Think about what

we call whānaungatanga. It means making and keeping good relationships. You're going to need to if you're planning on sticking
round this town."

"I don't know what you're talking about."

We'd reached the library. She stopped and let go of my arm. I
was sure there'd be a bruise there. We were the same height, me
and Stella, and she looked me directly in the eye.

"I heard you got a job. Means you might be round a while.
Means you need good neighbours, not ones with a grudge against
you. Might lead to utu. That means someone hurting you back."

The scar on her face was still purple, still raw. I wanted to add
another one, slosh her across the face and open up the other side.
Why people think your sex life is for anyone to pass opinion on is
beyond me. My life was none of her business but a good journalist
never gets offside with possible contacts. I swallowed hard and tried
to smile at her, but she didn't smile back, just narrowed her eyes.
After a long look that shrank my smile and drilled her message in,
she turned back to the Town Hall and the long wait.

Shit. How was I to know he was someone else's man? He sure
didn't act like it, not when he looked at me that way, not when he
undressed me with his eyes. He certainly wasn't worth crossing this
woman for and, anyway, I was over him.

The library was pretty much empty when I went in, just me
and Notta and that boy Ray leaning over the computer in the back
room. I'd managed to keep Notta on side when I'd confessed to
having a job. Well, she hadn't asked me to leave. I'd played the informant card, saying that I'd be spying on what the management was
doing so that I could tell her. Notta had squinted at me, scratched
her nose and not said anything. I hadn't said it was me getting an
income and a track record back into employment, but then, we
didn't have much of a track record for telling each other the truth.

She'd probably told Leo. He wouldn't have bought the informant
story. Still, I didn't need his approval, even before the conversation
with Stella.

Notta looked up from the computer.

"Oh, it's you," she said. "Meeting started?"

"I think so. Everyone's inside, anyway."

"Do you remember Jim?"

"Jim Knox, you mean? FOL?"

"No, the boy called Jim who went to the zoo."

I shook my head. Sometimes I just didn't understand Notta. She seemed to live in the fantasy worlds that surrounded her, all those stories, all those books. She handed me a small paperback by Hillaire Belloc, open at a poem I remembered from sometime in our childhood. It was about Jim, who slipped his nurse's hand and got jumped by a lion, who "hungrily began to eat/The Boy: beginning at his feet." We used to act it out when we were little, with Notta as poor Jim and Dad being the lion, tickling her as he pretended to gobble her up. I was usually the lion keeper.

"I was wondering about what can be learnt from this," said Notta.

"What do you mean?"

"About being Jim and about getting into the lion's den."

"You mean Leo and the pulp and paper workers in the meeting?"

"No, Ima, I don't mean them."

I had no idea what she was on about, especially since, when we were little, she'd always insisted on being Jim. I really didn't know who she was imagining as Jim now. As I said, she lived in a fantasy world. She'd turned back to the card file. It seemed that was as much as she was going to say and I was just not prepared to try and get inside her scrambled little head.

There was a commotion at the door and in came Stella's daughter and the crowd she was hanging out with. Five of them. There couldn't have been many kids at school. Miriama made them hush; Notta had trained her well in how to behave in the hallowed company of the written word. The trouble with that was they all heard what she had to say.

"Miss Williams. I saw my mum giving you the old behave your-self talk."

I raised my eyebrows at her. I was not going to say anything.

"She warning you off the man with the busy dick?"

"Miriama!" It was Notta.

"Sorry, Miss. It's just your sister doesn't know what she's messing with."

"Maybe," said Notta. "But that doesn't mean you can be rude about him. He's a good man."

"Oh yeah," said Miriama. "According to who?"

I thought it was time I left. Both of them were staring at me as if I was supposed to take sides with one of them. I just shrugged and headed for the door.

Once outside I was left thinking about the lion and I couldn't quite see who he was or who he was eating.

Chapter Thirty-three
Miriama McLay

"Who's the busy dick you talking about, Miriama?" asked June.

"Well, it could be any number of fullas in this town, don't you reckon?" I said.

"Nah, not me," said Jason. "Wish it was."

"You keep your dick pretty busy," said May. "Just it has to do solo."

"All of you, out. I'll have none of that dirty talk in here. Go on, out."

Miss Williams came from behind the desk and shooed all my mates out, like we could've upset all the invisible people in there? They all went, just left me and her.

"How are things going, Miriama?" she asked.

"Dunno, Miss," I said. "Not very good, I reckon."

"What do you think will happen today?"

"Wish I could say we'll be staunch, Miss, wish I could."

"You think they'll give way, the pulp and paper workers, I mean?"

"Most people don't care anymore, Miss, they just want to go back to work."

"And how's the Old Man?"

"I'm worried about him. He got the whisky bottle out again. He must've bought a new one, 'cos I emptied the last one down the sink when he was out of it."

"You're a good girl, Miriama, but it shouldn't be your job to look after the Old Man."

If it wasn't mine, whose was it? Mum wasn't there anymore. The Old Man was real hōhā about her and Leo. That morning he hadn't wanted the porridge I'd cooked. He'd just sat down at the table next to the window with the whisky. He wouldn't talk, sat there staring at the grass outside, but I knew what he was thinking about. His face looked all sad and crumpled up, like a paper bag someone screwed up and threw away. He shouldn't have to look like that, not when he's so staunch.

I was just about to go and join my mates outside, maybe have a smoke, when Rainbow-man came out of the back room. I wanted to hit him and hug him both at the same time so I pushed my hands into my pockets instead, with my fists clenched up.

"Oh, you still here, then?" I asked.

"I'm trying to finish the software for the catalogue, Miriama."

"Isn't that kind of him? It'll make a big difference to my job, I can tell you."

"I need to run a title through to see which fields will operate, Miss Williams. Any preference?"

"How about "Here Today, Gone Tomorrow," I said.

"That's a song. I need a book title."

"Here's one, a Mills and Boon."

I handed him a paperback that was sitting on the returns trolley. It was called *The Abandoned*. He took it without even looking at me, just disappeared again to the back room and his computer.

Crap.

I tried again for the escape route. I thought I'd catch up with my mates, have a smoke and stop this big sore lump in my chest, but Miss Williams wasn't letting me off the hook.

"So what about the musical, Miriama?"

"Depends. If your back room assistant decides to leave, we're in the shit. No Danny, no musical."

"He won't let you down, will he?"

"Dunno. You ask him."

She called him out of the back room. He was staring at the

Mills and Boon book when he came out, like maybe he got what I was trying to tell him, or more like he didn't want to look at me. When she asked him about the show, he just shrugged his shoulders.

"You know how important this show is, don't you, Ray?" she said.

"Yeah, like if you do a runner it won't happen, Danny-Boy," I said.

"And I thought you had another project you were working on too, not just the catalogue, Ray. I think you know what I mean."

"Yeah, finding Kiwi Keith, what happened to that?"

He put the book down on the front desk, next to the whirly chair. He still wouldn't look at me or Miss Williams. He was staring up at the skylight. I couldn't help it, I looked up too, so there was me and Miss Williams and Rainbow-man, watching the sun shafting in, watching the dust light up then disappear.

"I've been thinking about fathers, about what a real father is," he said.

"And?" I asked.

"How come you don't want anything to do with Leo? When he's your real father?"

"That's none of your business, Pommy boy."

"Ah, they've finally told you," said Miss Williams.

Did everyone know about my hōhā family? So every time Leo came in the library, she knew he was my father, well, the sperm donor.

"It's a good question, Miriama," she said. "You should make up with Leo and your mum. I bet she's worried sick about you."

"My Old Man's sitting at home. He's the one who's staunch in this whānau. He's my dad, not Leo."

"So you'll understand I have to go home to Harry, then. He's dying, Miriama. I need to be there."

His eyes were all bright, like he was trying not to cry. If he started, I knew I would. We'd be two tangiwai, two crybabies together, and that wouldn't help anything. I opened my mouth to say something but I was too scared of what he might say so before I started to cry I was out the door, before I could ask him about him and me, before he could say too bad; I was outta there.

Chapter Thirty-four

Leo Harris

Dave bloody gets me out of bed. It's only bloody seven o'clock. No Stella again last night, I waited up till past midnight. He doesn't ask where she is, just comes in and clears the empties, puts the kettle on. He's stirring a pot of porridge when I'm finally dressed. I can smell it, it's catching on the bottom and the milk is burning.

All these weeks of being at home turned you into a real house-wife, I say.

Fuck off, he says.

We're sitting out on the deck having a cuppa when I tell him about the cat. He reckons I should tell the police about the shoot-ing and the cat. I don't think so. He says his missus is driving him crazy, says this morning she was going on about the power bill and how they're gonna get cut off any day, says he's sick of having to listen to her moan.

On the way to the meeting, I get Dave to detour into the mill. No one else is turning up that road, just us. The car park's got a lot more weeds in it than it used to and there's dirty great tyre marks crossing over each other. Someone's had a great time doing wheelies. It must've just been last night, I can still smell the rubber.

Stupid pricks, says Dave.

Got nothing better to do, I say.

Yeah, well this is a waste of time too, he says.

I've been doing this every day, reporting to work, even when I should be on days off, just to show the bastards, even when I have to walk all the way down the straight because I haven't got any wheels. But this morning there's only one smoke stack fagging it into the sky, half a dozen cars outside the office building and the security office at the gate's all closed up. All I can see in the tinted windows is my own ugly mug and even though we bang hard on the door no bastard shows up. We leave a note on the door.

9.10 am 1/10/86
LEO HARRIS AND DAVE CRABB.
WE CAME TO WORK.

By the time we get to the Town Hall there's fuckin' crowds. I reckon the whole town's turned out, well, the workers and their families anyway. There's not a suit to be seen, of course. There's plenty of journalists, with cameras and blokes in their work greens climbing the steps, going in the big glass doors. We all got told off for wearing our work boots because of the carpet in the Town Hall. Fuck them.

And there's Dave's missus on the steps with Stella, with bits of green branches in their hands and on their heads, waiting to do the old haere mai number. The welcome's not for us motley crew in our work clothes, we're not the visitors. They climb out of the car just pulled up on the main road. The car that's got a police escort with its fuckin' siren going. Out they get, the two of them from the back seat, old Jim and not-so-old Ken. It's the Federation of fuckin' Labour and two other fullas with big boxes full of paper.

Paper. Brought their own.

The four of them are standing looking at our sheilas on the steps up there and don't seem to know what to do. Then Hemi steps forward, one of our union exec, and he waves them up to the steps to be welcomed by our wāhine.

Because we're the ones on strike (or so the company insists) we have to stop by a desk at the door and sign for a voting paper. I stuff mine in my swannie pocket. By the time we get in, there's already a block of the pulp and paper workers, all in their greens, sitting together on the left. Solidarity. I reckon we nearly make up one third, even though we're not the biggest union. I reckon there must be a couple of thousand men in here. For that many men, there's not a lot of noise, just a quiet kind of hum, like when you first go on shift and you put on your earmuffs and the high pitched whine of a thousand bits of machinery banging against each other goes real quiet. Except I haven't got earmuffs on and I can hear it. It doesn't sound friendly.

Whoever set this up had the good sense not to use the stage. There's one long trestle table on the floor at the front, with the old king of the FOL and the new king-to-be settling themselves in with their two lackeys and piles of paper. Me and Dave are shuffling our way in to some spare seats when Hemi beckons us over to him. The pulp and paper workers exec are in the front row, in the cheap seats, right in front of the FOL. We nod to each other, sit down and fold our arms. One block. Solidarity.

The commotion starts at the back, like a wave. It starts with the very back row. Someone's come in the door, just as they were going to close it. Whoever it is walks slowly, you can tell from the noise that's following them, it takes a while to get louder. I'm craning my neck to see past Dave's fat head but all I can see is that old lady, Freda. She's got on her best hat and she's leaning on her stick and walking up the middle of the Town Hall. Stuffed if I know why that should cause such a racket. She's almost halfway when I see him.

It's the Old Man. He's walking very slowly, putting one foot carefully in front of the other, maybe it's so he doesn't bang into the old lady, but I don't think so. It seems to me he's concentrating on making those feet work, like they might give way on him. Freda keeps on coming, almost like she doesn't even know he's behind her, with the noise carrying the two of them forward. They get up close to the trestle table and Freda stops. She waits. The Old Man wobbles, catches up with her, almost stands on her heels, stands next to her. He's swaying. She swaps her stick to the other hand

and very carefully tucks her arm in his. The noise behind them dies down and the two of them are standing there, steady. Freda turns them both round, to face the crowd. Freda in her long black skirt and the hat she wears for weddings with its big red rose. The Old Man in his suit, without a tie, with his jacket all buttoned wrong.

Freda bangs her stick.

E noho, she says. Sit down, you fullas. We'll have a prayer.

I'm sure the blokes at the back can't hear her but, like a wave, everyone sits down. They bow their heads and she prays. First in Māori, then in English. She prays for peace in the town, for forgiveness, for understanding. As the amens fade away, she pulls the Old Man to the nearest seat. The spare seat's at the end of the big table where the paper shufflers and the FOL decision-makers are sitting. She sits him carefully down on the seat. Without a word to the suits sitting up there she turns round and walks back down the long aisle. There's silence. Not a sound as this one old lady takes herself past all those blokes in their steel-capped boots.

I try to catch the Old Man's eye but he's staring at the table. He's made a bad job of a shave, I reckon, and he's cut himself. There's a white patch where he's stuck some toilet paper on. He looks old. Him and Jim Knox, both. The old men. I don't know whether to scream at him, or cry.

Jim Knox clears his throat into the microphone sitting in the middle of the table and he starts. He says the reason for getting everyone together is so that we can all hear the latest the company is saying. He says that he'll talk to that, there'll be time for questions and then everyone except the pulp and paper workers'll leave the Town Hall. The pulp and paper workers'll submit their votes and they'll be publicly counted. One of his lackeys has emptied a box of paper and sits it in front of the microphone. An empty box, the star of the show.

The Old Man's still staring at the table. He reaches into his pocket and takes out a coin. He starts it on the back of his hand, across the knuckles from his little finger to his forefinger, then back again.

Jim's talking about the conditions the company wants. We know every single one: new technology, labour-saving machinery, changes in manning levels, changes in duties, responsibilities and classifications. In other words, fewer jobs. Then he says there'll be no forced redundancies for six months, no intention of redundancies, if there's cooperation.

If there's cooperation. Fuckin' veiled threat, that one.

So the company hasn't shifted.

There's a pause. The Old Man flips his coin. It spins in the air and he snatches at it in midair, his fist punching up towards Jim. Jim squares his chin to the crowd, flick go his eyes to the Old Man, flick back to the crowd. He leans forward on the desk, flick go his eyes. He asks if there are any questions.

Then it starts. How long does the Pulp and Paper Workers' Federation intend to keep this town out of work? Who's going to pay for my kids to go and see their sick aunty? When are those fuckin' commies going to stop banging everyone's head against the wall? Jim repeats his rule. Questions about the company's offer only, please.

So the pulp and paper workers exec have a go. How are the changes to manning levels going to be determined? What about the changes in duties, responsibilities and classifications? That's bound to affect hourly rates, how is that going to be determined?

So we learn that there'll be a special disputes committee set up, to deal with any grievances around changes the company make. No mention of negotiation between management and the union, no mention of any power to the union, just enforced redundancy if we don't cooperate.

There's some muttering after those answers. One of the delegates from the Engineers' Union stands up and asks how the decision of redundancy is made and by whom? Jim puts up one hand, behind it he's having a whispered consultation with his handmaiden, Red Ken. The Old Man has gone back to nudging the coin across his bare knuckles. The whispering carries on. The blokes start getting a bit on the restless side.

Then Red Ken has a turn. The redundancies are tied into cooperation to improve productivity, he says.

What the fuck does that mean? I ask.

It means if the company loses production, men will be laid off, he says. The company sees production as a joint responsibility of management and labour. You don't put out the goods, you don't have a job.

And I thought that bastard was a socialist. What kind of power does that thinking give the workers? Jeez, it's a sellout, that's all I can say, a sellout.

Some wanker at the back's asking about that woman Sally Wihongi, the wahine who started it all.

She's to get her job and, if anyone has issues with it, it's to go to the special disputes committee.

That means anyone can take stuff to the disputes committee. That means unions are sidelined.

The Old Man hasn't shifted from his endless shuffling. Back and forward goes the coin. Back and forward.

Jim calls the meeting to an end. If there were any more questions, it's too bad. Everyone except the pulp and paper workers get up to leave. It takes a while. Chairs flick up, steel-capped boots scrape at the carpet. One fucker yells across his shoulder as he leaves—You do right for our town.

The Town Hall looks empty without all the workers in it. We're not such a big block after all, just a few blokes trying to keep some power for the working man. Our so-called allies, the FOL, are sitting down waiting. All we have to do now is vote. I pull out my voting paper.

It's got two lines of writing on it and two tick boxes. The writing says: I agree to return to work, upholding the conditions outlined in the company's offer dated 30.9.86. There's a yes box and a no box, no maybe box, no only if box. Just a yes box and a no box.

Dave passes me a pen. He's already folding his bit of paper. I've got the pen and the paper and I look up one more time at the Old

Man. He's staring at me, right in the face. His eyes are bloodshot and his stare is like one of Dave's bloody pig dogs, letting its prey know this is it, this is the moment.

I make my mark. I fold the paper up. I file behind Hemi and Dave and post my folded-up paper into the box.

None of us say anything as we walk outside to the foyer. It's jam-packed but there's a parting made for us, right the way to the door. That's where we stop, on the steps, with a sea of faces staring at us.

It's a long ten minutes. Dave's wittering in my ear about getting a letter from one of his kids asking if he and the missus want a bit of a holiday, a break away from the town. I'm not answering.

Then from behind us come the four—Jim and Ken and the two box carriers. They get down to the bottom of the steps before they say anything. They wait for quiet.

I try reading their faces but they're stony. There's not a flicker to say who's got the victory. Jim clears his throat. He's holding a single sheet of paper, foreign paper, not from our mill. He adjusts his glasses halfway down his nose. You could hear a pin drop.

The vote is to return to work, accepting the company's conditions. That's what he says, old Jim. The crowd passes it on, hand to hand, mouth to mouth. Behind us, inside the foyer, a haka breaks out. A great roar of a shout with hands slapping on thighs and chests and steel-capped boots thudding on the carpet.

It's over. The mill is to roll again.

There's a knot of journos with microphones and TV cameras and the whole shebang over by the corner of the building, surrounding Jim Knox and Ken Douglas, getting the word out. Not one of them is over on the steps with us, the union exec. The rest of the workers are leaving, coming out through the big glass doors, and they pass us without a word: carpenters, maintenance crew, fitters, mechanics, all smiling, all trying not to see us standing there, most heading for the pub to celebrate.

Then there's just me and Dave left, waiting for our womenfolk. That's when the Old Man comes out, when everyone's left. He stands next to me, pulls out a fag and lights it. As he lets the smoke out into the sunlight he starts talking. I'm not sure if it's me he's talking to, or me and Dave, or just himself.

Know what this means, he says, the start of big corporation in this country, labour as something management buys for as cheap as it can. No more security for the working man. No more negotiating the work place or the work conditions. Welcome to the brave new world.

He drops his fag and steps on it.

I'm leaving town for a while, Leo. Union's all I know. I'm needed elsewhere. Besides, there are folk here who wish me ill. I want you to take Miriama home, to you and Stella. Keep her safe.

He's got one hand on my shoulder. If I didn't know better, I'd think there was a shine to his eyes.

And by the way, he says, what did you vote?

Before I can answer, he's turned his back on me and is walking back across the green to the supermarket.

Chapter Thirty-five
Stuart Duncan

The cafeteria seemed almost full. That new woman Fred employed scooped up quite a few. There were half a dozen photographers clicking away and the noise was unbelievable. I never could understand why a media briefing couldn't be run civilly, without all the shouting. No one can hear themselves think, let alone answer a question sensibly. Fred managed to quieten them down. He put one of his big hands up in the air and quiet and order descended. The tables had been moved to the side and there was a scraping of chairs as the photographers and reporters sat down.

That was when I saw her. She was standing at the back with her cameraman and sound technician, all three of them leaning on the wall. She was staring at me. I nodded, my neck stiff. Before we could lock gazes, my eyes slid away. I was rattled, badly rattled. The only way I could cope was by pretending she wasn't there and watching the scribblers in the front row settle in with their notebooks and pens.

Fred and I had decided it would be a joint press conference. He'd answer the more local issues, I'd do the big picture. I'd rather not have even been there because Jennifer had said she'd be back but, as Fred kept reminding me, I was the one with whom the buck stopped, the one who would have had to close the mill if the federation hadn't backed down.

The new woman stepped up to run the meeting. She introduced herself as Miss Williams, Assistant Communications Officer. I didn't remember having been consulted about her employment but then Fred always knew he had free range with operational matters. She was good. She insisted that they hold up their press badges if they had a question, as if they were kids in school. She said she would give priority to questions from the local press because they had been so diligent in their reporting. You could see the locals preen, especially when it was coming from a blonde in a tight skirt and high heels.

The questions came in rapid succession, about how much the strike had cost the town and how long it would take for it to recover. Fred spoke about the new enterprise park that was about to open and how that would bring new business in. I spoke about the bigger picture: the revenue loss, the need to have a workforce that was cooperative so that production could be increased. The reporter from the *Sentinel* was obviously only interested in scuttlebutt. The light glinted off his glasses as he poised his pencil over his pad.

"Mr Duncan, what do you think was the game changer? I hear the president has left town. Do you think there was dissension in the rank and file?"

I almost said that he should ask the federation that question but that new woman, with a very subtle raised eyebrow, reminded me that we wanted to stay in control of the media.

"We can safely say that the people of the town got tired of no wages. Many of the workers in this company are looking for more cooperation between management and workers. They're not interested in union politics that are one hundred years out of date. That same feeling is shared by many of the pulp and paper workers."

"Are you expecting some individuals not to cooperate?"

"Some extremists may see the new agreement as a victory for capitalism and a loss of union muscle," said Fred. "We are confident that the bulk of our employees have faith in their company. This town is good at getting on with things. There is enough of a groundswell of goodwill, both ways, to ensure that everyone knuckles down and gets things moving again. One of the first things we need to do is move that pile of wood chips. It's a danger to all the workers and the company recognises that. I'm sure the union will agree."

The blonde woman asked for questions from the national media. There was a pause. I was half expecting Jennifer's TV crew to jump in but she didn't move. An older man, red-faced, his tie askew, waved his press pass.

"Do you envisage this as the last big strike?"

"I certainly hope so," I said. "After all, the reality is that this company is a fair, generous and modern employer."

"And what do you see will happen when blokes are told they no longer have jobs?"

"We have set up a disputes committee," I said. "It's a joint enterprise between management and workers. We'll work through the de-manning together."

"And you don't think this will lead to more strike action?"

"We will all do our level best not to have that happen, but this company needs to make a profit. That's the bottom line. No production, no profit, no jobs. I hope that's clear."

"Time's almost up," said the blonde woman. "I'd like to thank you all for coming. One last thing: you may notice I am a woman." There was laughter, and one catcall. "The woman who was employed at the beginning of this strike starts her first shift at eight o'clock on Monday. Thanks for your time."

I laughed, along with the reporters. It was a great finish and well-timed.

The cafeteria emptied, with Fred ushering the press out and keeping up a banter about the company team pulling together. All except for Jennifer and her two assistants. I picked up the file I'd left on the table behind me and tried to keep my face neutral.

"Miss Price has requested a television interview, sir," said the blonde Miss Williams.

"Has she indeed," I replied.

"She wants a more personal statement from you."

"Really?"

"We could all move to your office, if you like. It would be more private there."

"No, no that's not necessary, here will do."

I sat down quickly. The sooner we got started, the sooner it would be over. I opened the file so that I wouldn't have to look at her. Inside was a balance sheet, except it didn't balance. Projected losses for the year had ballooned.

"I just want a little of your time, Stuart," she said. "That's not too much to ask, is it?"

Too much to ask? It was more than I had to give, to her, anyway, but Sir Ron Trotter's words about reviewing my performance were echoing in my ear. I had to do this interview.

"It will be my pleasure, Jennifer. We might as well do it here, don't you think?"

She hesitated a moment. I smiled, or at least, my mouth did. She nodded.

"OK boys, light's not the best, but looks like we'll have to do it here."

I opened the file again while she pulled up a chair and her sound technician got her to speak into his furry microphone. The figures on the page took on a life of their own. There seemed to be far too many sevens. Seven was always Paul's lucky number: seven presents by his plate every birthday, seven posters on his bedroom wall. Until that night. The seventh of January, at seven in the evening.

"Are you ready, Stuart?"

I closed the file and blinked myself back to Jennifer motioning the cameraman closer.

"Of course I am, Jennifer," I said.

"Can you look down at the file a moment, Stuart? We need to get a few seconds of lead-in."

I opened the file again, from the back, so that the page I was looking at was blank.

She began with an introduction, while I continued to stare at the blank page. She said the strike had resolved and she was about to get a personal statement from the CEO.

"Mr Duncan, this was a close call. I understand you almost announced that the mill would cease production altogether. How did it feel at that time, when it looked like closure was a reality?" she asked.

I looked up. It wasn't Jennifer Price the television reporter I saw. It was the ashen face I'd met when she'd woken me in the hospital that day. She'd made me jump, a guilty startle. I'd fallen asleep by Paul's bedside.

"None of us like to face such difficult times," I said. "Least of all when you know lives are at stake; the future of many lives."

"How are you feeling now, Mr Duncan, now that a resolution has been found and the mill is about to start up again?"

She'd had a bunch of flowers in her hand. They were bright yellow sunflowers, so bright they'd hurt my eyes.

I couldn't help it. I laughed.

"You know, part of me thinks this whole thing has been a big farce. Just a bunch of theatrics to make some kind of obscure point."

I stood up. Jennifer gave a hand signal to the cameraman.

"Can I suggest we do another take here?" It was Miss Williams. She came and took my elbow and sat me down again. I was shaking.

"Can you give us a few minutes please, Miss Price?" she asked.

Jennifer nodded. She jerked her head at her assistants and they went out to the hallway.

"Are you OK, Mr Duncan?" Miss Williams asked.

"Sorry, it's all been a bit much, I suppose. Just give me a minute, will you?"

I went over to the window. Downstairs was my BMW. How I just wanted to bolt down there and drive off forever. I had a thumping headache coming. I wanted to escape the headache, escape the job, and more than anything else, escape Jennifer and the heavy unspoken misery of it all. I couldn't. That was not an option. I breathed in through my nose and tried to make myself present by looking at the scene out there, in the car park. I noticed that next to my car was another one, its twin, in red.

"That's funny," I said. My voice was almost under control.

"What's that, Mr Duncan?"

"There's a car down there just like mine," I said.

"Oh, yes, well, that's mine."

"You must have good taste," I said.

She smiled at me. Nice smile, not a bad-looking woman.

"Are you ready to start again?" she asked.

I nodded.

I don't know what I said. I remembered some of the key words we'd discussed, me and Fred: cooperation, solving the future of the company together, something like that.

Jennifer's motley crew were already packed up and waiting in the foyer. She had the door open. She made a comment that froze me where I was, leaning on the table, half-standing, half-sitting.

"My ethics really require me to use the first take, Stuart, not the revised one."

I made some kind of non-committal noise. I looked up and our eyes locked. I might have imagined it but it seemed to me there was softness there.

"Please," I said.

"I won't do that," she said, "use the first take, I mean. For old times' sake."

Her mouth clenched and she nodded. It was decided. She turned and joined her crew and I collapsed back in the chair.

"Mr Duncan, you look terrible," said Miss Williams. "Let me get you a cup of tea."

Day Seventy-seven

Some statistics for you.

> Length of strike: 86 days
> Number of workers locked out: 1,000
> Number of pulp and paper workers voting to continue strike:
> Unknown
> Number of management conditions agreed to: All
> Number of jobs to be disestablished: 91
> Number of jobs the union has successfully negotiated to keep:
> 17 (91 – 17 = you work it out)
> Number of union members on "special disputes committee": 3
> Number of management members on "special disputes
> committee": 4 (if you include my turncoat sister)
> Number of rats living in the pile of woodchips:
> 2,349. None of them voted to return to work.

So it's all over. They're back at work. Reluctantly, some of them. Leo would say they had faces as long as a donkey's arse but you'd probably see a lot of happy faces as well. The digester gets stoked up first and then there's the pile of rotten wood chips that needs to be moved. The first paper comes off the machine within the week.

On a Sunday.

But it's not all over until it's over.

Chapter Thirty-six

Stuart Duncan

"He's doing a good job, Stuart," said Fred.

"If you say so. I didn't think there'd be adequate access for a wheelchair myself."

"He's just taking mail and messages to those he can get to. I checked them out before I sent him, no use frustrating him. He can get into Dispatches, and he can access the paper machines."

"Right. Thanks for that, and for negotiating with Crossley. It's a blow that young Ray fellow's going back to England. At least Paul hasn't lost the time with the computers."

"Yes, well. We couldn't do it without good old Stan. He helps get Paul up the stairs."

The last couple of days it seemed as if Paul was settling in. Not that I'd been seeing much of him for a few weeks now. With the weather a bit warmer he was out of the house a lot more. He'd got some weights delivered to the house and I heard them thumping down on the floor in his room. He still wasn't forthcoming with me but he was civil at mealtimes, at least. So things were looking up. I wished I could have told him we were heading back to Auckland any day, but I couldn't see my way clear to do that yet.

"These production figures look excellent," I said.

"Don't they? That firm hand paid off, Stuart. We did it, old son. We did it."

"Let's hope we're on the way. I'm concerned about number one paper machine. It's been down more than expected, I see."

"Roller damage. Some foreign body on the belts. Turned out to be tools each time."

"Do you think they were dropped accidentally?"

"Probably, or worse, something like that could be intentional."

I'd feared something like this. It had been a dream start-up. There'd been a lot more maintenance required because the shut had been so prolonged, but the new computer analysis had been helpful. Morale seemed to be OK; at least there were no reports of difficulties. I was very surprised by how cooperative the pulp and paper workers' representatives had been when they'd had to work with the disputes committee. There were no signs that they were taking out hard feelings. Sabotage was a possibility, though. Better safe than sorry.

"I want a full report, Fred: times, who was on, how long the machine was down, how much loss in production occurred. If there is something going on, we need to nip it in the bud."

"I'll get on to it. I believe Miss Williams wants to meet with both of us this morning. Nice-looking woman, Stuart. Smart, too."

I looked down at the production figures in front of me. I didn't want him to see that my face was hot.

"Yes, well, do you think you could ask her in, Fred?" I asked.

We'd been for a drive in my car the first time and stopped for a drink in a nearby town. It didn't pay to fraternise with staff right under people's noses in this town, but there was no harm in a drink. We'd talked about our cars, mostly. She was good company, a good listener. Good enough to repeat the exercise, in her car. The conversation had been more wide-ranging the second time.

She sat down on the edge of the chair. She had good legs too and she knew that I knew it.

"Good morning, Stuart," she said.

"I think we'd better stick with Mr Duncan, if you don't mind, Miss Williams. In the work situation, I mean."

Fred snorted. I looked back at the production report. Ima, I mean Miss Williams, looked as if she was trying to suppress a smile.

"Right, Mr Duncan," she said. "I've an idea I want to talk over with you. My sister, the librarian, wanted to set up classes on the history of the unions and on the rights of workers, in the library. She wanted to work with Leo Harris, you know, he's the president of the Pulp and Paper Workers' Union now."

I knew Leo Harris. Surly chap, only just cooperating with us. I had to say he wasn't much improvement on his predecessor, although he didn't seem to have such a rigidity about him. I nodded at Ima.

"Well, this manual that we got from the British Council has a whole section on educating workers about the economic realities of the workplace. I was just thinking it might be a good idea for this company."

"Education about what?" I asked.

"What's involved in the economics of making paper, global influences on pricing, that sort of thing."

"Stuart," said Fred, "this could be a really good initiative. Especially if it was planned cooperatively so that the unions got to run some of the sessions."

Told you she was smart, his look was saying to me. I didn't let on that I'd already worked that out.

"It would go down very well with the board, I think," I said. "Fits with their intention of clear and open communication. It's got potential. I like it. How do we move this forward?"

"How about Ima and I work on the company curriculum first, just in general terms?" said Fred.

"Then we bring it back to you, and decide how to work with the unions," said Ima. Miss Williams.

"I'd also like you to think about who should attend this education programme," I said. "My feeling is that we should start with middle management, supervisors, I mean. Pilot it with them then move down the ranks. I'd like to see every worker engaged in this."

You would have to say that Ima's smile was radiant. She smoothed her skirt as she stood up. I don't think I was supposed to see the wink she gave Fred as he opened the door for her. He was still holding on to the doorknob when he turned towards me.

"Good to see you're in much better spirits," he said. "Miss Williams is an asset, isn't she?"

"Fred, it's got more to do with the end of the strike. She's a colleague, that's all."

I would have to say that the smile on his face as he left was just a little smug.

Chapter Thirty-seven

Ray Parlane

"Liz, it's me, Rainbow," I said.

"I knew you'd ring today. Mercury's been retrograde. It's been difficult but it's fine now and we can talk. We couldn't last week, you know."

I wished my mother spoke English like other people. I wished she were like other people in lots of ways. I was just about to ask the next question, but I stopped. If I didn't, then I wouldn't know and maybe it would all be some bad dream and Harry would just be skinny old Harry putting his hands on my shoulders and kissing me, left cheek, right cheek, left cheek again. It came out in a rush.

"How is he?" I asked.

"Who, darling?" she said.

"Harry. How is he? I haven't heard from anyone."

"He's reached some blessed state, darling, you can see he's communing with another plane."

"Do you mean he's got worse?"

"I wouldn't call it worse, darling. He's facing it all with such courage. It's an inspiration, really."

"I'm coming home," I said. "I'm leaving tomorrow."

"Really? That'll be nice, Rainbow. I'm sure Stan will be pleased to see you."

"I won't be too late, will I?"

"Too late for what, darling?"

I gave up. I'd have gone right then if I could, but I could hear

Harry telling me off and telling me that the show must go on. The show would go on, one performance, that night, and I had to be there. For Harry. For Miriama. There was still one more piece of unfinished business to deal with. I gave it a try.

"Liz, can you please think for a minute. Is there anything else you can tell me about my father?"

There was a silence. There usually was a silence. Then her voice became a thin thread.

"Sorry, Rainbow. Please don't. I'm feeling somewhat fragile."

The phone beeped again. I put my hand up to the slot to feed in some more coins, but there was no point.

"Right," I said. "See you in a couple of days."

I was speaking into a phone doing a one-note song. I'd heard it before. It said no one home.

My feet took me without my permission. They carried me over the cracked footpath. All the footpaths in this town seemed to crack, break up and tip at all sorts of crazy angles. You had to be careful where you put your feet.

I was going past the bus station. I'd leave with my suitcase and bequeath my computer to the library, to Miss Williams, for her kindness and her help in trying to find Kiwi Keith, the elusive father, the shadow somewhere who gave me the shape of my nose, maybe. The shoebox of letters would go back with me in my suitcase. Somewhere in the world, maybe in this town, there just may be another shoebox of letters written by another boy. The one I used to be.

The following week would be my birthday. I wanted to spend it sitting at Harry's bedside and writing a letter to him, a letter that said I love you and you're my real father that I could put in his hand, not in some postbox somewhere at the other end of the world.

My feet carried me to the bridge over the stream. It was cold under the shadow of the willow tree and the water was so clear. I could see the pumice bottom shifting with the current and it was hard to know how deep the water was. Water flows faster on the surface, where everyone floats along. It's the depths that go more slowly.

Maybe one day I'd be able to make sense of all this.

By the time I got back to the hall Miss was opening up the door.

"So, we still have you," she said. "Thank God for that. Look, Ray, this won't be anything like up to the standard you're used to. We haven't even got costumes properly organized but at least we're putting it on."

"Show must go on, and all that," I said.

"Have you seen Miriama since the meeting? Is she all right?"

She bustled into the hall and didn't seem to notice that I didn't answer her. I hadn't seen Miriama since the day before yesterday, in the library. She'd been really strange and we hadn't known what to say to each other.

By the time I got inside, Miss was setting up the sound system. She was rabbiting on about how kind it was of the school to lend it to us and what a difference it would make to the sound quality. I wasn't sure if that would help me and Miriama.

"Shall I set up the chairs?" I asked.

"Would you? Thanks, Ray. You know, you've been a real gift to us in this town, what with the library catalogue and the musical. I do hope you'll keep in touch when you go back to London."

"Oh certainly, I will definitely do that."

I knew I was lying.

The others arrived all at once. June and May were wearing skirts. Full skirts and socks, bobby socks, the Americans call them. They looked very strange, almost as if their legs weren't used to being out in the fresh air. Davey and Jason were in the same get-up as me, jeans and a white shirt, except that Davey's shirt was hanging out at the back. I supposed that wouldn't matter.

There was no Miriama.

The show was to start at five so that kids could come. *Songs from Grease,* we called it, because we hadn't had time to pull a full musical together. It was free, a sort of celebration for the mill starting up again, a sort of peacemaking.

I was peeking out of the curtain, looking for her.

The first of the audience arrived at quarter to five. Davey's family took up nearly a whole row; they seemed to be trying to set up a dynasty. Then there were everyone else's little brothers and sisters and cousins who sat on the floor at the front. People were streaming in and by five-to-five the hall was full and it was standing room only.

Near the middle, with his arms crossed, was Leo. Miriama's mum, Stella, was with him.

But there was still no Miriama.

We held the curtain. We were all backstage except for Miss who was down on the floor of the hall by the little kids, operating the music. June and May were whispering, wishing they could have a quick smoke to quieten the nerves. I was biting my little fingernail.

By five past five the noise in the hall had got even louder and there were some wolf whistles. I was sure we'd have to make an announcement soon; to say that the show wouldn't go on because we didn't have a leading lady, but the wolf whistles weren't to hurry us up. They were for the woman who'd come down the aisle right up to the front of the curtain. She'd washed her hair and it was held back with a hair band, lying on her shoulders, smooth and shiny. She was wearing a dress with a flared skirt and a petticoat underneath that made her look as if she was floating. I caught my breath, like some fool in a bleeding movie seeing his true love …

There was no time to think about it. The music started and that was what I was carrying in with me.

We started the first song and the girl and boy met and fell in love and we worked together. We worked. We brought the house down, as they say.

When she sang her devotion to me, she had tears in her eyes and I had to blink very fast too.

Then it was my turn. I felt like a hypocrite begging her to stay when it was me going. I suddenly didn't want to leave.

Everyone cheered except Leo. He still had his arms crossed.

I was staring at June on the stage. She was getting everyone to join in with the hand jive song and she only had three of the movements: hands one on top of the other in front, bang the elbow with the other hand and make your hands cycle one over the other, just like my stomach was doing. Miriama's hands were fluttering up as if she was trying to will June to do it properly, to fill in the blanks. The kids in the front wound up wrestling, the aunties yelled out you forgot this one, girl, and Leo didn't unfold his arms. We had to do the number twice.

By the time we were all singing the last song, the whole audience was singing with us about togetherness and being as one.

In the middle of the hall Leo stood up and it started a wave until everyone was standing and clapping and carrying on singing, but Leo was pushing past them to get to the door. Miriama started towards the steps as if to follow him but I pulled her back round to face me, to sing my last line.

Chapter Thirty-eight
Miriama McLay

I felt like that dumb Cinderella running away from the ball or something stupid like that and I didn't leave a shoe behind either, just that dumb stiff petticoat in the rubbish bin by the door. I couldn't stay, not so that everyone could be all happy and say well done to us and make me feel all hōhā. Mr Rainbow-man never was Prince Charming anyway.

Leo had gone. I couldn't see Mum, but Leo, he was out of there. It must've been that stuff about being one. No one was gonna be as one, not me and Rainbow-man, not the whole town. Not ever again.

I jumped on my bike and my legs were cold and I wished I'd brought my trackies. The shops were all shut and there was no one to tell me off, so I blasted through the middle bit that the flash people call the plaza and nearly ran over that stray tomcat that was always in the bin outside the fish shop. Down past the bike track, empty, all the kids were at the great show, the only show in town that night. Then there was the one long road home and the last bit of sun on the mountain, like it was kissing the mountain top goodnight, or maybe goodbye. Maybe it was just that I was going fast and the wind in my face was making my eyes water. Yeah, must've been.

There's a time when the last of the sun's gone and the night hasn't quite started, when the light goes all strange. Each thing seemed to stand out, the bench near the streetlight, the wrecked car sitting on the front lawn of that house where the fulla lost it that night, the hedge around our house. It was like each thing'd got a special life all of its own and no one thing was part of another thing. The opposite of whakawhānaungatanga. The opposite of making connection.

Our letterbox was standing up like it had divorced everything else. Maybe I should call it my letterbox. There was a letter poking out of its mouth; it was doing a pūkana at me. When Jason and them do that in the haka I always feel like doing it back but I can't, I'm a girl. I just picked up the letter and opened it.

Dear wee lassie,
I'm staying with the Walker family. You'll remember them
from that time we all came to Auckland. I'm doing some work
with the Seamen's Union. They appreciate my work. I won't be
coming back to the town. I want you to go and live with Leo and
your mother. They'll explain everything.
Your father.

He used to call me wee lassie when I was very little. When I climbed up on his knee, he'd lift me up in the air and put me down on the floor.

Away ye go, wee lassie, he'd say. Away ye go.

There was no return address.

It was dark in the house and it was getting cold. I turned the heater on in the lounge but not the lights.

I was wrapped up in a blanket in front of the heater when he came. He didn't knock, he just walked in like he knew I was there, on the floor. He didn't even say anything, just sat behind me, with his legs and arms and his duffle coat wrapped round me in my blanket. I leaned back on him and his breath smelt of rum. He reached into his coat pocket and pulled out the bottle. The top was hard to get off but when I did and took a swig, it was so strong it caught my throat and I was coughing and crying and the rum bottle was on the floor tipping over everything and I was hanging round his neck and I didn't want to let go.

Somehow he got his duffle coat off and put it down on the floor. Me and my blanket wound up on top of it. He'd got one arm up under my neck and his other arm was pulling my skirt off. There was a moment when I wanted to tell him to fuck off, I wanted to run away and never see him again, then he was kissing me again and the taste of the rum was sweet on his breath and I couldn't.

He was in me as soon as his pants were down and his belt buckle was clanking on the floor and he was pushing like he wanted to nail me to the floor, except I was rising with him, up in the air and arching into him like I wanted to swallow all of him into me. Harder and faster. Fighting for some kind of togetherness that couldn't ever be broken. We flooded into one.

He wound his fingers in my hair and I sobbed on his shirt. I couldn't help it. I was sobbing because we got to be one person and I was sobbing because my body didn't want it to stop and I was sobbing because we were two separate people again. We'd never go back, never.

Except we did. The next time it was slow and it was gentle and he fitted himself inside me like he wanted to live there forever. He kept very still while my insides reached up to him and drank him in. He kept very still.

I was drifting in some sort of in-between sleep, one that was full of soft black darkness and humming. I was listening hard to try and make out the tune but it was too big and too much of all of me to catch. I rolled over to try and hug him, my Rainbow-man. There was the duffle coat, rough on my skin, and one of the duffle buttons dug me in the ribs. But there was no Rainbow. He'd gone from the sky.

The tune in my head arrived. It was "Ten Guitars." My tune. My birth tune.

I pulled myself up from the floor. My skin could still feel him, feel his fingers on my belly and his mouth on my neck. He was still with me. I pulled the duffle coat on and shuffled my way out of the dark house.

I went across the field to the river, where we swim in summer, where I go when I don't know what to do next. The water knew; it just kept on going. There was no moon, not yet, just the clouds that wrapped the sky up. I walked in the cold grass, my feet going numb. My mother taught me about this darkness. About te pō-uriuri, the deep night. And I took my Ūenuku with me, my Rainbow-man. He was on my skin, he was inside me. We both went into te pō-te-kitea, the night in which nothing is seen.

I could feel the sandy bank of the river with my bare feet. The water was slow just on this bend, and black. It talked. It told the story of its journey from the sky to lie in the lake where the reeds stroked it and the swans drank it. Then from the lake into the dreaming place where it could become river, or stay as lake. That was how this little bay was, here where we swam. It could be lake again or it could rush away like the other side of the river.

There was no moon on the river, not even starlight. The ruru gave its screech to tell the world it was waking up, but it was so dark that it must've gone back to sleep. There was no ruru crying back to her mate to say she would go out hunting with him. I couldn't see my hand in front of my face. I only knew the water was there by its speaking, by its resting there and its rushing.

He was going the next day, back to his home, back to that man he said had really been his father. He hadn't said anything about me. He hadn't. This Rainbow that was printed on my skin was all that I would have. I didn't want to cry, not yet. I didn't want to be a tangiwai, not while he was still warm on my skin. Maybe he would stay like that forever. Maybe. Painted on me, pressed in under my skin so I would always have a Rainbow.

I felt her coming more than heard her. She was silent as she sat down beside me. She didn't hug me, not like she used to. She just sat beside me and something was different. We weren't mother and daughter any more, we were two women. I shuffled along the sand on my bum till my toes were in the water. It was so cold that they ached and the ache started in my toes, up my legs and deep in my belly, where he was. Still I wouldn't cry—I'm staunch. It wasn't the time to be sad.

The water just kept going.

When I stood up, I could see her walking back to the trees. The clouds had unwrapped the sky and the starlight was showing us the way. Me and Mum, we had to find the way from this time. We had to turn back to now and find the way, through this dark where nothing is seen.

She walked ahead of me, across the grass, back to the empty house where she used to live.

"Haere mai, e kare. Come with me, Miriama," she said. "You can't stay here by yourself."

So we got in the car. It wasn't Leo's old ute for a change; it was a proper car. I didn't ask who it belonged to.

"Tomorrow we'll come and get your things," she said. "The house needs to be cleaned out. The bank's going to sell it."

I just looked out the window at the lights on in the houses and at the people settling down to their usual lives. I pulled the duffle coat closer.

"Miriama." It was Mum, on the other side of my bedroom door. "Come and have breakfast with me."

"Just you?"

"Just me. Leo's gone to work."

The alarm clock said eight o'clock. Me and Mum needed time together, to sort stuff, but I was so tired. It must've been the show and all that and it would only get worse with that long bike ride down the straight to school and the library. I stretched and remembered it was Saturday. My Rainbow-man would be gone. He would've got on the bus that morning, then a plane to go to the other side of the world.

My eyes were leaking.

The wind caught the scrim on the walls. It was such a decrepit old house it still had scrim on the walls. Last night Mum said we'd pull it all off and put up proper wallpaper. Leo said there was nothing wrong with the house as it was. I said I didn't care. As soon as I could I'd be out of there.

"Got the bacon cooking, girl," said Mum.

She had the radio on. It was some kind of talking stuff. I stretched again and pulled myself out of bed. The smell of the bacon was coming through the walls.

Leo's house always smelt stink, all old and mouldy. And there were rats in the ceiling. Last night they'd held the rat Olympics up there, marathon, I reckoned, and high jump. It'd kept me awake. Another reason why I was so tired.

Mum was wearing Leo's dressing gown, one of those old towelling ones. We'd have a sort of pyjama party, just the two of us.

"You want your bacon crispy?" asked Mum.

I pulled out the chair at the kitchen table and held on to it, hard. The floor felt like it was moving up to get me, swallow me up. It felt real weird.

Mum was cracking eggs into the frying pan. She didn't see me sit down and put my head in my hands. I just wanted to cry. That was the other thing with feeling so tired, I just wanted to cry.

Mum turned around with the frying pan in her hand.

"You OK, e kare?"

The tears landed on my empty plate on the table. I sniffed.

"You missing Ray already?"

I nodded. The only place he was now was in my dream last night. Those grey eyes were shifting all over the place like they were looking for something, searching. They'd soon be on their way to the other side of the world.

And I was on this side of the world, tears plopping in the little lake on my plate without my permission. I couldn't stop.

When I looked up Mum was sitting there, all blurry. I blinked but the tears just kept leaking out and making her all fuzzy. She reached out for my hands.

"You got an address for that boy?" she asked.

I shook my head.

"I suppose the people he stayed with, his whānau, will have?"

"Yeah, but I don't want to be the one who starts first."

"You'll have to tell him he's going to be a father, e kare. I suppose it's him?"

"Oh, shit."

That first night, on the floor in the Old Man's house, when we got to be one person, not Miriama and Rainbow, but one person, when he left with the light.

I started shivering, crying and shivering. I'd felt he was still there with me in the night when I woke up, he was still on my skin. I suppose some part of him was still here, but the truth was that most of him was already far away.

"E kare, we'll work it out. Your baby'll be all right. There's plenty of whānau and plenty of aroha."

I just cried some more. Mum pulled me up from the chair and put her arms round me and I leaned into her and felt like an oozy, wobbly jellyfish.

"You supposed to be going to work today?"

"Saturday. I'm supposed to be at the library."

"I'll take you in and we'll explain to Miss Williams. She'll let you off work, I'm sure."

I nodded and wiped my nose on my pyjama sleeve.

"But we'll have breakfast first. Got to feed my mokopuna, got to feed his mother."

After breakfast, in the shower, I washed my belly and my boobs real carefully. I still had him, my Rainbow-man, deep inside me.

When we got to the library Miss Williams was just opening the door with all her keys we always joke about. I counted them once, there was one for every day of the week. She'd only got to number three when we came up the steps.

"Not on your bike today?" she asked.

Mum explained about the baby and Miss Williams got all excited and gave me a big hug and my boobs got all squashed and I was all excited too.

"You can keep working here, Miriama," she said. "Finish this year of school then work here until the baby's due. Doesn't need to affect your education, you know. A baby can fit in with your life."

She kept on talking as we went in the door.

"You might get a bit tired, but that's OK. There are other things you can do than lug that heavy returns trolley around."

Mum leant down to pick up the mail off the floor. Miss Williams was going on about me being able to sit down and mend books and how good the new computer programme was that Ray had left behind and how I could learn to use it, when Mum passed me an envelope. The front of it was addressed to Miriama Harris (e kare). It didn't have a stamp. He must've put it in the hole in the door. On the back he'd drawn a great big rainbow and inside the rainbow was an address for London, England.

And I was crying again.

Chapter Thirty-nine
Ima Williams

It had taken me a while to work out the best place for us to meet. I thought he might be intimidated if I suggested upstairs in one of the management offices, but then, I didn't want it to be on his terms, not in his union office. The best I could manage was the cafeteria. It wasn't private, but at that time of day it was pretty much empty, except for that young man in a wheelchair.

I heard him before I saw him, the squeak of his wheels on the polished floor. He was practising wheel stands. He was good at it too, holding a point of balance for several seconds. He hadn't quite mastered the descent; it was more of a crashing down. I did wonder what it was doing to his wheelchair. I'd seen him watching us when I'd dropped his father home one evening, rocking his wheelchair backwards and forwards, no greeting, no acknowledgement, he probably needed his hands on his wheels. We hadn't met and we needed to.

"Hi. Paul, is it?" I said.

"Yeah, that's me."

"Pleased to meet you, I'm Ima Williams, Assistant Communications Officer." I held out my hand.

He didn't reciprocate, just turned his wheelchair between two tables and leant over to try and push away a chair.

"Let me," I said.

"Someone needs to write a manual for the public for when they meet a cripple. It should say always let the cripple, sorry, I mean disabled person, be as independent as possible."

That stopped me in my tracks. I had no response for it, so I chose a table at the other side of the room and put down my files. It wasn't a promising start. I'd have to find some way to make a connection.

The door opened. I tried to quieten my breathing. Meeting with Leo would be difficult; I knew that there was unfinished business between us and some of it might re-trigger my traitor body, all that adolescent heart-pounding, the memory of us rearing towards each other and the taste of my bruised lips. Last time we'd had any real contact had been in the supermarket when I turned it all into rage and managed to pretty much tell him to go to hell.

"Got a strong man for you, Paul," said a voice from the doorway.

It wasn't Leo. When I turned around, it was plump little Colin Hopewell looking at me.

"Leo Harris is meeting with you, I believe, Miss Williams. He's just going to help get Paul upstairs to the computer suite. He'll be a couple of minutes."

"Sorry to steal your man," said Paul.

I opened my mouth to say he wasn't my man, but Paul was already wheeling himself to the door.

For the want of something better to do, I watched them man-handle Paul up the stairs. Colin had a plan of operation worked out. He and Leo made a seat with their hands then Paul put his arms around their necks and manoeuvred himself onto their hands. They must have forgotten the brake on the wheelchair because it began to move backwards. I went to help hold it but Paul yelled at me.

"Get away!"

I pulled back as fast as I could. I suppose being dependent on three people was too much.

They carried him up the stairs. At the top, a man in a white coat had wheeled an office chair onto the landing and Paul was deposited on it. He looked down the stairs at me.

"Stay away from my dad," he said. "Blonde women like you are lethal."

The force of it nearly knocked me over. I held on to the handrail while the wave of his intense, well, it wasn't exactly hatred, more like panic, rolled over me. I was left feeling confused. There must have been other blonde women in his life, and his father's life, the history of which I wasn't aware. If I wanted a relationship with his father, getting past that history and past Paul was going to be a challenge.

So when Leo came back down the stairs I was already messy. He led the way into the cafeteria and held out a chair for me and asked if I was all right, as if he was in control of this situation, rescuing the maiden in distress. That was when I got coldly professional, to take back the lead. I ignored the chair he was holding and sat down across the other side of the table.

"Thanks for your time, Leo," I said. "I appreciate that you're still settling back into the rhythm of work again and rebuilding the trust between you all as workers."

"Trust," he said. "Yeah, you could say that. You know all about trust, I suppose."

I felt like slapping him for assuming there was still some kind of grounds for being so familiar and for ignoring me when I was making it quite clear this was a professional meeting.

"That's what I want to talk to you about, trust-building between the union and the company," I said. "You notice I didn't say rebuilding. This is an entirely new approach."

He sat down on the chair he was holding and folded his arms. He put his chin down on his chest and squinted at me from under his eyebrows. I felt like the adult facing up to a truculent teenager.

"Some time ago, I believe Notta talked to you about an education outreach on the history of unions in this country and workers' rights."

He leant back in his chair and sucked in air through his teeth.

"Stuart, I mean Mr Duncan, and I have been discussing this. The concept has got the blessing of the board of directors. We're proposing a joint education venture with both the union and management putting in sessions."

He leant one arm on the table, scratched the back of his head and rested his chin in one hand. There was black underneath the nail of the finger that worried at one stubbled cheek. He stuck his chin out and ran his fingers back and forward over his mouth. He narrowed his eyes.

I waited, completely still, with my head on one side and my face neutral. I was completely in charge.

"Why?" he asked.

"I think you know the answer to that, Leo. Because this is a new era, because the rules have changed, because the old approaches don't hold water anymore."

"What's in it for the men?"

"Knowledge. Knowledge is power, Leo. It's a share in the information that feeds decisions."

"Not a share in the decisions?"

"No."

He leaned forward on his chair and put his elbows on his knees. His head slumped and his hair fell over his face and I couldn't see his expression. There was another long silence.

"S'pose we've got fuck-all else to lose," he told the floor. "When do we start?"

I tried not to smile. I nodded as if he was the greatest sage who lived and didn't let it show that all of me felt I'd won.

Chapter Forty

Leo Harris

Stella's hair smells of something sweet and sharp at the same time, bit like her, sweet inside, sharp as a needle outside. She's always softer after a bit of how's your father. That's when I get that feeling like this is where I'm meant to be, with my woman and with my girl. She'll come round, I know she will.

The fuckin' phone stops me just as I'm about to move into kissing my lovely Stella on her delicious left tit. Loud as hell, that phone is.

So I get myself free of Stella and the sheets and stagger out into the hall. It's Dave. Him and me are supposed to be on at four this afternoon. Why he has to ring at, what is it, just before eight in the morning, I do not know. It's hard to hear him over the racket even though he's shouting. Seems he was just being Dave this morning and gave one of our mates a ride in. Seems that there's some trouble at the security gate. Seems he's using their phone and I'd better get down there fast or else.

Stella's gone back to sleep anyway so I take a leak on the lemon tree outside, pull on my work gear and get on the old bike. No brakes. Lucky it's a flat ride down the straight. Lucky it's not been raining. The day's clear as a bell. The digesters are already on their way. The air's got a whiff of sulphur. I sniff it up as my legs are going hell for leather.

I don't bother putting my bike in the rack, just ride right on up to the security gate. That's where the trouble is. Usual suspects, you could say, making all the noise. Dave and the two blokes in uniform, the security blokes who're union, who've been on strike with us, who should now be in the security office. It's a lot of noise for a small number of blokes. The rest of the shift, the paper machine workers, who can get started now the ground wood pulp is up and running, are just standing to one side, like they're waiting for the fuss to be over. Funny the things you notice. It's their clean, pressed work gear that gets me. Looks like their sheilas have gone all out. Never seen a sharp crease down the leg of a pair of greens before.

The two ring-ins doing the security blokes' jobs are standing at the window of the security office. Both of them've got their arms folded. One of them looks like the All Blacks've just lost a series test, his face as long as a donkey's arse. It's the other fulla who's joining in the racket.

You can't be serious, he keeps saying. You can't be bloody serious.

Our union fullas, that's the two real security blokes, are in there boots and all. You don't bloody know, they say. You're just bloody contractors. You're not even union. You're bloody scabs. That's what they're saying over and over and bloody over. I get that sinking feeling in my guts, like I've been here before.

I've seen the Old Man in situations like this. When feelings are running high and the wheels are spinning. So I tap each of them on the shoulder and suggest, very quietly, that we just move to one side out of the way of all the eyes.

In two minutes me and the two ring-ins agree the shift can go in. When I go over to break the news, there's just silence. One of our pulp and paper workers gives a sullen kind of shrug and turns his back. No comment at all from any of them. Jeez, I'm used to this from the other unions but not our own. They walk in that gate like the fight's all gone out of them.

That just leaves the six of us, me and Dave and two sets of security guards. One of the pretend guards tells me they've sent for Mr Grant. Should've known it wouldn't start well for us pulp and paper workers, even though the rest of them've gone in like lambs. Should've been down here this morning to settle things down. Me and Dave offer to stay, to sort it out, even though we're not meant to be here till later this afternoon.

The two of us are crouched down in the sun outside the security building having a fag when Mr High-and-Mighty Grant turns up. I take my time standing up. I'm all courtesy when I suggest we can go over to the union building to talk things through, maybe even have a cuppa together.

He's too busy, he says. He wants to know what the problem is and he wants it fixed. Now.

I remind him that the security blokes have always been part of our union, that the two who are on now are not. They're contractors brought in to man the gate while we were all locked out. I ask, very politely, why the two men who should be in there working at their normal jobs are standing out here, still locked out.

He looks at the sky while I'm talking. He's a tall bastard at the best of times and I'm feeling like he wants me to be just low life, crawling down here on the dusty pavement, so I ask very politely.

He tells the sky about this being a transition time and about wanting to keep some continuity and that these contractors have been doing the security work for the last three months. He says there's a need to phase the original (he means unionised) labour back in.

I look at my boots and don't say that I think this is because the bloody management doesn't trust union labour. They want us back running the digesters and the paper machines because no one else can, but they don't want us at the gate checking up on our fellow workers to make sure they haven't fuckin' pinched anything. Never know, we might walk out with a couple of rolls of toilet paper.

That's what I don't say.

I've watched the Old Man. This is what he'd say: Yes, transition. Good idea. Let's make that a true transition. You have your contract labour and we'll have our unionised labour shadow them, to get a true transition.

That's what I say but I'm expecting a flat-out refusal.

What I get is: good idea. Each side gives a little and we can get back to equilibrium. Equilibrium. Got some sense of equality in it, hasn't it? Can't help saying that. It slips out. He ignores me. Well, that's settled then, he says, and he's off back to his office.

Just like that.

The contracted security blokes look very pissed off with this. Say they'll probably have to join the contracting team coming in to shift the rotten wood chips.

Mr Fred Grant only gets halfway across the carpark when he's got me at his elbow. When I tell him it won't go down well to bring more contractors in, he stops, and the fucker listens for a change. When I tell him we'll shift the mountain of chips, we'll work round the clock to shift it, he narrows his eyes. I can just about see him doing the calculations in his head about how much it'll cost in overtime compared to paying bloody contractors. I'm expecting him to refuse my generous offer. He stares at me for a full minute. I take a breath through my nose, my mouth firmly shut and put my hands in my pockets. I'm not going to look away.

The steam comes across from the digester. It'll need feeding with fresh wood chips and the rotten wood chips need to be removed as fast as possible. I can see him adding that to his cost analysis. We'll iron out the details later, he says. You set in motion finding the labour, I want to start today. This time he marches right back to his office.

Just a little more fuckin' equilibrium has been established.

I borrow a hard hat from the smoko room and head in to the floor of the paper machine. The monster was started last week, just to give it a trial run, but there've been problems. I heard a rumour it was tools being dropped. I've no comment. That young fulla with the wheelchair is coming across the access way. I don't think he's supposed to be in here and I wait for him down the dry end where the big rollers are spinning. The little bugger is coming straight at me and I have to dive to one side. I'm on the floor and there's a flash of something flying out from his hand as he lurches away, just missing the paper speeding by.

There's a scream from the machine and the paper rips and flies off the rollers and flaps like a fuckin' great pterodactyl. It's knocked him over. I pick myself up and get in under the paper piling up on top of him and rip and tear. He's trying to talk but I can't hear a fuckin' thing over the fuckin' racket. The paper's all tangled round his wheels and I can't shift him. He's not helping, grabbing at the wheels and trying to turn them. I slap at his hands and a whole lot of monkey wrenches fall on the floor.

He's looking at something over my shoulder and I turn round and there's the top roller tipping in slow motion off its rest and I'm frozen watching it come through the paper screen and one end hits the floor and the concrete crashes into bits and it's close and it's moving. I give the wheelchair a mighty heave. It rockets off with its streams of paper. The roller tips and sways and I don't know what the steps of this dance are …

NOTTA'S NOTES (8)

Sometimes the maverick escapes and leads a life of freedom, according to its own rules. More often than not it's shot, or recaptured and put back in with the herd. It takes more than a lone maverick to stem a tide. Look what happened to King Canute.

The overhead crane was retired eventually. A new one was bought, more efficient, shifted more logs, stacked them more neatly. The logs kept stacking up and the digester kept eating its way through the pile of wood chips. The rats went to live somewhere else.

So what happened to all these people you ask, all these folk who lived in this town, who worked together, fought with each other, and kept silence when it was needed?

The Old Man continued his activism, mostly with the Watersiders' Union. He kept them true to the path and suffered more defeats.

Ima moved in with Stuart, temporarily, to start with. Last I heard they were both in New York because Stuart had been offered a job with some big corporation there. We don't communicate, Ima and me.

Paul stayed behind. He got a job in the computer suite. He lives in a little flat in town, completely independently. I hear he's got a girlfriend.

Fred and Cynthia are still here. Fred oversaw the restarting of the mill. Apparently it was a joint effort and all the unions pulled together.

Miriama had a baby boy. She called him Ūenuku. He slept in a bassinet in the nonfiction section when Miriama was at work. He loved the peace of the library. He never got to meet Leo.

Leo wasn't meant to be working on the Tuesday when it happened. Paul was wheeling himself along the floor next to the paper machine. He shouldn't have been there either. It was banned to all but that day's shift workers. He said afterwards he had an urgent message to deliver.

Something caught in the granite rollers. Normally the machine would just close itself down but for some reason the top roller came off-balance and tipped. Two ton of granite was heading straight for Paul. It was Leo who ran to help, shouting as he dodged the wildly snapping paper. He pushed Paul to safety, but the granite roller got him. It broke most of his bones, including his spine. Dave told me later that a pile of tools was found near his body. Dave hid them, in case people thought Leo had been sabotaging the paper machine.

We buried Leo two weeks later. He never came out of the coma. He had a big tangi at the marae, was hailed a hero because Dave told everyone he'd saved the life of the CEO's son. Stella was magnificent. I sat next to her and Miriama with his body, as the grieving family. He didn't look like Leo. Once he was dead, he could have been anyone.

After the tangi, Stella and Miriama and little Ūenuku packed up and moved to London. Stella is working in New Zealand House. Miriama is attending library school. They're living with Ray and Stan. They manage their relationship with Ray's mother quite well, by the sounds of it.

I was left to clean out the house and sell it. They didn't take much with them, even left a photo sitting on the china cabinet in the lounge. It was Leo with Stella and a little Miriama. Stella's laughing because Miriama's poking one small finger into his eye. He's squinting, just the way she does.

In the bedroom that Leo and Stella shared was a big old wardrobe. You know the kind, heavy oak wood with mirrors on the doors. I was pulling Leo's gun out from the top shelf when I saw it, underneath a photo album. It was an old poster, for Woodstock, with a ticket stapled to it. The edges were worn and the paper was grimy. It looked well-travelled. Leo must have been to the States, in the 1970s.

When the death certificate for Leonard Keith Harris arrived in the post, I couldn't help wondering, but then truth and fiction are not always the same thing. I put it in my bottom drawer. One day, maybe, I'll give it to the family.

All this is true, every word of it.

Acknowledgements

I would like to acknowledge the following people who helped with
this novel.

My family: David for emotional and financial support, Robin for creative
conversation and design.

My technical assistants: Harold Appleton for long conversations
about unions and for sharing his comprehensive records, Garry Mace
for discussion of the role of management, Barry Joyce for technical
support around pulp and paper manufacture.

My mentors and readers: James George for the best help with concept
and style, Cynthia Rogerson for supportive mentoring, Maggie, Glen
Erik and Dave for reading the manuscript, my writing buddies for support
and feedback.

My professional assistants: Sue Reidy for assessing the manuscript,
Patricia Bell for editing, and proofreading, Cloud Ink Press (especially
Mark and Dione) for support in publishing and publicity.

Many, many thanks.